Accidentally in Bloom

LOVE IN FAIRWICK FALLS

 BOOK ONE 

ELISE KENNEDY

ISBN 979-8-9883664-0-9

For content warnings about this book, please go to https://elisekbooks.com/books

For the ***Weird*** *Girls,*
For the ***You're Too Loud*** *Girls,*
For the ***You Might Intimidate Him*** *Girls,*
For the ***Don't Be a Showoff*** *Girls.*

For all the girls who thought they were somehow too much and also not enough.
You deserve swoon-worthy love.

Chapter One

ROSE

Rose Parker balanced precariously on the hood of her rental car, her stilettos sinking into the dented metal. She raised her phone above her head and hoped like hell for a signal.

"Damn these valley hills." Rose glowered at the rolling, spring countryside of western Pennsylvania. It had taken her two plane rides and four hours by car to get from LAX to ten miles outside her hometown of Fairwick Falls.

AKA, the middle of fucking nowhere.

As Rose contemplated her odds of lighting her rental car on fire if she tried restarting it for the fourth time, a FaceTime call miraculously came through. She swiped up as if her life depended on it, almost losing her balance on the car hood.

A grainy video of her youngest sister popped onto the screen. She was wearing a hydrating sheet mask that reminded Rose of serial killers.

"Rosie Posey! Why aren't you heeeeere? We miss you." Lily giggled and held up a bubbling champagne glass.

"Oh my god, are you guys drunk already? It's eleven a.m."

Violet, their middle sister, popped onto the screen beside her. "You are very late, and Lily convinced me to open the champagne to get the Parker Sisters Hang Session started early."

Rose bit her tongue to keep from exploding at her adorable, but currently very fucking annoying, sisters. "Guys, I'm stuck on the side of the road. Come get me."

"Where are youohhhhaahhhh—" Violet's voice went mechanical, and their faces froze.

"Vi? Can you hear me?" Maybe she could text them the address. But what the hell was this road even called? Rose had driven on it so many times as a teenager she never bothered to learn its name.

"You are—uh—the—" came the stuttered response through Rose's phone, and then the call dropped.

Shit.

The backroad was nestled between the rural rolling foothills of the Allegheny National Forest. Tall oak trees stood in thick brackets all around her. *Blocking the fucking signal.*

The crushing weight of anxiety that came and went found its way onto Rose's chest for the millionth time in the last twenty-four hours. She coached herself to breathe.

I'm not dying. It's not a heart attack. It's just my sympathetic nervous system trying to tell me what I already know: I am stressed the fuck out.

She couldn't deal with a panic attack on top of a car in the middle of a two-lane country road. Not today. She needed to manage the life crumbling down around her.

Make a list. The safety of a simple, ordered list always made her feel better.

Top reasons I need to GTFO of Fairwick Falls ASAP

Number 1: Neolithic Cell Service.

"If what's-his-face can pop up to space for vacation, why can't I get a signal next to a field of cows?" she grumbled.

Number 2: Looming Irrelevance of My Professional Life.

Rose thought about last night — had that only been fifteen hours ago? — when she'd been called in for a "quick meeting" with HR before she left for her three-week vacation. Of course, they'd used that opportunity to fire her, the cowards.

She should've known better than to report sexual harassment to the bro-tastic HR manager. When a low-level employee reported an executive, the executive was never punished at her toxic male bullshit consulting company.

It had taken years for Rose to claw her way to the middle of the high-profile consulting firm. She'd regularly worked hundred-hour weeks and deferred every vacation.

She'd also finally — *finally* — built up a solid following on her podcast side hustle. She needed to maintain her hard-earned identity as the Fortune 100 Got It Covered strategy consultant. How could she face her audience when she'd been fired?

A ball of tension radiated in Rose's chest as she stared at the second item on her list.

The list. Keep going.

Number 3: Chemical Dependence.

There's probably not a decent latte in the entire county.

Rose had a deep, committed relationship with her emotional support Nespresso, and she already missed it.

She'd only stayed in Fairwick Falls for forty-eight hours for the funeral a few months ago. The last time she'd really visited her hometown had been over ten years ago, and the only places open then were watered-down, drip-coffee-swill-from-yesterday diners.

A chilly wind whipped around her, causing her teeth to chatter.

Number 4: There is *weather* here.

How could it be this cold in March? Maybe I can get the estate settled in 2 weeks instead of 3.

The family lawyer had been extremely particular that Rose be there in person for her father's will reading.

And so, here she was, on top of a car hood in the cold, sunny March morning.

Rose thought back to the last time she'd seen her dad alive. It had been almost ten years ago, and they'd barely spoken since their final fight. Her haunting, awful words to him still rattled in her head.

Rose pulled her thin khaki jacket around her as she peered up and down the back road that connected the highway to her small hometown. No sign of cars.

Maybe if I stand on top *of the car, I'll get a cell signal.*

She scrambled up the windshield to the roof, giving herself a few extra inches. *Maybe* there was a signal bar coming.

If she didn't get service, at least someone would stop to ask if she'd lost her goddamn mind.

There was a farm off in the distance, but it would take an hour to walk through muddy fields to get there, and who knew? Maybe it was a farm of murderers.

Or worse, cult members. Maybe they'd innocently ask her to drink their homemade buttermilk, and she'd wake up in chains...

A low roar interrupted her thoughts, and a lone motorcycle barreled down the empty back road toward her.

As the bike came closer, the rider's broad shoulders and thick muscular arms became hard to ignore. An idiotic physical reaction of need rippled through her.

Fuck. She was still on top of this stupid car hood. Her feet slid underneath her.

Don't fall in front of the hottie, don't fall in front of the hottie.

Could she get down without falling to her death? *No, just stay put and see if he stops.*

She'd always had a thing for guys on motorcycles. There

was something sexy about a guy who would make you feel reckless.

She tossed her long hair and struck a damsel-in-distress-but-I'll-kick-your-ass-if-you-try-anything pose.

On top of her fucking rental car.

The bike slowed and pulled in behind her. The rider had a wide expanse of chest, covered in a leather jacket, and a dark helmet obscured his face. He cut the engine and quiet rang out over the countryside.

His jeans and jacket were designer if a little beat up. What the hell? What were European-cut jeans doing outside of nowheresville, PA?

He stood up, and she took in his thick, muscular thighs and noticeable height. Rose was a healthy 5'10" and always wore heels (it was a power thing). She guessed she still wouldn't quite meet his eyes if he stood next to her.

He flipped his helmet off and tossed back his dark hair.

Holy. Fuck.

His storm-green eyes pierced her from where he stood, and his square jaw was dotted with a shadow of stubble. Strands of his dark hair caught in the breeze, and she stupidly envied it for being able to run its fingers through his hair.

Had he walked off an Armani photoshoot, hopped on a vintage bike, and decided to come rescue her?

"Hi? Do you need help?" The smiling hot rider spoke loudly and waved at her, trying to get her attention.

Oh my god. I've been internal monologuing this whole time.

"Yes, sorry. I was...distracted." *And probably drooling.*

He hopped off the bike and removed a backpack. As he

swung it around, Rose realized there was a *dog* in his backpack. A small, floppy-eared hound mix sat patiently in the bag with goggles on.

A hot man on a bike.

With a dog.

Wearing goggles.

Rose wiped at her eyes to double-check she wasn't hallucinating.

The rider set the bag down, and the dog hopped out. "No, don't bother the cows. Go over there," he muttered to the dog.

Hot Biker Dog Dad grabbed the goggles from the dog's head and pointed at the opposite field.

Rose watched the dog hop the ditch. "Was he...was he wearing goggles?"

"Doggles, actually." The rider walked toward her. Delicate line tattoos ran the length of his hands and disappeared into the cuffs of his leather jacket.

She rolled her lips together and tried to stay focused.

He stopped in front of her and peered up with a charming smile. "That's a funny way to drive a car. What seems to be the problem?"

You're probably married?

"The car started smoking, so I pulled over. I couldn't get a cell signal to call for help."

He chuckled, and his eyes danced with laughter. She wanted to permanently take up residence in the moment when he looked at her like that.

"That *totally* explains why you're on the roof, then. Here." He raised his arms, his hands on either side of her knees.

"What are you doing?"

"You gonna drive your car from the roof?" He dropped his arms and cocked his hip to one side, smiling at her. Rose felt her cheeks flush, and goose bumps slide along the back of her neck at his smile.

"I can get down on my own, thank you."

Probably.

He bit his lower lip, and she swore she saw the faint glimmer of a laugh as his eyebrows raised.

Rose doubled down and shoved at her hair. "I can. I'm very strong; never miss a Pilates class." She was babbling, she knew, but she had to maintain control of the situation.

"Sit-ups or no sit-ups, four-inch spikes," he gestured to her heels, "and windshields don't mix. But please, show me how wrong I am." He crossed his arms and watched her with a smile.

She ran her tongue across her teeth and considered the dust-covered roof.

These are new jeans, damn.

Rose huffed out annoyance and bent down so her bottom hovered over the roof.

He angled an eyebrow, challenging her. "That a special Pilates move?"

Now she *really* wouldn't accept his help. She placed a hand down and planned to gracefully slide off the roof...

...but her heels had other plans.

Her feet slipped out from under her, and she launched herself from the roof *at* a 6'3" wall of muscle.

Her life flashed before her eyes, and sadly it was mostly a

montage of Zoom meetings of her saying, "*You're muted, Rob.*"

Until she felt a vise wrap around her hips.

Hot Biker Dog Dad *caught* her.

Rose peered down in shock and admiration into the sculpted face staring back up at her.

Those stormy eyes locked with hers, and her breath caught. He was in no hurry to put her down, apparently.

"I might suggest taking *off* the spikes next time."

His eyes roamed her face, and she could almost feel their caress against her cheek.

Her feet dangled in the air; her shoes had flown off in the slip and slide off the car.

Rose felt a solid wall of muscle pressing against her stomach and was pretty sure one of his hands was perched on her ass.

"Sorry for almost killing you," she said softly. Her eyes had locked themselves on his lips. Why couldn't she take in a proper breath?

He slowly — painfully, excruciatingly slowly — slid her down his body. She felt every ripple in his chest, then abs, and *phew*, thighs.

The stranger gently lowered her to the ground. He held her in his arms, pressed close to him.

He smelled like pine and leather, and... was that lavender?

The heat of his arms radiated through Rose, and she was sad to leave them when he stepped back.

A ghost of a smile played across his lips as he bent down, grabbing one of her shoes and holding it out for her.

A gorgeous man was on bended knee in front of her, holding a thousand-dollar pink heel out like a roadside Prince Charming.

For the first time in her life, Rose Parker became tongue-tied.

He slipped her shoe on and held her hand so she could balance as she slipped on the other.

He held onto her hand as he stood but let go after a second. "Do I get to know your name since you almost pancaked me?"

"I'm Rose..."

Wait, don't give him your real name. The hot ones are always murderers. Even if they do buy doggles.

"Ah...bertha," she finished lamely.

A grin appeared as he dusted off his knees. "Roseabertha?" He snorted as he walked to the hood of her car. "That's an awful fake name."

He nodded to the hood. "Let me take a look. I'm Gray, by the way. The 'bertha' in my name is silent."

He reached out a hand for her to shake, and she grasped it firmly, meeting his eyes briefly. Rose swallowed a smile, feeling utterly thrown off her game.

It was probably the jet lag, right?

"Are you a mechanic, Gray?"

He peered over the engine of the car. "Nope, but I've kept that hunk of rust over there working." He opened a gasket cap, looked in, and replaced it. "Why didn't your boyfriend check this for you before you left?" He peered up at her with a smoldering smile.

An actual smile that was fucking smoldering.

Tingles flooded her body. *Down girl. You do not have time for whatever distraction this might be.*

She wasn't dead, though. She could still flirt.

"No boyfriend." She sent him what she hoped was a sultry smile. "And this is a rental. I'm just visiting. Can you imagine *living* in Fairwick Falls?" She sent him a conspiratorial laugh. With designer clothes and that handsome face, he had to be passing through too.

Rose sent him a mischievous look, but she was met with icy silence as his eyes narrowed back at her, the smile falling from his face.

Ah, shit.

Chapter Two

GRAY

Gray Roberts stared at the stunning brunette who had gripped him by the balls since he first laid eyes on her.

Her killer smile had knocked him sideways when he'd hopped off his bike. Long chestnut hair fell in graceful layers and framed her heart-shaped face. She was tall and leggy with curves that he wanted to linger on.

He'd have given his next three-acre crop of dahlias to press her up against the car and steal that smug look on her face right now with his lips. Run his hands against her hips, her ass.

But as her mocking words rang in his head, he thought maybe this goddess of perfection might not be so perfect after all.

Gray crossed his arms and considered her. He leaned

against the car, less willing to help now. "What's wrong with Fairwick Falls, Bertha?"

Her mouth set into a smirk, chin jutted out in defiance. "Too many things to name? It's nothing but mindless farmers, one stop light, and a barren wasteland of taste."

"Barren wasteland?" *Snob.* He put his hands in his pockets and sent her a sharp glare.

He'd only lived in Fairwick Falls for a few years but adored the quirky little town tucked into the countryside. They'd taken him in, no questions asked, after he came out of rehab licking his wounds.

He pushed off the car, done with her game. "I'd rather be a mindless farmer than a know-it-all snob who thinks she's too good for everyone else." He glared at her and walked to his bike.

She clenched her jaw, but panic glinted in her eyes.

He ambled over to his bike and called back over his shoulder. "Your engine needs water. Too bad I'm just a mindless farmer, or I'd remember I have some extra water with me."

"Wait. I'm," she paused, gulping.

He turned to see her mouth turn down in disgust.

She closed her eyes and opened them slowly, chewing out the words. "...sorry. For what I said."

"Was that physically painful for you? Cause it looked like it."

"...No," she said, clearly lying.

He paused, weighing his actions. Damnit, he couldn't leave her out here even if she was a snob. He walked back to the car with a large bottle of water.

"This should get you to town. Maybe you can find two yokels and explain what a horseless carriage is so they can fix your radiator leak, snob." He dumped water into the reservoir.

"I can't be a snob. I grew up here."

"You sure can. Case in point, look in the mirror."

"Just because I made something of myself?"

"No, sweet cheeks, you bought things and put them on yourself. There's a difference." He nodded to her shoes.

"These are adorable, thank you very much." Acid hit on her every word.

Let's have some fun. "Sure, for something that was three seasons ago."

He held in a laugh, biting his lip at her indignant yelp.

"These are not three—you know what? I'm not arguing fashion with someone who was given a haircut with garden shears."

He let the car hood slam down and stalked toward her. "Don't pretend you didn't rake me up and down with those big caramel eyes and practically drool into a puddle when I hopped off my bike. I know your type."

"Too good for you?" she scoffed, crossed her arms, and stepped closer to him.

"You're so high and mighty, but you want some big strong man to come and take charge." He stepped closer to her, contempt in his tone, but his heart thrummed a million miles an hour.

"Oh, yes," she huffed. "I definitely dream," she waved her hand in front of him, "of slumming it with a farmer from the middle of *fucking nowhere* with his big, strong man hands and his tiny little man brain."

Gray saw red at the corners of his eyes. He had a few raw nerves left after years of therapy, but she managed to hit every single one.

He took a step towards her, now nose to nose with her. "Slumming it, ice princess?"

"Princess?" She yanked back as if she'd been slapped.

"Yeah, you're an ice princess." A slow smile spread on his face. He'd found her raw nerve in return. "You think you're so sexy, but there's just a cold, shriveled heart inside that doesn't give a shit about anyone else." He backed her up to the car, boxing her in.

Her eyes narrowed at him with hatred. "You think you know me because I wear designer shoes? Because I left this redneck cow-filled county and experienced the world? That makes me a heartless, dried-up old shrew?"

"If the Louboutins fit, my friend." He sucked in a breath and tried not to stare at her full lips, covered in some gloss that made him want to run his mouth over hers.

He fucking hated that he wanted nothing more than to take her pouting mouth with his.

She turned so fast that her hair flipped into his face, a cloud of apple blossom and vanilla wafting around him. He shoved his hands in his pockets to keep himself from yanking her back so he could pin her to the car.

"You're welcome, by the way," he yelled as she stalked to the driver-side door.

"We'll see if it starts. I sincerely doubt someone who's

happy here has the computational brain power to fix a car engine."

Her cheeks were flushed, her eyes bright with fire. She vibrated with crackling energy, and he hated that he found her even hotter. If the crazy woman on the car roof was gorgeous, she was nothing to this fire goddess in front of him.

"Oh, and please." She shot a molten look over her shoulder. "Go to hell." She slammed the door behind her.

"Don't worry, princess, I've already been there," Gray muttered.

She attempted to turn the car on, but it only made a whirring sound. She sent him a victorious "I knew you couldn't fix it" laugh, but then the engine roared to life. He saw the self-satisfied look drain from her face, and a laugh bubbled out of him.

Her eyes shot daggers at him as she ripped the seatbelt from the holder and buckled it with fury. He half expected her to peel out with a middle-finger salute.

Just to fuck with her, Gray motioned for her to roll her window down. She huffed at him but rolled it down an inch.

"Sure you don't want my number, princess? Mindless farmers are the best at melting ice off you in the sack."

He sent her a wink and an air kiss. Her jaw fell open in outrage.

He hadn't been this delighted in a long time.

She slammed on the gas and left him standing in the dust, bent over with laughter. He walked to grab Duke, who was sniffing a tree.

If Gray was lucky, that would be the last time he saw the most irritatingly beautiful woman in Fairwick Falls.

GRAY PULLED his bike into Canon's Diner and killed the engine. The diner, a Fairwick Falls institution, sat on the corner of the town square, looking out onto the gazebo and nestled between the hardware store and the Maroo Law Office.

He'd planned to treat himself to a full breakfast and pancake stack for his four-year sober anniversary before running into the gorgeous hellcat on the road earlier. Nothing said celebration better than Pop Canon's apple pie pancakes.

In college, Gray had discovered a knack for fashion photography. It led him to beautiful places and even stronger drugs until the unthinkable happened in front of him. Sobriety had been hard fought at first, but he'd settled in by throwing himself into work. He walked a thin fucking line between boredom and exhaustion every single day.

He let Duke down from his backpack, and as they walked to the diner, Gray thought about all the projects he had in the hopper. The flower farm was doing well. He could plan more expansions, but he should wait until the deal with Frank, well, Frank's family, went through.

His mentor, Frank, had been the first person to welcome him to Fairwick Falls. He'd helped Gray turn his grandparents' ramshackle hobby farm into a profitable floral business.

Gray's heart still felt heavy at the unexpected loss of his

friend. He and Frank had always celebrated his sober anniversary at the diner with the most disgustingly sweet thing on the menu. Gray's eyes pricked with emotion at the thought of doing it without him this year.

Just outside the diner's door, Gray's phone buzzed. Seeing the screen, he took a deep breath to steady himself before he answered.

Maybe she remembered the anniversary this year?

"Hi, Mom."

"Sweetie, do you want pork chops or spaghetti for our monthly dinner?"

A deep sigh hit Gray. How was it comforting to know he wouldn't be comforted? To *know* in his bones that he'd be disappointed?

"Either's fine, Mom."

His parents only lived two towns over, but sometimes even that felt too close. His father still resented Gray for his addiction, and his mom was trapped in the middle.

"Let me know if you change your mind. What are you up to today?"

"I'm just..." Should he remind her that it was an important day? *Nah.* "Just heading into Canon's for some apple pie pancakes."

"On a random Tuesday?" His mom sounded distracted, chattering to someone that passed by her in the grocery store.

A bone-deep sigh escaped his lips. He had to accept that he couldn't change her. Had to depend on himself for everything. Including celebration.

"Yep...just felt like pancakes. Look, Mom, I've gotta go."

"Okay, sweetie," his mom chirped in her sing-song voice. The phone went silent before he could respond.

Gray closed his eyes and took a breath. There was comfort in having your hopes constantly dashed. At least his parents were predictable.

"C'mon. Let's get some lunch," he called to Duke. Pop Canon, the geriatric diner owner, had a soft spot for Duke's hound dog eyes and insisted Duke come in to get his own pup-sized plain hamburger.

Gray and Duke walked in, and the clatter and conversation hit him like a wave of warmth. Canon's was a small, cozy, casual diner with buttercream walls covered in soccer team photos and had vintage 1960s tables tucked close together, each with a small votive of fresh flowers.

He spotted Nash already in a big booth, and Gray waved to a few friends as he strolled over. Gray clocked Nash's three-piece suit that stuck out like a sore thumb in the humble, cozy diner. Duke settled down by Nash's feet and promptly fell asleep.

"Lord Donnelly." Gray bowed as he slid into the booth. "You didn't have to get all dressed up for us peasants." Giving his friend shit was one of the few pastimes Gray still had time for.

Nash shook his head even as he grinned back at Gray. "Some of us have office jobs. We can't all be as lucky as you."

Nash had been a trader on Wall Street but moved back two years ago to step in as CEO of his family's bank. He also took over the title of Fairwick Falls' most eligible bachelor, much to Gray's relief.

"What's this?" Gray flicked a small paper bag in front of Nash.

"Happy four years of sobriety. Have some carbs." Nash shoved the bag toward him.

Gray opened it to see a pile of Fox & Forrest Cafe's famous cinnamon donut holes. His eyes went wide at the powdered sugar heaven.

"I thought they only made these in the fall." Gray popped two into his mouth and closed his eyes, savoring the melt-in-his-mouth goodness.

Fuck yes—this was like Christmas morning, but better.

"Aaron and Nick wanted to do something special for you. I'm just the messenger." Nash pointed at someone behind Gray.

Pop, who rarely left the kitchen, hobbled toward their table with a plate of caramel pancakes topped with lit candles.

"This one was Pop's idea, but I get credit for the candles." Nash sent Gray a shit-eating grin.

Pop slid a big plate of pancakes with four lit birthday candles in front of Gray. "Happy whatever, kid," Pop hit Gray on the arm and sent him a sly wink before scooting a small plain hamburger on a napkin under the table.

Gray felt an equal mixture of embarrassment and gratitude. *Is this what family is supposed to feel like?*

"Candles? C'mon, man. I'm not a teenage girl, and it's not my birthday."

Nash stared back at him with an open-mouthed grin. "Now, now. I worked very hard on those two-dollar candles. Blow 'em out, Roberts."

Gray rolled his eyes in embarrassment, but smiling, expectant faces stared at him around the diner.

God, he loved this town.

"Jesus, fine." Gray blew the candles out and heard a smattering of claps. He narrowed his eyes at Nash, who chuckled into his coffee.

"You're the worst." Gray tucked into the gooey pancakes.

"Stop it, or I'll blush. Oh..." Nash pulled out a folder. "Before I forget. Here's the hard copy of the loan approvals. Congrats."

Gray grabbed the thick folder full of headache-inducing paperwork. "You're at least gonna pay for breakfast since I owe your bank eighty grand, right?"

Nash snorted as he speared a piece of bacon. "I'll pay when you beat me in a one-on-one game."

Gray leaned back, taking a break from shoveling pancakes in his face. "Can't. My schedule is crazy this week. We have a new planting of dahlias going in, and I meet with the head of product for Bailey's Home Improvements soon. Trying to get my stuff in all their stores."

Nash's eyebrows shot up, and he nodded with approval. "Wow, those guys are a national chain, right?"

"Regional, but it's a start." Gray rubbed his eyes. Pop didn't have enough coffee in this entire building to combat how tired Gray felt in his bones.

"You guys are expanding like crazy. I don't remember when you weren't." Nash's face was neutral, measuring Gray.

Gray was ultra-aware when someone was trying to babysit him. He needed to be self-sufficient, no matter how well-meaning his friends and family were. He shrugged and stabbed a pancake. "Work keeps me grounded."

"You'd tell me if you ever needed my help, right?" Nash said suddenly.

"Why would I need Lord Donnelly's help?" Gray's eyes playfully narrowed.

"Gray cut the bullshit. Work isn't everything. You don't have to prove anything anymore, you know? Live a little. You work more than anyone I know."

Gray gazed into his coffee, not wanting to get into it.

"You okay?" Nash's face now plainly displayed his worry.

Gray busied himself, wiping dirt off his jeans so he didn't show the emotions clutching at his throat. He nodded and finally met Nash's eyes.

"Yeah, I'm okay. Thanks for checking." His skin crawled even admitting that much to his closest friend.

He desperately needed to change the topic away from himself. "Speaking of bullshit, you'll never guess what happened to me on the drive into town."

"Rosie Parker," Nash yelled to someone behind Gray. Nash was already out of the booth and headed to the door as Gray glanced up.

Gray turned to see who it was, and his stomach fell as he clocked the man-eating ice princess wrapped around Nash.

Chapter Three

ROSE

Rose threw her arms around her childhood best friend as he lifted her off the ground. She squeezed her eyes closed, savoring a bright spot in what would otherwise be a pain-in-the-ass trip home.

Nash set her down, and Rose took in the restaurant.

Her eyes landed on a recently framed picture of her father. It was clearly a memorial to one of Canon's most loyal customers. She ignored the lurch in her stomach.

The place hadn't changed a bit. Her eyes scanned the restaurant but came to a screeching halt when she locked eyes with a familiar sneering glare.

What the hell?

Nash sent Lily and Violet friendly waves and gestured to the booth with the brooding asshole. "C'mon, sit with us. Let's catch up."

"No, that's okay." Rose ripped her gaze away from the

asshole and smiled back at Nash. She'd missed her childhood best friend, but it was impossible not to see Gray's steely glare shooting back at her.

Talking to him again would be a disaster.

Get out, get out, get out. "We don't want to interrupt. Maybe we should leave. We have a lot to do."

"Come on, Rose," Lily said. "It's rude to refuse an invitation." Lily smiled up at Nash and couldn't take her eyes off him. *Interesting.*

"Oh my god." Gray rubbed a hand over his face. "Just sit somewhere."

Don't get distracted. Don't engage with the asshole.

Rose narrowed her eyes at him but tried to keep her anger in check. "We have a big list of things to do today, and we're just getting coffee and pancakes to go." When Rose finally got to Vi's cottage, both sisters were three mimosas deep and wailing to karaoke. She needed to get some caffeine and carbs in them so they could start on her GTFOOFF List.

"Come on, Rose. Plans don't have to be set in stone." Violet nudged her arm with a happy, buzzed smile.

"It's officially three against one." Nash took Rose by the arm and led her to the deep booth. Violet and Lily slid in next to Gray, and Rose slid in next to Nash.

"Hey Vi, hey Lily." Gray sent them friendly nods. "Rosa Bertha, we meet again." He glared back at Rose with a sizzling, challenging look in his eyes.

"Rosa what? Wait, you know each other?" Nash pointed a finger between them.

"No," Rose said as Gray said, "Yes."

A beat hung in the air as Gray crooked an eyebrow at her.

"Go ahead, Bertha." Gray nodded his head in deference.

Rose took a deep breath and felt the anger rise inside her chest. "We met briefly earlier today."

Lily gasped. "Gray's the hot asshole?"

"Lily!" Violet smacked her arm.

"What? That's what she called him."

Rose kicked Lily underneath the table, and Gray let out a snort of derision.

"How did I end up with such violent sisters," Lily muttered, rubbing her shin.

"Wait a minute." Gray's face changed. "You're Frank's oldest?" Gray's eyebrows came together with concern.

"The Bertha is silent in my name, too," Rose drawled.

He scrubbed a hand over his face. "Ah, fuck. I'm sorry about your dad. I was out of town for a few weeks when everything happened. I hated missing the funeral. He was the best."

Gray's earnest look only made Rose madder. "Let's not talk about my father." Her ice shield was back in full force.

Gray let her sentence hang in the air, sending her a wary look.

God, stop sounding so shrill, Rose. Not everyone needs to know your shit.

He continued. "I know Vi a little bit from around town and met Lily because she's hard to miss. Weren't you upside down when I first met you?"

"I like to do yoga in the middle of the park." Lily shrugged and hiccuped.

"Sorry, I didn't catch that you all were sisters." Gray's

eyes moved to each of them as if trying to find the through line.

That wasn't his fault; they looked utterly mismatched. Violet had riotous auburn curly hair and curves for days. Lily was short with long honey-blonde waves, whereas Rose favored her mother, who'd been tall and lanky.

Nash stretched his arm behind Rose. "What brings you into town?"

Rose caught a flash of heat in Gray's eyes at the motion. It was innocent enough; she'd known Nash her whole life. They'd been childhood best friends, and there had never been any spark between them, even though Nash was a perfect fit for her on paper. And in all that perfection, she saw nothing that appealed to her.

Just for fun, though, let's screw with him.

"Well, I'm so excited to run into my oldest friend." Rose grabbed Nash's cheeks and smacked an innocent, friendly kiss on one side. She saw a muscle twitch in Gray's jaw.

Ha.

"But I'm here to deal with the will. Mrs. Maroo insisted the will reading be in person, and she kept rescheduling it for some reason. I had to move my flight twice."

"That would be" —Gray threw a hand up— "my fault."

"What?" Her head snapped around.

"I'm the reason we had to reschedule twice." Gray fiddled with a creamer on the table, never breaking eye contact in a challenging glint.

"Why are you sitting there with a little smirk talking about 'we' had to reschedule?" She hissed through her teeth.

"Mrs. Maroo said I had to be there too. Video

conference, phone call, talking to her later... nothing would do. I had to be there in person. And work kept getting in the way." Gray shrugged as he twirled the creamer in his hands. "Guess I'll see you there, ice princess."

"Stop calling me that." She yanked the creamer out of his hand.

Rose was baffled. The man sitting across from her was the complete opposite of her father. Why would a smoldering, tattooed farmer be at his will reading? Her dad had been lax and carefree, always looking like he was on the way to a Jimmy Buffett concert.

A dull ache thumped behind Rose's chest as she remembered her father sitting across from her in a booth just like this. Before she'd finally lost her temper after he missed Lily's tuition payment again, and all the horrible things she'd said to him spilled out of her.

"Hiya, kids." Margie, the ancient waitress at Canon's, popped over and interrupted the tension simmering in the booth.

Rose raised three fingers. "Coffees to go, please."

"Actually." Lily made a show of pulling up a menu. "We'll have the waffle combination. Extra waffles, extra gravy. Hold the sausage on mine."

"The hangover special?"

"We're still buzzed." Lily giggled with Margie.

"On it." She snapped up the menus from the waiting hands and zoomed toward the kitchen.

Anger threatened to boil over as Rose stared at the irritatingly hot pain in the ass across from her. He stuffed his face with pancakes and sent her a mischievous smirk as he chewed.

"So," Violet said sweetly, trying to cut the tension at the table, "how's work, Nash?"

Gray winked at Rose with a smirk, and she wanted to dunk his smug face in his pancakes.

Nash glanced from Gray to Rose. "Uh, it's—"

"Why do you have to be at the will reading for *our* father's will? Did you trick him into giving you all his Hawaiian shirts?"

Gray leaned forward, spite on every word. "All I know is I have to be there just like you do. Your dad was one of my best friends."

Rose glanced at Violet, who shrugged and nodded.

"Then why did you change the will reading twice, farmer?" Rose snapped.

He leaned back, a cool look on his face. "What's it to you, ice princess?"

"It's about five hundred dollars in flight changes, you Neanderthal. And I am no one's goddamn princess."

Lily and Violet bit back laughter, and Nash's eyes ping-ponged between Rose and Gray.

"Well, Rose." Gray leaned back, enjoying himself. "Sometimes, I can't spare even thirty minutes of daylight when planting a crop. I'm just a mindless farmer if you remember."

Gray reached for his pocket suddenly, pulling out his phone. "Fuck. I gotta take this. Duke, stay here," he called below the table. Lily and Violet scooted to let him out, and he walked out the diner door with a phone pressed to his ear.

Her father had a best friend who was twenty-five years younger than him, was that hot, and that annoying?

Figures.

Rose turned to Nash. "You have atrocious taste in friends."

Nash twirled his coffee cup around the table, trying to hide a smile. "Gray's all right. Seems like you got off on the wrong foot."

"Hopefully, I won't have to endure his presence beyond the will reading."

Three plates steaming with syrupy gravy goodness slid onto the table, and the ancient waitress toddled off as fast as someone half her age.

Rose's stomach turned at the thought of eating. She'd been up for almost twenty-four hours and already couldn't wait to get back where she belonged: the hell out of here.

GRAY

GRAY TRIED to follow the man on the phone, but he was driven to distraction. The thud in his chest hadn't stopped since Rose had walked through the diner door.

He'd been thinking about the glint of the sun on her hair as she walked in, backlit with sunbeams. The joy on her face had transformed the ice princess into something magical and radiant as she'd locked eyes with an unexpected friend.

Her smile could have powered the fucking room. He was desperate to see it aimed at himself.

He tried to keep his thoughts straight as he listened to Bill from Bailey's Home Improvement.

"I'd love for you to come in a week earlier."

"Uh..." Gray had lost track of the conversation.

Focus, Roberts. "Yeah, that should be fine to come in this week. Wait..." *Fuck. His trip to see Alex.*

"You have a problem rearranging your schedule to meet with us?" Bill's voice was stern.

Gray had been itching to move his business beyond mom-and-pop suppliers. Distributing throughout an entire regional chain would be the first step in proving he could handle a larger load, especially after his failure last year with that fucking lavender crop that nearly ruined him.

"Yeah, that's no problem. I'll move some things around."

He'd planned to fly to Montreal to visit his son, but he'd have to push it to the next weekend. This meeting was a once-in-a-life chance to take the next step for his business, the business he wanted to leave to Alex someday. His stomach churned at disappointing his little buddy, but he had to sacrifice for a better future.

"Great. Good to hear. See you then."

Gray hung up and sent off a flurry of text messages. Alex's mom wouldn't be happy he was moving his trip, but it wouldn't be the first time. He ran a growing business that required his full attention.

It was only Gray running the show; he had a part-time employee, but no one he felt like he could trust. He'd trusted Frank, and Frank had filled in for him when needed, but...

Emotion clutched at Gray's throat, thinking about how Frank had filled the void in his life as a best friend, father figure, and mentor. It had been a rough few months without him.

And that goddess inside had the nerve to ignore one of the best people he'd ever met. It had eaten Frank up inside that he'd fallen out with his oldest daughter.

Gray glanced at the diner door and thought about the viper pit that waited inside. And idiotically, he'd wanted to grab Nash by the throat when he put his arm around Rose.

Gray desperately wanted to be in her orbit even though she irritated the hell out of him. She locked him by the throat with those molten caramel eyes fanned out with lashes so long they should be illegal. She'd glared at him with undeniable fury, and Gray had found it so hot and so irritating at the same time.

A laugh burst out of him. How the fuck was that woman related to Frank Parker?

Gray threw open the door, and though the familiar wave of comfort washed over him, he could feel Rose's eyes roasting him. Lily got up to let him back in the booth.

"Don't get up. I'll just sit right here." He slid in next to Rose. He easily fit on the long bench seat but made sure to slam his body up next to hers. "There's plenty of room, right?"

Rose slowly turned her head to glare at him. "We were just finishing up."

Every syllable out of her mouth hit him like a blow to the cock.

"Looks like you haven't made a dent there, princess. Those LA influencers getting to you?" He picked up a piece of toast from her plate and chomped on it.

She grabbed the bread from his hand and threw it down. "We are not friends. I don't know who you think you're talking to." She threw fifty bucks on the table and shoved him to move out of the booth. "But we're done. I have a long to-do list, and you're in my way."

He stood but crowded her as she got up. "I'm not on your to-do list, princess?" Gray smiled back at her, the innuendo flying like a checkered flag between them. *Game on.*

She leaned in close. His breath caught, and his entire body stiffened in surprise. He felt her hot breath whisper against his skin.

Her lip brushed his ear as she spoke low. "You will never, ever, under any circumstance, be lucky enough to be inside my to-do list." She turned on her heel and glided out the door.

A searing heat spread through his body. *That woman will be my downfall.*

The will reading couldn't come soon enough.

ROSE

Rose threw open the door of Canon's and waltzed out of the diner. She hoped Gray's jaw was still on the floor.

Rose pulled up her long To-Do List and clicked away on her heels toward her first stop.

"Holy shitballs." Lily laughed as she jogged out of the diner.

Rose desperately wanted to change the subject away from Gray. No need to think about him or their irritating conversation that still had her blood boiling.

"Have you guys been to the shop yet?" Rose charged down the sidewalk.

Lily yanked her to a stop. "Uh, first we're gonna talk about whatever that was." She threw a thumb back toward the diner.

Violet caught up with them. "How did you manage to piss off the nicest guy in town?"

"Nicest?" Rose shook her head to clear it. "Are you shitting me? That man is a menace."

"Gray is the best." Violet sent Rose a smile. "He's seriously so nice. You should've seen him at the Food Bank's Valentine's Date fundraiser. I thought one woman was going to swoon with how sweet he was with all the older ladies."

Gray was the town's heartthrob? What planet were they on? "We have a lot to do today." Rose shook her phone at them. "Gray is a bump in the road that I don't have time to think about. He'll be at the will reading, hear about whatever trinket Dad left him, then be gone forever."

Violet shrugged. "I don't know. He and Dad were close."

Rose snorted as she lowered her head to her phone and swiped through her never-ending list of tasks.

"They could have dated for all I care. I just need us to get through my 'Get the Fuck out of Fairwick Falls' list as soon as possible."

Lily shook Rose's arm to get her attention. "But you said we'd hang today. My nails desperately need sparkles on them." Her lip puffed out in a tortured pout.

Shit. That pout was Rose's kryptonite.

"We'll do nails later. I want to see Dad's shop. We have to decide what to do with it while I'm here."

"Okay, but we get thirty minutes of no list time." Violet held her hand out.

Rose rolled her eyes to the heavens and dropped her phone into Violet's hand. "Ugh, fine."

They started toward their father's flower shop on the other side of the square.

Having no distractions, Rose took in the greenery of the town square with surprise. Fairwick Falls had grown so much in the ten years she'd been gone. It was now, dare she say, adorable.

The town square was a patchwork of blooming grass and sidewalks. Early spring flowers showed bits of purple and pink as they fought to bloom in the early March chill. A new white gazebo sat in the middle of the town square lawn, and a young family sat in it, blowing bubbles. The soft glow of the early afternoon sun spilled over the building tops, illuminating the quaint little shops lining each side of the paved streets. Buildings that had been empty when she was a kid now had cheerful storefronts.

It was all very Instagrammable.

"How's the shop?" Rose asked as if seeing her hometown for the first time.

"Lil and I haven't gotten up the courage to go in yet since...." Violet bit her lip with worry. "Well, since."

Lily had been in Fairwick Falls for a few weeks helping Violet sort through the junkyard that was their father's house. Lily was a freelance designer based in Brooklyn and worked wherever suited her mood.

Violet had opted to stay in Fairwick Falls after college and was close with their father. His death had hit her the hardest. She was a landscape designer and supported their father's flower shop with her small greenhouse.

Rose thought about the business that might be piling up. It had been three months since the funeral.

"I guess the shop never did brisk business, and everyone's aware that he...that the shop is closed." Rose cleared her throat.

They stopped on the sidewalk, looking up at the flower shop sign. No one wanted to walk in first.

Bluhm's Flowers had been a Fairwick Falls institution for over a century. Their great-great-grandparents started the shop in the late 1800s, eventually passing to their mom and dad.

The building faced the town square, a prime location for foot traffic, and was nestled between the Fox & Forrest Cafe and a bookstore. The tall three-story building still had the original large display windows with ornately carved trim.

Piles of leaves and dirt collected at the front entrance. The dingy windows looked like they hadn't been cleaned in years, and Rose felt a tickle of dread in her stomach.

Lily pulled her coat tighter around her to stave off the chill of the early-March wind. "I don't have a good feeling about this."

The brisk wind whipped at Rose's legs, and she bit the bullet. She held out her hand to Violet for the key. "Now or never, ladies."

"Just so you know, it's not great." Violet's eyes were lined with worry.

The black front door was covered in cobwebs, but the original hand-carved flowers around the door handle were still there.

It's dirty but gets a 10/10 for potential.

"We can always sell or lease the building, right?" Rose stuck the key in the rickety, rusty lock.

She turned the antique key and shoved at the door. The shades had been drawn down over the windows, and they filed into the dusty, dark showroom.

Rose flipped on the single gray light, and a wave of moldy stench hit her.

"Jesus Christ," Lily said. "He didn't die in here, did he?"

"Lily..." Rose elbowed her.

Lily covered her nose. "What? It smells terrible."

"It's just the old building smell." Violet rolled her eyes at them.

"And the fact that he never cleaned, and there's water damage somewhere," Rose muttered.

The three of them stood in the entryway of the barren store, jaws hanging open. The bones of the store were the same as Rose remembered, but it was so, so much worse.

The walls were painted a floor-to-ceiling kelly green, and the windows were covered in a heavy layer of dust. Display cases blocked the light from the windows and held dusty, out-of-fashion ceramic figurines and fake flowers.

Wilted flowers sat in small glass vases, waiting to be given a home in the nearly empty coolers. A thick layer of dust sat on the old balloons and cards next to the register.

The shop was, to put it bluntly, pitiful.

Rose's mind raced. No sane person would come in and think business was going well. How had he let it get like this? Did he even have customers? They were the only flower shop in town, so people *had* to come here, right?

The high ceiling was covered in a thick layer of grime that obscured the original turn-of-the-century ornate tin tiles.

Rose's heels echoed on the old, worn wooden floor that was gorgeous but in desperate need of some TLC.

As Rose walked through the showroom, a wave of nostalgia hit her. She'd practically grown up here, playing in the back room while her father ran the store. She ran a finger over an empty display table, and a pile of dust collected on her finger.

"We can't sell or even lease it in this condition. We'd hardly make any money."

Violet shrugged at Rose. "A building across the street sold for about $200,000 last month, but it was in good shape."

"Have you been up there?" Rose jutted her chin to the loft overlooking the store. It was a cute little space that overlooked the store with a spiral staircase coming down from it.

"Not in a long time," Violet said. "He never wanted me to meet him here."

"I guess, maybe...maybe he was embarrassed." Lily's eyes welled up. "Just think of him all by himself in this moldy, old place." A tear spilled over and down her face.

Violet wrapped her arm around Lily's shoulder. "No wonder he was always out visiting other people. He didn't want to stay here."

Rose had to ignore the emotions bubbling inside of her. If she broke down now, she might not recover. She wandered to the original marble and wood checkout counter that had been there since the store opened.

"I wonder if he even had any customers." It was safer and easier to focus on business, not the complicated emotions running through her.

"Violet, would you mind taking stock of the plant situation in the back? Lily, can you go to the third-floor apartment and see what we're working with?" Rose had to take control of the situation. It made her feel safe to be in command and make progress even in the worst of times.

"On it, boss." Lily sent her a salute. Violet nodded and wordlessly went to the back prep room.

Lights blinked on the old answering machine, and Rose hit play. A handful of messages were condolences, but the rest were people placing orders for upcoming holidays or calling about store information. Her dad never had a website, and Google didn't know the business existed.

A thought tickled at the back of Rose's head. The shop still had tiny bits of income because there weren't any other flower shops in town, despite the showroom looking like a horror movie.

Rose had always wanted to redesign the store when she was a kid. She could see a better way to do things, but he wouldn't listen to her. Couldn't seem to care they were barely hanging on.

Her dad had wanted to keep things the way they'd been when her mom was still alive. Even in elementary school, she could see they were losing business and Rose hated her father for it.

Lily clomped down the tight spiral staircase.

"Third-floor apartment is fine. Lots of spare boxes, but otherwise empty."

Violet rounded the corner from the back. "The prep room needs a little love and a lot of cleaning, but it's serviceable. A few dead plants are in the back coolers, but it's bare. He didn't have backstock."

Their father had died in his sleep unexpectedly, but Rose wondered how much of this was his original plan, to let the business dwindle down to nothing.

"We'll have to figure out what to do with it. Lease it, sell it, blow it up, start all over; something." Rose slapped her hands together to wipe off the dust.

Violet wiped the tears from the corners of her eyes and re-tied her mound of curly hair into a top knot ponytail. "Does your to-do list include lattes?" Violet handed the phone back over to Rose.

There were dark circles under Violet's eyes, and Lily wiped her tears with the back of her hand.

This was enough for today.

Sometimes Rose forgot other people hadn't mastered the art of shoving down their emotions as well as she had.

"I would give my right heel for a good latte." Rose smiled at her sisters. "We can take the rest of the day off. The list can wait until tomorrow."

Just this once.

Laughter danced in Lily's eyes. "Do you think your list will be able to stand the heat between you and Gray tomorrow? Or will it burst into flames from all that hottie hot tension?"

"Oh no," Rose countered, "if you're teasing me about that fool, then we're definitely talking about whatever that was between you and Nash."

Violet mouthed a big "I know, right?" behind Lily's back and Rose swallowed a smile.

Lily spun between them, eyes narrowed. "Oh, stop that, you two. He barely knows I exist."

"Want to try Fox & Forrest?" Violet asked. Violet's best friend, Aaron, had opened a new adorable cafe next door, and Rose had been itching to try it.

"Sure, I'll meet you guys there. Just going to finish up here."

This would be the perfect moment to record a short message to her podcast followers so she could control the narrative about her career. She'd let her listeners know she'd decided to take some time to reconnect with her roots. It wasn't lying if she omitted part of the truth, right? Publicly admitting her failure could crumble the reputation she'd built.

Violet and Lily walked out and shut the large front door behind them.

A haunting silence rang out in the old, stalwart building. An infuriating sob clawed at the back of her throat, but no. *We don't have time for that.*

Rose let her eyes wander over the space. It had potential. It had *always* had potential. The back room had plenty of storage space, and whoever bought the building could probably host events.

She was jealous of the person who'd buy it from them. Rose loved making something out of nothing. She loved counseling her clients on creating a new line of business to solve their customer needs. Despite what her former employer thought, she'd even been pretty good at it.

As for what to do with this place? She was the big sister. Always in charge, always had to have a plan. She'd think of something.

She opened her camera, wiped the exhaustion from her

face, and pressed the record button to tell her followers she was taking a trendy break, ignoring the breaking of her heart.

A THRUM VIBRATED through Rose's thighs as she gripped thick motorcycle handles. Wind whipped around her, tossing her hair over her shoulder as it snaked down and caressed her back.

She drove over the open road, or was she flying? A throb was insistent between her legs, and she ground her hips into the seat to relieve the pressure in her aching clit.

"You want me, don't you, princess?" A rich, velvet voice whispered in her ear.

She looked down, and the bike had transformed into Gray underneath her. She straddled him as he vibrated under her. He was shirtless, and his muscles rippled as he gripped her ass, guiding her up and down as she rode him. "Put your hands above me, princess; I want to see you over me."

Yes. She wanted him so badly.

She gripped the low headboard above him, her back arching over him. A wicked grin transformed his face, and he sucked on her nipple.

"You like it when I'm in charge, don't you?"

She wanted to say no. She wanted anything but what she felt. A pulse of need for him inside her. A guttural moan ripped out of her as her pussy came around his cock. "Yes, Gray, yes."

Rose shot up with a start in the guest bed of Violet's cottage and slapped her hand over her mouth.

She'd woken herself up *by moaning* from a fucking *sex dream*. After returning from the flower shop, she'd laid down for a quick nap, but it had accidentally turned X-rated.

She caught her breath; hopefully, Lily or Violet hadn't heard her moan his name. *How mortifying.*

She lay back down. *Honestly, Rose. A sex dream with the most annoying man you've ever met.*

Okay, the hottest and most annoying.

She punched her pillow, reforming it and getting out her aggression at his smirking face that now literally haunted her dreams. She closed her eyes and willed herself back to sleep.

The throbbing between her legs pulsed as a flash from her dream appeared. *No, no, no. We are not going to fantasize about him.*

A picture of him staring up at her from the roadside lodged in her mind, his smile broad and happy. His eyes danced with amusement, and he looked fucking delectable.

Shivers started at the base of her spine and spread through her. Those fucking tattoos. On that body.

Her pussy still throbbed.

She wasn't going to get any sleep in this state. She huffed out an annoyed sigh.

Fine, just this one time. But this cannot be a habit.

Rose slid her fingers down to her panties, and of course, they were already so wet. Was it possible to angrily masturbate? She was so pissed. Pissed that he'd invaded her dreams and made her want him even more with that smirky mouth of his.

This is my fantasy, so I'm in charge. She pictured Gray shirtless and sweaty from working outside, with drops of moisture gathered along his shoulders and abs. She imagined what tattoos he might have across his chest, and she'd kiss his broad expanse of muscle, breathing in that intoxicating scent she caught today. It had to be pheromones, her attraction to him. It would explain why she wanted to bury her face in him and huff like he was oxygen.

He'd take her mouth firmly, pulling on her hair to expose her neck and nip and suck his way down to her breasts.

Then he'd haul her over his shoulder, and suddenly she'd be under him in his bed. His cock would be rock hard against her, and he'd rip down her blouse, exposing her breasts, tonguing a nipple as she watched.

"You like to watch me, don't you, princess?" She sucked in a breath at the nickname she wanted to hate, but her pussy clenched as she thought of him whispering it in her ear.

Her fingers rubbed a lazy circle around her clit as she pictured his head traveling down her body and shoving her legs apart. He'd take that wicked mouth and run it along her pussy, teasing her with his tongue.

Rose rubbed faster, imagining his thick head of hair between her thighs, scraping his rough stubble along her pussy. He'd pin her down with both arms, so she had to take what he gave her as she climaxed again and again.

She circled her clit back and forth, imagining his mouth sucking on it as he buried his face in her.

Rose felt the curl of need hit the base of her spine as she came hard against her hand with a muffled groan into her pillow. She caught her breath, and goose bumps cascaded down her body again.

Okay, Parker, fantasy over. From here on out, he was an annoying asshole only.

Chapter Five

GRAY

The next morning, Gray leaned against his bike outside Mrs. Maroo's law office. The sunshine warmed his shoulders, and birds chirped in the cheerful, blooming spring trees.

Gray wished he was anywhere else on the fucking planet.

He swallowed hard, suppressing the lump in his throat. Frank had been the nearest thing to a supportive dad that Gray had ever known. His father had always expected him to be more, do more. Frank accepted him for who he was and understood everyone fights their own battles.

The whole thing was worse since he'd have to see the prickly, know-it-all she-demon he'd met yesterday.

Speak of the ice princess. He saw the familiar old BMW rattle into a parking spot.

Frank's three girls got out, looking like a bouquet of mismatched flowers. Lily had on a cropped, flowing top and flowery bell-bottom pants. Violet wore her landscaping company polo shirt and work khakis.

His eyes lingered on the third, most annoying one. He tried to convince his dick to pay less attention to Rose's long legs and fantastic ass. She was a vision in tight black jeans, a designer coat, and a blouse that fit so perfectly that he had to force his eyes up from staring at her breasts like a creep.

Christ, he was going to a will reading of his close friend, and he coaxed every nerve in his body to remember that.

She glared at him from behind her sunglasses as she slammed the car door shut. He could feel her projected wall of "fuck you" from where he stood.

Time to get this shit over with. He ambled to the front door and held it open for them.

Lily walked through. "Thanks, Gray." Violet kept her eyes downcast and sent him a shy smile.

He waved Rose through. "After you—"

She stuck out a finger at him. "Don't you fucking dare," she hissed through her teeth and stalked through.

"What? I was gonna say Rose." He sent her an innocent shrug. "Or do you prefer Bertha?"

She glared over her shoulder, and he chuckled as he meandered in behind her.

The old wooden floor creaked as they walked through the cozy cottage that had been converted into law offices. Frank's lawyer, Mrs. Maroo, stood in the back hallway waiting for them.

Mrs. Maroo, the unofficial grandma of Fairwick Falls, was one hundred pounds soaking wet, had white, tightly curled hair close to her head, and left a cloud of perfume wherever she went. She was one of the spitfires that kept Fairwick Falls running.

Gray fucking adored her.

She waved them into her doily-laden law office. "In you go, my dears." She sent Gray a wink from behind enormous rhinestone glasses. "Hiya, handsome."

He'd gotten roped into a charity date auction for the local food bank, and Mrs. Maroo had been vicious in her battle to win him. He'd taken her out to her requested evening of a biker bar and tequila shots—though his were just Sprite—and they'd been good friends ever since.

Gray sent her a winning smile as he leaned down for a quick hug. "How am I going to keep my head on straight with all those sparkles you've got on?"

Mrs. Maroo shimmied her shoulders and sent beams of light around the cottage from her sequined jacket. "You just keep your eyes on those pretty ladies in there, young man." She swatted him into her office.

Gray couldn't take his eyes off Rose in the small office, which only irritated him more. She stared straight ahead, ignoring him. Gray needed to bury his growing attraction to her. He'd never been so drawn to someone he needed to forget so much.

Mrs. Maroo closed the door and power-walked to her desk. "Let's get down to business, shall we? I'm sorry to see you all here, but know that Frank always planned ahead."

Mrs. Maroo adjusted her rhinestone glasses and straightened her back. "Frank had an unconventional request, which is why I wanted you here in person. I'm sure you've heard of an executor of a will? The person who handles someone's affairs to close out their estate?"

All four of them nodded back.

"Frank named two executors. Unusual but not unheard of. Just like Frank." Mrs. Maroo's eyes went misty, but she blinked the tears back quickly.

Shit. Two sisters would be in charge, and the last one would be left out. Why did Frank ask him to be here for this?

"The two executors are Rose" —Mrs. Maroo cleared her throat, seeming to hide a small laugh— "and Gray."

Mrs. Maroo steepled her hands and sat back, hiding a smile.

Gray's eyes shot over to Rose with surprise.

"Did you do this?" she spat, eyes shooting venom at him.

"Why would I want *more* work, princess? I'm busy enough." Goddamnit, she was frustrating. Like he had time to coerce his friend into writing him into his will to babysit his absent daughter?

"In the case of the co-executorship, Frank was very particular that you have to sign off on all decisions together. The decisions of what to do with his property, finances, everything."

Gray glared over at the fuming, bossy, gorgeous know-it-all and cursed under his breath. The next few weeks of his life would be absolute torture.

If Frank weren't already dead, Gray thought he might kill him.

~

ROSE

Fuck. Her life just got seventeen times more complicated.

"What do you mean we have to sign off on decisions together?" She never took her eyes off the pain in the ass across the room.

"I mean," Mrs. Maroo said, "you're a partnership. You're in it to win it. He's peanut butter, you're—"

"Cyanide," Gray muttered at Rose.

"I'm sure," Mrs. Maroo continued, glaring at Gray, "you'll want to consult with Violet and Lily, but ultimately you both have to agree on what to do with Frank's house, his greenhouse, his business, including the building, and finally, another very unfortunate piece of information."

Rose's stomach sank. What could be worse than working with her newly found enemy, smoldering three feet away?

"I'm not pleased to tell you this, sweets, but you're in deep shit." Mrs. Maroo took a deep, resigned breath and pulled out a folder.

"Did she say 'deep shit'?" Lily glanced around the room in confusion.

"Yes, ma'am. Deep, deep. Frank was a good man, God rest his soul, but not one for handling money." She spun around to Rose with a pained look on her face. "I'm gonna give it to you straight. Your dad and his business owed a lot of money to the IRS."

Rose heard a small gasp beside her and saw Violet's eyes widen behind her glasses to the size of saucer plates. Rose reached for her hand, and Violet squeezed it like a lifeline.

"It's fine, we'll be fine," Rose said quietly, squeezing Violet's hand back.

Rose felt her fingers tingle with panic, but she reminded herself she could handle it. She'd made a good living and had some savings.

How bad could it be?

"Ok..." Rose took a deep breath. "Owed how much?"

Mrs. Maroo peered at her computer screen. "Three hundred and forty-seven thousand dollars and fifty-seven cents."

Rose gasped and confusion echoed in the room. She pushed her hands through her hair. "How? He's had the house and the shop forever."

Mrs. Maroo removed her large glasses and steepled her hands in front of her. "He couldn't keep up with the tax payments, and then they accrued faster due to the late fees." She shrugged. "I think after a while, he just ignored it. We were in the process of discussing bankruptcy before...."

Before he died.

The county had ruled his cause of death as a stroke that took him while he was sleeping. Had the stress of this caused it?

"What if..." Violet started but bit her lip. "What if he was the borrower on my house loan?" Her skin had gone pale, and her hand trembled in Rose's.

Mrs. Maroo's eyebrows shot up. "He was the primary borrower on your loan?"

A tear fell down Violet's cheek as she nodded. "I was so young when I wanted to buy the house. It was our grandparents'. In the family forever. I didn't have the credit, so he got the loan, and I was the cosigner."

"The IRS is usually pretty lenient when people die, right?" Gray offered Violet a small smile, and his eyes met Mrs. Maroo's.

She shrugged. "Honestly, Frank's finances were so intertwined with his business that it wouldn't surprise me if they acted more harshly. They'd have every right to. I'm sorry, sweetie."

Violet started sobbing, and Rose scooted her chair so she could lean Violet's head on her shoulder.

"I've gotten letters with Dad's name on them. Some have been in pink and yellow paper." She hiccuped through her sobs. "I thought maybe they were a scam?" Violet peered up at Rose with a helpless vulnerability that gutted her.

Rose bit her cheek to keep from tearing up. She pushed Violet's head on her shoulder and begged her body to keep her emotions together.

Gray's eyes bored into hers, and she felt like grasping his hand from across the room, she was that desperate for a lifeline.

"We'll get it figured out, Vi." Lily patted Violet's back and crouched down beside her.

That house meant everything to Violet. This was just like her father. *Damn him.* He'd had an "everything will work out" attitude her whole life, and who picked up the pieces behind him?

Her.

The oldest sister. Part family therapist, part cruise ship activities director, part mother, part friend.

What part was left over for herself?

Rose felt tears starting at the edge of her eyes, but she pushed aside her feelings.

She'd get back to them.

Eventually. Probably.

"We've got time, right?" She did the math in her head. The sale of the house, the greenhouse, and the flower shop could make a big dent.

Mrs. Maroo held up a finger. "The payment was already way past due, and taxes are soon, sweetie. Whatever you can send sooner rather than later will help."

Rose took a deep breath and straightened up. *Get down to business and deal with your feelings later.*

Rose stood up and held out a hand. "Thank you, seriously. I'll follow up in a few days once I'm able to process everything."

"Oh, don't be silly. I need hugs." Mrs. Maroo scooted back, hobbled around her desk with surprising speed, and caught Violet and Lily both in a hug and then Gray. They filed out of the office, leaving Rose behind.

Rose glanced over her shoulder to make sure they were alone. "What's the deal with Gray? Why did Dad put us together? It doesn't make any sense."

Mrs. Maroo nudged her with her elbow. "He's not hard to *look* at, that's for sure. And knows his way around a dance floor." Mrs. Maroo sent her a wink. "He's a good man, but be careful; he's quite the charmer."

Rose scoffed as she gathered her things. "I'm immune to whatever charm he thinks he has."

"Give him a chance. Could be fun to work with him,

especially if you catch him walking away long enough." Mrs. Maroo bobbled her eyebrows, and Rose let a skeptical smile sneak through. "You'll figure something out, Rosie. I just know it. You let me know the second you need anything, okay?" Mrs. Maroo caught Rose in a fierce, bony hug, gave her an extra squeeze, and finally released her.

"Will do, thanks." Rose threw her a wave and tossed on her sunglasses, mentally putting on her armor to deal with Gray. He was waiting outside the cottage for her.

Ugh, he *was* a nice view from behind. He'd worn his omnipresent leather jacket and dark designer jeans that hung perfectly on him.

Rose walked outside and nodded to Lily and Vi. "Why don't you guys go grab a coffee? Gray and I need to talk."

"And miss an epic fight? No way," Lily snorted. Violet grabbed her arm and pulled her to Fox & Forrest.

Gray leaned against his bike and eyed her with a solemn face. "I didn't know about any of this." His voice was quiet and hinted at something she wanted to ignore. Something like kindness.

She rubbed a hand on her breastbone, willing away the Clydesdale-sized ball of anxiety sitting on her chest.

Why did it sound so good to be wrapped in his arms again? She wanted to bury her face against his chest—hell, anyone's chest—and forget everything crumbling around her. If he could catch her from a car roof, maybe he could catch her in the freefall she was in right now.

"I'm just sorry you got roped into this. My father..." She shook her head. Not sure where to even start.

"Was one of the best friends I ever had. Despite the age difference, or maybe because of it."

A smile ghosted over Rose's lips. "It's hard to imagine a tattooed motorcycle-riding millennial being best friends with a guy who looked like Santa Claus on a tropical vacation." She imagined them marauding through town and had to admit it made her just a little happy.

He ran his tongue over his teeth and sent her a wary look. "Just so you know, I'm doing this for Frank. I want to make sure his legacy is taken care of. I owe him that much, at least."

Rose saw the very clear line that he was drawing between them. "Fine. We'll divide and conquer and—"

"Nope. Sorry, sister, you heard the rules. I'd love to never see your pretty face again, but we gotta work together. Frank's orders." He sent her a thunderous look, daring her to contradict him.

God, this man.

He stood up and grabbed his helmet. "The first thing we should talk through is that I was in the middle of buying Frank's greenhouse. Meet me there on Saturday to go over everything?"

No way. She had to get out of there as soon as possible. "We should meet tomorrow." Rose took a step closer and held her chin up. She usually intimidated men with her six feet of height in heels, but his gaze bore into her, daring her to speak.

Her breath caught in her throat as his unwavering stare held her. The muscle in his jaw ticked, biting off unspoken words.

She cleared her throat, irritation gaining steam. "I'm not here for long and need to deal with this now."

He snarled at her. "Saturday. I can't bend my schedule to your whims, princess."

"And you think I'll sit on my ass all day, waiting for you?"

He glanced around her. "Based on what your ass looks like, I bet that's not true." He winked as he put on his helmet.

A stupid, idiotic flutter landed in her belly, and she willed it away.

"Violet should have my number. Text me what time you're available. On Saturday." He turned on his bike, revved it, and sent her a victorious smile as he flipped his visor down.

That's how he wanted to play? Then he'd vastly underestimated her.

He rolled out of the parking spot, and she hated that seeing him straddling his bike had dirty thoughts dancing through her head. Like what he might look like if she were under him instead, tattoos rippling as he gripped her and told her exactly what to do with his smart mouth.

She hated that she found the bike hot. That she found *him* hot.

She hated this entire fucking thing.

Spinning on her heels, she stormed to Fox & Forrest. She needed an IV drip of coffee to get through the next two days.

Chapter Six

ROSE

The next day, Rose positioned her laptop camera and checked her makeup in the onscreen video. She psyched herself up for the first podcast episode since she was fired, and the ruby red lipstick she was applying helped hide her insecurities.

She'd architected a semi-professional-looking background in Violet's cozy cottage dining room. A row of original white, built-in bookcases arched behind her, completely stuffed with Vi's romance novels. Lazy vines of philodendrons hung from the approximately one bajillion planters Violet had tucked around the cottage. It was like living in the coziest plant store on earth.

Lily and Vi were both out of the house, thankfully. She hadn't muscled up the courage to tell them she'd been fired yet, and luckily they didn't listen to her podcast. The bad news from the will reading yesterday was still so fresh, and they were counting on her. She needed to carry her burden alone.

Well, alone and dragging a 6'3" hunk of annoyance behind her.

The last twenty-four hours swam through Rose's head. *Three hundred thousand dollars. Dad's estate. New job search. Stupid fucking farmer Gray. Don't let anyone know you've been fired.*

"Hey, hey. You ready?" Angela, her co-host, hopped on the video call and sent her a wave.

"Almost." Rose checked her teeth for errant lipstick marks.

They produced a podcast with video, and Rose had to look her best today. She needed a distraction from the growing imposter syndrome that threatened to overtake her sanity.

People who give business and coaching advice don't get fired. You're an absolute failure, Parker.

A bubble of anxiety clutched Rose's stomach, but she ignored it. "Ready."

"Starting now," Angela said. "And we're live in three, two, one."

Rose plastered on a smile and greeted her listeners. There were already several hundred queued up for the live episode. "Hey, all. This is Rose Parker and Angela Lin. In this week's live small business Q&A, I'll answer some of your previously submitted questions, and we'll see if Angela or I can't solve some of your problems."

Rose loved sharing what she'd learned from the inner sanctum of the top companies she'd consulted with. She loved creating a community and an ecosystem of people who believed in themselves and played by their own rules.

"All right, Rose," Angela said. "First one's for you. User GottaBeClosin asks: what if I don't want to have my business forever? Is there some sort of escape hatch if I want to try something else?"

"That's a great question, GottaBeClosin. There are lots of parachutes for small businesses. Maybe you end up just closing it, and you enjoy your profits. But," Rose sent the video camera a winning smile, "you could also plan to get acquired, like selling your business to a competitor. This could make you an even bigger profit because you built up an amazing reputation and client base with your hard work, and someone else gets to run with it."

"Great point, Rose." Angela added how the caller could think about marketing their business for acquisition.

Oh my god, that's it. Why didn't I think of it before?

The flower shop and building were worth nearly nothing now. Both were so out of date that they wouldn't make much money if they sold it as-is. But what if they cleaned the building? Or hell, re-designed it?

What if the three of them spent a few weeks of blood, sweat, and tears flipping the building? She could make the financials work. Lily had an amazing design eye, and Violet knew enough about what a floral shop would need.

Or... Chills ran down her arms. What if they reopened the shop and sold it to a competitor in a few months?

Rose felt excitement thrum in her chest for the first time in a long time. She'd enjoyed helping her clients, but ultimately, she'd helped somebody *else's* business thrive. She'd never had the time, capital, or energy to make something of her own. What if this was her one chance? Her heart beat faster at the possibility.

What if she could use all her experience, save her little sister, and bail her dad out one last time?

Rose quickly answered as many caller questions as she could, counting the minutes until the podcast ended. She spoke faster and faster as she and Angela were batting ideas back and forth off their callers' questions.

"That's all for us. Be a badass today and a rich badass tomorrow." Rose waved, and Angela hit the end recording button.

"What the hell was that, Rose? Did you do a line of coke before we started?" Angela slumped over on the video call, winded.

Rose burst out laughing. "No, I just need to go. I'll talk to you later, Ang."

Angela waved as Rose closed her laptop and dove for her phone. She opened her favorite group text.

ROSE

I have big news.

LILYBUG

oh 💩

VI

are u tryingggggg to kill me right now rose

ROSE

No - GOOD big news. Meet me at the flower shop at 6.

LILYBUG

OUR NERVES CAN NOT TAKE THIS

VI

maybe she found a secret pile of cash I
forgot about?

Rose smiled at her phone and tossed it across the room so she wouldn't be distracted. She opened her laptop and furiously started her research. As she opened a flurry of spreadsheets and web pages, Rose saw her reflection on the laptop screen and realized she was *smiling*.

Oh my god. I'm having fun. She'd forgotten what it felt like to dream up an amazing future you couldn't wait for. She was the mistress of her own destiny.

Gray's face flashed in her head. Shit, well. If she could convince Gray to sign off on her plan for the shop. He'd probably be high and mighty about eventually selling the shop to someone else.

Rose chugged her bucket-sized cup of coffee and glanced at the clock. She only had an hour before her clandestine meeting at her dad's greenhouse.

Time to get to work.

"Miss Parker, do you know where exactly your land ends?" The stocky, shy, bald man in a work vest peeked his head out of the well-worn greenhouse.

Rose stood outside, trying to get a better cell signal to

email real estate agents. She needed to get her dad's house listed for sale ASAP.

She flipped open her folder and combed through the paperwork she'd found in the depths of her dad's shop. "It looks like the rest of this country block. About two acres."

"Got it. I should have my report in about fifteen minutes."

"Perfect." She sent her most genuine smile back at the real estate evaluator. He blushed, scratching his head as he went back into the rusting greenhouse.

Rose wasn't above using charm to get a higher evaluation for the property. If she could get the estimated price before negotiating with Gray, she'd have the upper hand. Her internet research said she could expect around $35,000, given the greenhouse was in poor but working condition.

She paced in front of the greenhouse door, tapping away at her phone. The drab sky was filled with clouds, and the air was thick with the threat of rain. A chill ran through her, and she pulled her trench coat around her tighter.

Her nerves were on edge from no sleep, too much caffeine, and not nearly enough food. Rose scrolled her "Get the Fuck out of Fairwick Falls To-Do list" and had the immense satisfaction of checking off one more box.

She didn't need to involve Gray, despite what the will said. She'd just do it her way, which would be faster and obviously better.

A rumble sounded through the valley that made Rose stop doom-scrolling her to-do list.

Why did that sound so familiar?

Rippling brown hair and a leather jacket came into view, and a motorcycle turned into the greenhouse.

Ah, fuck.

Gray's eyes were dark as thunder as he scowled at her. He parked next to the evaluator's van and cut the bike engine.

The evaluator wandered out of the greenhouse, pencil behind his ear as he flipped through his papers, finalizing his report.

"What the hell are you doing?" Gray barked at her.

The property evaluator's eyes flew up out of shock, and his clipboard went flying.

"Don't worry about him." Rose placed a hand on the evaluator's arm and picked up the clipboard. "He's just mad because I didn't invite him to play."

Gray hopped off the bike and marched toward her. "What are you doing here? Hey, Abe." Gray threw the man a nod and a quick smile. Abe waved back with a nervous smile.

Of course, Gray knew everyone. Rose rolled her eyes. "Just moving forward with my to-do list."

"Oh, the fucking to-do list." Gray wiped a hand on his face. "We're supposed to do this kind of thing together. Abe, did she con you into anything?"

"Don't answer that, Abe." Rose turned to the evaluator whose face was looking more nervous by the minute. She stepped toward Gray, nearly nose-to-nose. "*Technically*, we're supposed to handle the estate together, but it will go much faster if you let me handle everything. I'm used to working at a much faster pace than you'd be comfortable with."

His nostrils flared, and a small rush of delight swept through her. She loved seeing the flint of anger in his eyes.

Gray towered over her. "It would be much faster if you told me what the fuck you were doing so we could do it together like the will states. Or do you not care about your father's final wishes?"

Abe backed away toward his truck. "I'm going to go. I'll email you the results."

"No, it's fine. You don't have to go." Rose turned, not wanting to lose momentum on the evaluation.

"I think I do." He glanced between the two of them and scurried to his truck.

"Great, now you've scared him." Gray shook his head at Rose. "He just started opening up again after his break-up with Susan."

"Why are you everyone's best friend except for me, huh?" Rose crossed her arms and raked him up and down with her eyes. "Which side is an act?"

"Princess, I'm not like those fake assholes you're used to in LA."

He stepped closer, and she stood her ground, fighting the urge to back away. *As if he would know anything about life outside of Pennsylvania.*

His voice went low. "I don't like how you treat people. I don't like how you talk about my friends or my town. I stand up to bullies."

A *bully*? She was protecting her family. Herself. "How dare you act as if you know me?"

He'd backed her to the greenhouse door and leaned over her, his hand on the doorjamb. "Oh, I know your type, better than you realize. And I can't wait until you crawl back to the Hellmouth you escaped from. So, the sooner we get this over with, the better. Frank and I discussed selling the land and greenhouse for eight grand. Deal?"

What the actual hell? She stuttered through a million emotions, namely fury.

She pushed at his chest to let her through, but he didn't budge. Goddamnit, why did that cause every nerve ending to sizzle through her?

"Asshole." She shoved him again.

Rose sidestepped him and wheeled around, hands on her hips, taking up space in the drizzly spring morning as if on the front lines of battle. "Ignorant, annoying, asshole."

Keep it together, Parker. Lure him in, and then hit him with the number you need. Never mind that his voice sent chills down your spine. Or that you'd rather punch him in his stupid sexy face than talk to him. Dig in, put on your iciest shield, and get through it.

GRAY

"What the hell is your problem, princess?"

Gray had initially been delighted to see Rose outside the greenhouse. He thought space away from everyone else would give them a chance to start over.

She had a tight, form-fitting skirt that hugged her curves, a blouse that showed a tantalizing hint of cleavage, and heels so high his mouth watered. He'd thought today wasn't starting out so bad after all, until he clocked Abe's truck and put it all together.

She'd gone behind his back.

Rose paced in front of him, and it made him madder that his eyes wanted to linger on her long legs.

She sent him an icy death stare. "My problem? Eight thousand dollars is ludicrous. I've paid more for plane tickets."

"You think *I'm* unfair?" Gray's temper thundered. This woman. Stalin would be easier to deal with. "Did you bother to ask any questions before throwing accusations?"

She stood straighter and paused. "How on God's green earth did you arrive at that number with my father?"

He closed his eyes, pressing the bridge of his nose, trying to stave off a headache. This was not how he pictured his morning going.

"Because Rose, that's what he would let me pay him." Opening his eyes, he pleaded with her. "I offered more, but he said the land and the structure weren't worth it. He would only take that much."

"Bullshit. Do you have anything to prove it?" She crossed her arms and cocked her hip with blind confidence.

"To prove...?" Who the hell did she think she was? He threw his hands in the air, fed up. "We live in a town of one thousand people." He was nearly growling now. "We shook on it, and that was it. You couldn't possibly be Frank's daughter because you don't know how things work around here—"

"—Don't pretend as if you knew my father."

Gray reeled at her. "You're the one who didn't speak to

him for ten years. Do you know how much that broke his heart? It's the only time I ever saw him cry. His last birthday, in case you care. You didn't call." He and Frank had often talked about how much Frank missed Rose.

"Oh, like you know anything I went through?" Rose took a step closer to him, nearly laughing with frustration. "Did he tell you how I raised Vi and Lily? I was nine years old when my mom overdosed."

Gray flinched. Frank had never talked about the specifics of his wife's addiction.

"My mom had been in the bathroom for a long time." Rose weighed her words carefully. "And after I found her and called 9-1-1, I had to hold Violet and Lily back as they cried, shielding their eyes. No one was there to shield me." She shrugged at Gray. "That's all. So, when you tell me that your best friend was this amazing guy, just remember that. He chose an addict over me, and I never forgave him for it."

Her stare burned a hole into him.

Gray's heart thudded in his chest. Did she know that he was sober? That he'd been addicted once, too? Did he need to tell her?

No. He didn't know all her shit, so she didn't need to know his. "I didn't know the specifics. And I'm really sorry that happened to you. That's fucking heartbreaking. I..."

He knew what it was like to watch someone overdose. He couldn't imagine seeing something like that as a kid.

They just had to figure out what to do with the estate, and then he'd be rid of her. He wiped a hand over his face. "But let's just leave it at Frank was my friend, and I want to do what's best for him. For you all."

She stood straighter, any shred of emotion leaving her face. "I am willing to let the land go for fifty thousand dollars, which, as you know, is a steal in this market."

Gray's eyebrows leaped off his face. "Fifty thousand? As in four zeros?" He burst out laughing. "Princess, you've gotta be kidding me. It's not worth half that."

"That's not what FX Enterprises said." A cat-like smile played on her lips.

Fury ran down his spine at hearing the name of his largest corporate competitor. "You talked to that conglomerate?" He spat the last word with venom. "The people polluting this county and causing cancer rates to skyrocket? Of course, you would."

He stepped closer to her as he railed. "They don't give a shit about this town like I know you don't." He stood nose-to-nose with her now, and they both stared furiously at one another.

He was so damn mad, and it made him furious that he couldn't stop imagining kissing her full lips, inches away from his.

He wanted to take her porcelain face in his hands and muss her up. Wanted to run his hands up and down every curve as she glowered up at him. What would she taste like? Probably tart and sweet. He ran his tongue along his bottom lip, trying to think about anything other than taking her mouth.

Chapter Seven

GRAY

Gray almost couldn't look at her; she was so radiant when she was angry. Her eyes crackled with energy. He needed to step away before he caved and gave her whatever she wanted.

His eyes searched hers, and she inhaled a fraction of an inch but turned away suddenly. Rose took a few steps away and gazed out across the fields.

"I care," she said quietly. "It's been a long time since I've lived here, but I care. My sister lives here. I have to take care of her, Gray."

She uncrossed her arms and walked back to him. He could see part of her defenses falling. "I'm sorry you got caught in the middle. I just need to take care of her. Of both of them."

She glanced up at him, this time calm and contrite.

Gray finally saw her—the real Rose. Tough, no-nonsense, but a good big sister. And that had to count for something.

His anger drained away as he considered her. There were dark rings under her eyes she'd tried to hide with makeup. Her clothes were loose, like she hadn't eaten much in the last few weeks. She'd lost her father and gained a lot of problems in return.

His eyes softened. *Maybe ease up on her.* Everyone deserves a second chance, right?

Thoughts of what he'd do in a different lifetime ran through his head in a flash. He'd pull her in for a hug, make a joke, ask her to dinner.

But it was too late for that.

"Frank was the best, but he was a dreamer. I can see where he'd make decisions not caring about the money. He wanted to make sure everyone else was happy." He held her eyes for a moment.

Gray shifted and gestured to the greenhouse behind them. "C'mon, let's do a walkthrough while we're here."

Gray ambled into the chaotic greenhouse. It was semi-transparent, with tables covering the interior and tools lying against the far wall. The overflow plants Gray had left here were doing nicely, despite the leaks he spotted. Grass poked through the dirt floor, growing now that they were safely out of winter's way.

"I practically lived here when I first started. Frank helped me get my sea legs when I converted my grandparents' farm to produce flowers."

Starter seedlings of black-eyed Susans sat on the long

tables. A few had started blossoming. "He didn't use this space except when business was booming. Which was rare."

"I gathered that last part," Rose said drily, looking around.

The soft patter on the gray transparent ceiling signaled the beginning of the first big spring storm. Good. His crops needed water.

Silence hung between them, broken by the gentle drops.

"You really liked him, didn't you?" Rose asked out of the blue.

He nodded as he looked around the greenhouse. "I know it's hard to imagine since you now see a pillar of strength and stability before you, but I was in a bad place when I moved back. Frank saw my potential. For the first few years, he was more of a dad to me than my own."

"I'm glad he had you." Rose ran her hands along a small flower petal, caressing it lovingly.

Gray fought an idiotic urge to bring her close to him.

"My sisters and I reminded him of our mom, I think. We couldn't connect."

Gray's eyes fell, not sure how to respond in a way that wouldn't set off another round of angry discussions.

Blades of grass wiggled under their feet, and a cute little garter snake slithered by Rose's foot.

"Rose, don't look down and move over by me." Gray calmly placed a hand on her arm to guide her.

Of course, she looked down and immediately screamed.

City girls.

She leaped at him, and he caught her before she toppled

over a table. “It’s fine, it’s fine. Just a garter snake,” he chuckled.

His hands grabbed her waist, steadying her.

Her hands clutched at his shoulders, and her fingers dug in, gripping him like a lifeline. Their faces were inches apart, their breaths intertwined.

He stared into the caramel depths of her eyes and felt himself teeter on the edge of something.

Get your shit together, Roberts. He held her close as she got her bearings. The heat of her body next to his felt like absolute perfection. “You okay?”

Their eyes locked, mouths a breath away from one another. The gentle sound of raindrops filled the air.

“Uh-huh,” she said, out of breath.

Neither moved.

She felt so fucking good in his arms, and for a moment he considered pulling her head back and taking what he wanted from the red lips that taunted him.

He stroked his thumbs against her waist and felt her breath hitch. Gray tilted a fraction toward her, and her eyes went to his lips. He could feel her breath on him.

A clap of thunder boomed overhead, and they both jumped apart. His heart felt like it might leap out of his chest.

Rose took a step back and shook her head. “I should...uh, go. Lots to do.”

Gray dropped his hands. “Yeah, this thing isn’t leak-proof yet. We should go.”

Before I do something stupid.

Rose ran her hands through her hair, getting her bearings again as they walked to the door. “Gray, I’m just trying to do what's fair. You know the tax bill we owe, and this could help a lot."

They paused at the doorway, and Gray took a breath, weighing his options. He needed the extra greenhouse space if he landed the deal with Bailey's. Building a new greenhouse would take forever, and this was right next to his farm. It was too convenient to ignore.

He glanced at her, and his breath caught. She was a perfect fucking picture in the doorway: hair tousled with her trench coat cinched on her waist and the rain falling behind her.

He crossed his arms so they didn't do anything dumb, like haul her to the nearest flat surface. "I know you're in a tough spot. But this is a big price change from what I was expecting. Can I text you in a few days? And then we can talk about what to do with the rest of the estate?"

"That only seems fair. I did ambush you." Her mouth curled into an *I'm not sorry at all for ambushing you* smirk.

"It's always a memorable day when I see you, Rose Parker." He stuck out his hand and wondered if she'd even deign to take it.

She grasped his hand, and the jolt of electric need spread through him again, turning into slow heat that went straight to his dick. He saw her eyes flit to his mouth for a fraction of a second, and his breath caught at the possibilities of that look.

"Bye, Gray," she whispered, and jaunted out to the car to avoid the pouring rain.

As he watched her jog away, he felt like something had been taken from him. He was entranced by her shapely, mouth-watering legs as they swished away to that damned old car.

She was the most intriguing woman he'd met since —*well, maybe ever.*

If she hadn't been such a pain in the ass, he'd have run after her right then. Kissed her in the middle of the rainstorm. He pictured taking that smart mouth just the way he wanted. He shifted, his pants now feeling uncomfortable.

Gray shook his head to clear it. *Keep it in your pants, Roberts.* He needed to focus on the deal and figure out what he wanted to do, regardless of his undeniable, utterly unfortunate attraction to Rose Parker.

~

ROSE

Get the Fuck out of Fairwick Falls To-Do Item #1:

~~Deal with The Flower Shop~~

~~Sell the Flower Shop~~

...Relaunch? The Flower Shop.

Rose nervously tapped her foot as she watched Lily and Violet walk from their cars to the front door of the flower shop in the drizzle. It hadn't let up since Rose had left Gray at the greenhouse earlier that day.

Lily swung open the flower shop door and shook the water off her coat and hair. "This better be good. I missed my mid-evening catnap for..." Her eyes went wide.

"Whoa, it looks completely different in here." Violet craned her neck around.

After putting together a passable draft business plan, Rose had used her burbling anxiety to give the shop a good scrub, including the windows. The old wooden floors now gleamed without the dark display cases blocking the windows. Despite the setting sun and drizzle outside, the shop practically glowed.

Rose beamed a smile at them. "It's amazing what happens if you just clean the place."

"Rose, you are a miracle worker!" Violet exclaimed as she turned around, dumbstruck. "Who knew it could be this bright in here?"

Rose took a big breath. *Now or never.* She had corkboards propped up with cloths over them to pitch her vision to Lily and Vi.

"I wanted you to see the store to imagine the possibilities. I've been thinking..." Rose glanced nervously between them. "We should re-open the shop. We could redo the interior and sell the business in a few months for more than it's worth now. But I would need both of you to help make it happen."

Hope blossomed on Violet's face.

"But aren't you going back to LA in a few weeks?" Lily's eyebrows drew together with confusion.

"I was..." A sick thud landed in Rose's stomach. She had to tell them. "Fired." Her voice wavered for a fraction of a second before she gained control of her emotions.

She didn't even like those assholes. Why did it still hurt so much?

Lily walked toward Rose for a hug. "Those assholes."

"I'm so sorry, Rose." Violet joined their hug.

"It's fine, really. A blessing in disguise. I want to prove I can do this." She dropped her arms, and they stepped back. "If I can turn around this scrap heap for a profit, and it also helps save my little sister, I'm all for it." Violet squeezed her hand like a lifeline.

Rose didn't tell them, however, that she'd say this was the plan all along when she announced the store project on her podcast. To her listeners, it would look like she was taking a trendy break from corporate America to relaunch her family's flower shop.

Rose's business reputation was all she had. It *was* her worth, all she'd ever worked for. Her reputation was the one thing she couldn't risk.

Time to start the pitch.

"An average flower shop makes around two to three hundred thousand per year here. If we got the business going again, someone might be willing to buy the entire business outright. It could make a huge dent in the taxes."

Rose lifted the cover off the first giant corkboard holding several paint swatches, sketches, and photo inspiration. "What if we reimagined the space so it was a modern, style-forward floral experience?"

The color palette was clean and bold. The combination of bright white, a pale, almost neutral pink, and a dark, rich teal created a fresh and modern feel. It was accented with pictures of rose gold lighting fixtures playing up the shop's high, turn-of-the-century tin ceilings. The old, wooden planked floor, rustic in its dark wood and rough finish, was blessedly back in fashion now. All the scuff marks and stains would be seen as character.

"The shop should feel fresh, light, and airy, with industrial accents in the shelving and light fixtures. I picture the walls a bright white, maybe using subway tile for part of it, and paint the lower wainscotting a dark teal."

They glanced at the walls now. A dull, lifeless, kelly green covered the walls and original trim.

Rose uncovered the next corkboard. "For retail, we'd still sell cut flowers but make more modern arrangements. Maybe the artist in the family could help?" Rose pointed to the reference photos, which were beautiful, rustic arrangements featuring a combination of ivy, wildflowers, and roses.

"These are gorgeous." Lily ran a hand over the photos. "They look lush and modern but still feel organic."

"I have dogwood branches that would look amazing in these," Violet added.

Rose swallowed a smile of hope. "We'd add gift items, like soaps and lotions, and start by selling on consignment. Give people a reason to come in more than just for Mother's Day. Oh, and a large section of houseplants."

Violet, not one for a poker face, clapped her hands with building excitement, her long curls bouncing. Lily considered the images in front of her. She hated being tied down to anything, and this was a big ask.

"Finally," Rose continued, "I think we should rebrand. What if, by selling all sorts of gifts, we encourage more people to buy flowers? What if we make our brand synonymous with a modern, excellent taste and a store experience that people love? What if" —Rose finally revealed the last board— "we updated the logo and branding to Bloom."

Violet audibly gasped. Rose had chosen a modern handwritten font that spoke to the future brand they'd build.

Lily's eyes narrowed as she smiled at Rose. "You live with a designer, you know."

Rose sent her a cheeky shrug. "I wanted to surprise you. This is just an example—I know you'd design something even better once we started."

Lily rolled her lips together and kept looking at the photos.

"It would only be a few months, Lil. Just until we can get interest in someone buying the business. Or even just the building."

Violet clasped her hands together, an eager smile on her face. "Lily, Fairwick Falls has nothing like this, and with the historic town tourism, it could support another gift shop."

"Especially one with recurring revenue like wedding flowers, funerals, and holidays," Rose added.

She'd spent so many hours as a kid dreaming about how she'd run things if given a chance. They'd be breathing new life into a piece of history. The building had beautiful character and was essentially the same since its unveiling in the late 1800s. It just needed a fresh coat of innovation.

Violet danced with excitement. "Rose, it's absolutely amazing. I'd love to order and manage the supply. I even have some potted plants we could use right now."

"Where would we get the money for the changes?" Lily frowned at the interior. "We're gonna need a shit ton of white paint."

"I have some savings, and we can get deals from people in town who knew Dad."

"Maybe your dreamy motorcycle hunk can help you." Violet shimmied her shoulders, teasing Rose.

Rose shoved at her hair. "That's the other thing. I need Gray to sign off if you're both on board."

"I bet he'll *loooove* that you're going to stay in town for a few more months." Lily made a face at Rose. "It'll give him more time to pin you against something and have his way with you."

Rose shoved her, and Lily burst out laughing.

"He still needs to get back to me about the greenhouse purchase. Maybe I can casually drop that we know exactly what to do with the business, and he just has to sign off." Rose flitted her hands in the air. "But what do *you* think about reopening the shop?" Rose looked at her mercurial little sister. Lily's design career kept her busy, and she hated being tied down.

Lily blinked back unexpected tears. "I feel horrible saying this, but I've been happier here the last few weeks than when I was in New York. Dad died and I'm happier? I think I'm a monster."

"Lily." Rose ran a hand over Lily's hair. "Living paycheck to paycheck would make anyone miserable. I need to get back to LA soon, anyway. What if we all commit to being here for just a few months? Would that be okay?" Rose asked Violet.

"Okay?" Violet's lip trembled. "You'd really stay with me? And help?"

"We'd never leave you stranded, Vi." Lily rubbed her arm.

"It's been nice to have you here," Violet's voice came out in a whisper.

"Then it's settled. We're relaunching Bloom." Excitement built in Rose's chest.

Violet laughed and enveloped Rose. She invited a bouncing Lily into their hug.

"I've done more hugging in the past four days than in the past four years." Rose tried for an annoyed tone but still laughed as her sisters snaked their arms around her.

Something happy and whole settled into her heart, and she took a nanosecond to appreciate having them beside her in a place so steeped in their history.

This was going to be the craziest ride with them ever. She squeezed her eyes shut and opened them, ready to dive in.

Okay. Gratitude nanosecond over.

"Vi, can you start researching the plants and cut flowers that we need? Lil, can you start drafting branding and floral designs? I'll handle the financial projections, the store interior, the business plan, the timeline, and start researching potential buyers."

"Oh my gosh, I'm so excited." Lily clapped her hands together. "The first time we're all working together." Lily squeezed them both. "To Parker sisters."

"To Parker sisters," Violet added.

"To kickass Parker sisters." Rose took in her two favorite faces in the world. *Together, hell or high water.*

Chapter Eight

GRAY

"Hey, Mom!" Gray called out as he wrenched open his parents' front door.

"Hi, sweetie!" Lula Roberts swirled through her kitchen, stirring a handful of pots on the stove.

"Is that a farmer tromping through my kitchen?" His dad bellowed.

Gray sighed. *It had already begun.* "Not everyone can be the mayor, Dad."

"Come in, come in. Do you want a drink?" His father offered a highball in his hand.

"George," his mother scolded.

"Oh, right. Sorry." His father stroked his chin. "Water? Some tea?"

"I'll get it." Gray ground his teeth. Reason number 184 of why he dreaded going back to his parent's house.

"How's business, son?" His father hooked a thumb underneath a suspender. His father would have been more at home in a southern gothic novel rather than Western Pennsylvania. He'd been the mayor of Cooperstown, PA, for twenty years, loving the power and the politics of it all. Gray didn't understand the appeal of greasing palms only to produce nothing of substance.

If Gray didn't see his own eyes staring back from his father's face, he'd swear they weren't even related.

"Business is good." Gray shrugged noncommittally. The less he told his dad, the better. George Roberts liked to have his finger in every pot, and if Gray told him too much, he'd meddle.

Gray grabbed a glass from the cabinet and kissed his mom on the cheek.

"Fixing your favorite, sweetie." She absentmindedly poked the pan.

"Thanks, Mom." She'd held their family together after Gray had almost gotten kicked out of high school after he'd been caught selling drugs. When Gray had tried to get sober, his mom had always been there. He never wanted to let her down again.

"No big partnerships or expansions recently?" His father sent Gray a questioning look, his bushy eyebrows dancing like caterpillars.

A tickle started on the back of Gray's neck. *He knew something. What was he playing at?*

"I might expand into Frank's old greenhouse."

His dad let out a snort but said nothing.

"And my crops are coming in well," Gray baited him. He could never wait to tell Gray how he'd interfered.

"No meeting with a regional distributor?" His dad tapped his fingers on the side of his highball.

Gray drank his iced tea and tried not to choke from the ball of anger that lodged in his throat. "How do you know about that?"

"Bill's an old friend. Thought you'd want the introduction so you can get your little flowers to a few more places."

"That was you?" Gray didn't need handouts, especially from a meddling father. Shame ghosted behind that anger. He'd been so proud when Bailey's had reached out. Felt like he'd started to see some traction, that it was because his trial with one of their stores last year had done so well, not because of a fucking handout from his pompous father.

"Just trying to help. I don't want to see you make another mistake like last year. No more lavender, right?" His father sent him a friendly shrug and chuckle.

Gray sent him a death glare. "Don't meddle with my farm."

"What meddling? I told my golf buddy my son could use some help."

"Help?" *Fuck.* Now Bailey's would think he was a risky partner. "I'm doing fine without any help." Gray thought back to all the "help" his dad had given him when he kicked him out of the house in high school. When he'd stopped talking to him for months because Gray had made him look bad during a re-election year.

"Gray," his mother warned. "We're just trying to support you. Sit down, plates on the table."

His dad chuckled as he downed the rest of his whiskey. "Don't want to have to bail you out again."

Heat crawled up Gray's collar, and he remembered why he only came here once a month. "That was twenty fucking years ago."

"Language," his mother chastised.

Gray sat on the edge of his seat, unsure if he could make any headway in the meal in front of them. His stomach turned with anger.

His dad stabbed at the pork chop in front of him. "I'm just saying, son, everybody could use some help. We're trying to support your little dream. You know, most farms fail, and maybe now yours won't."

"Little dream?" Gray sat back. He crossed his arms to give himself a barrier of protection. "I own ten acres of land. I have an employee—"

"Part-time." His dad huffed out a laugh.

"You want to know why I spent so much time with Frank?"

"Because he was a useless busybody?" His dad shoveled peas into his mouth as he spoke.

Gray leaned into the table, pointing at his father. "Because he believed in me. He believed that everybody was allowed to make mistakes."

"Probably why he died so young." His dad laughed at his own joke as he took another big bite.

Gray scooted his chair back and grabbed his keys. "Bye, Mom." He placed a kiss on her cheek. "We're done."

"Gray, he's just trying to help, and he's not very funny." She sent her husband a scathing look.

Gray wrenched open the door. *I do this without anybody else's help if it kills me.*

CHRIST, Gray hated these meetings. He tugged his collared shirt and blew out a breath. *These guys aren't better than you. They don't have to know you've been a colossal fuck up your entire life.*

He glanced at himself in the rearview mirror of his SUV. He'd properly shaved that morning, removing the stubble he usually liked to keep.

Don't fuck this up. He blew out a breath and shoved open the door. He'd parked outside of Bailey's corporate offices and wandered into the gray box of a building.

He'd convince them he could produce flowers. This would be fine; flowers were his business.

Shit.

He walked back to his SUV and grabbed the pot of tulips he'd forgotten.

Damn, was this cheesy? He thought about tossing the gift back in his SUV but walked in with it anyway.

He visualized them saying yes to his request. *Yes, Mr. Roberts. We'd like to pay you a fuck ton of money for a whole bunch of flowers.* He shoved open the door, greeted the receptionist, and sat waiting for Bill.

His skin crawled from the anxiety of reaching beyond what he thought possible. *And this goddamn shirt*. He moved his shoulders around to ease the discomfort.

What would happen if Bill said yes to two times the number of roses ordered last year? What if he really needed the greenhouse from Frank's estate?

And like a lightning strike, Rose's face flashed in front of his eyes. The fiery storm he'd seen in them yesterday haunted his memory, making his blood course a little faster. His hands itched, remembering what her waist felt like underneath them. *I desperately, stupidly, wanted to kiss her senseless.*

Fucking Frank, he chuckled. He did this on purpose. He knew exactly what he was doing putting Gray, who had a problem with authority, with Rose, the bossiest woman God ever made.

"There he is!" boomed a smarmy voice. Bill, a portly man in his 60s, peeked around the corner of the hallway and waved Gray toward him. "How the hell are you, Roberts?"

Gray stood up and grabbed the plant. "Hi, Bill," Gray strode confidently toward him and shook his hand. "Brought you something from the farm."

"Lovely. Let's go to my office."

After exchanging pleasantries, Bill thankfully cut to the chase. "Your dad said you needed some help fulfilling orders?" Bill's bushy gray brows drew together in concern.

He could throttle his father right now. *Later*. "The opposite, actually. Last year, our knock-out roses sold well in one of your stores."

"I remember." Bill leaned back in his chair, hands behind his head. "Couldn't keep the damn things in stock."

"Should we double your order this year for the entire region? We're expanding the farm, and I wanted you to have the first pick before we reached out to other distributors."

Lies, lies, lies. He didn't have any other major distributors, not at Bailey's scale.

"All right, what are we talking about here? Exclusive rights?"

"Sure, for a fee."

"All right. Let's say ten times last year's order and 1.2 times last year's price."

Gray pretended to have enough confidence to have this kind of discussion. "I'm afraid I can only do 1.5, given the cost of inflation on fertilizer."

Did Rose do this kind of shit for a living? How wasn't she dead of a heart attack? Gray wondered if Bill could see the beads of sweat on the back of his neck and silently thanked himself for not getting a haircut yet.

Bill slapped the table. "Sounds like a deal. Just make sure to have those ready by early September, or...hell, as soon as you can." Bill stood up.

Guess their chat was over. That was success, right? He got what he came for. Gray thought he'd get out while the getting was good, shook the man's hand, and hurriedly walked out to his truck before he barfed all over the floor.

He let out a long, slow, controlled breath as he hopped into his SUV. He just made the biggest deal of his life, bringing in $80,000. His existing contract with the company meant he'd get paid half on signing, half on delivery.

He wished he could call Frank. This is exactly the kind of thing he loved to tell Frank about. He'd have made a huge fuss, probably because he'd known Gray's parents wouldn't understand.

Thinking about Frank, Gray realized who would be next on his call list.

He found the number Violet had sent him and chuckled as he started a new text.

GRAY

K Princess Bertha. I'm ready to talk money.

He snorted to himself. Using the nickname she hated was a particular form of enjoyment. He heard the ding of his phone before he put the car in drive.

PRINCESS BERTHA

You forgot to add 'your highness,' farmer.

Gray laughed.

GRAY

Your Highness, Crown Princess of Pains in My Ass: I would like to pay you a shit ton of cash for that pile of rust that passes for a greenhouse.

He sent it and wondered with a smile what she'd say back. He saw the three dots appear, disappear, and appear again.

PRINCESS BERTHA

Meet me at the flower shop at 7 tonight.

He let himself laugh, let himself feel the joy of things working out for once.

Wait, wasn't he supposed to loathe her? She irritated him to no end, but maybe he smiled because she was both a thorn in his side and an excellent verbal fencing partner.

Wonder what she'd have cooked up for him next.

ROSE

Rose checked her watch; 7:13, and he still wasn't here.

She scrubbed the baseboard with fervor in the empty flower shop and pretended it was Gray's face she punished with a Brillo pad.

Lily and Vi had gone home after a long day of deep cleaning the showroom. Rose leaned back on her bottom and wiped her brow.

She was caked in filth from cleaning the decades of grime on the walls and felt gross but victorious. The place now shone. If Gray agreed to reopen the flower shop, she'd start painting the first coat of primer in the morning.

Chugging from a bottle of water, she peered out the large front window and saw Gray coming out of Fox & Forrest holding two lattes in a to-go holder.

He stopped to say hello to three different people. She shook her head in disbelief. *How is the bane of her existence beloved by the community?*

It was a warm night for March, and he had only a Henley layered over a white shirt. He'd pushed up the sleeves, exposing his forearms and the detailed tattoos that wrapped around his arms.

Wanting him hit low in her belly and she took a mental snapshot of those forearms against the contrast of the dark Henley.

Rose's mouth salivated at watching him walk, his thick thighs eating up the ground and his broad shoulders thrown back as he stopped to chat with somebody *fucking again*. He pressed his hands through his hair and Rose felt an annoying tug of attraction. His hair was a little too long, which meant he was constantly flicking it out of his face.

He joked with the woman and child he'd stopped to talk with. Why did everyone else get that sparkling smile, but she didn't?

He finally ambled over to the front door of the flower shop, and Rose realized with a start that she looked like a dust-covered piece of shit. She checked her reflection in the window before she hopped up. She was wearing yoga pants, trainers, and a sports bra with a tank top thrown over it, but it was too late to make herself more presentable.

He's a potential buyer for the greenhouse, she rationalized as he wrenched open the door. That's definitely why she cared so much.

"You're late." She sent him a cool smile as he shut the door.

"Didn't realize we were punching timecards, Bertha."

She politely smiled back. "You said you're ready to talk, so talk, Roberts."

"If you're mean, you don't get the latte I brought you." He held out a to-go cup to her.

She took it with a small smile. He was clever. Free lattes were the paved path to her heart.

Gray's eyes traveled the length of her body, taking in every inch. She saw him lick his lips and his eyes came back up to meet hers with hot intensity. Goose bumps ran down her arms.

His eyes ripped away from hers as he took in the empty,

cleaned showroom and let out a little whistle. "Did you get robbed?"

She took a sip of the latte and let herself revel in the creamy goodness for a second. "They were that special kind of robbers only interested in dirt."

"Hilarious, Parker." His work boots echoed on the wooden floor and bounced around the cavernous open space.

Rose had managed to clean everything out, including the coolers, so they could paint the walls tomorrow. "We're reopening the store."

A flash of anger passed through his face, but he fixed it into a neutral expression. He bit his lip as he wandered over to the counter, taking in the changes.

"You didn't talk to me about this." His low voice cut into her. Gone was the smiling, happy-go-lucky hometown hero she'd seen outside. "This is the second time, Rose. You said we'd be partners in this."

"I never said we were partners. I said I'd think about it," she countered, walking toward him. God, why did she feel like a moth drawn to his flame?

"Are you aware I work in the flower business?" he thundered. "Let me help you."

"I don't need your help."

He sat his coffee down on the marble countertop. "No, but you do need my cooperation."

Her face couldn't betray the goose bumps forming on her arms and heat curling in her belly from this spikey side of him. "You wouldn't dare hold up reopening the business just because your little feelings got hurt."

He huffed a small, mirthless laugh as he peered at her, looking disappointed. "Sounds like you need me to sign off on this fancy new plan you have, and looks like I just got more leverage in our deal." He sent her a sizzling smile, but his eyes narrowed. He was cooking up some sort of strategy.

Those damn storm-green eyes reached into the depths of her soul, and she was afraid he could see who she truly was, someone who wasn't good enough, who didn't have it all together and was just trying to put one foot in front of the other. She could fool most people, but she had a feeling she couldn't fool him.

He twirled his coffee cup on the marble counter as he leaned back on it. "Tell me about this vision you have for a shop that could barely do any business." He looked like a dessert spread laid out just for her as he crossed his ankles and peered up at her.

Game face, Rose. Stop staring at those fucking forearms.

"We have big plans to reimagine the shop. My sister is a creative genius, and I have full faith we'll turn this place into something amazing. We've already fielded investor interest." Rose kept an even tone as she lied through her teeth.

She met his eyes with feigned confidence.

Neither of them broke eye contact and Rose started feeling a flutter in her chest.

"So," Gray started. "You're right that eight thousand dollars was unfair for the greenhouse."

Smug satisfaction tickled Rose's throat, but her face couldn't betray her.

Gray took a breath and met her eyes. "I'm prepared to offer thirty thousand on the condition—"

"You wasted my time for thirty thousand?" A spark of fury ignited in her.

His grin was quick and hot. "I don't think spending time with you is a waste, princess." His eyes roamed her body in a comical come-on.

His broad shoulders taunted her in the tight-fitting Henley shirt. His wicked grin played on his face, and she couldn't stop staring at his jawline. Heat crept up her cheeks. While her body might be interested in something more, her brain knew better. "I'm out of your league, Roberts."

He shrugged. "I just like to fire up the ice princess." He took a deep gulp of his coffee. "How about twenty-five thousand and six months of my flowers at cost."

She volleyed back quickly, her pulse jumping. "Are your flowers made of gold? A year and forty thousand."

His chest rose and fell faster. Hell, to be fair, she was probably doing the same.

He stepped closer to her. "Forty thousand," he paused, "and ten percent ownership in the store."

"What?" Rose shook her head, completely thrown. "I don't have time for games." Rose turned and walked behind the counter. She was done with today. Done with him. If he couldn't be reasonable, she had other things to do.

He followed her around the counter, eyes narrowed. "You don't have time for money? For building a business? Only have time for shoe shopping?"

She spun on him. "I have time for serious conversations with people who know what they're doing."

Gray laughed. "You are such a snob. Called it from day one. You're a little," he boxed her into the back counter behind the register, "big-city, spoiled, bossy, know-it-all who thinks she's better than everyone else."

Rose seethed at him and his fucking wall of muscles. Just like a man to underestimate her. "Spoiled? How dare you."

Her toes hit his as she pushed back on his chest. She stuck her chin out and tried to ignore his lips inches from her face. "I've worked for everything I've ever gotten, you mule-headed beefcake. You wouldn't know a P&L from a W2 if it hit you in the head with a protein shake."

"Snob." His chest heaved in front of her, and his hips pressed her into the counter, eyes searing into her.

Lust overtook her sanity, and she pressed back against him.

"Hayseed." She gasped for breath and couldn't stop staring at his goddamn mouth as he scowled down at her. He smelled like spice and sawdust, and she wanted to bury her head against his shirt and inhale it shamelessly.

"Condescending man-eater." His voice was a low growl that vibrated through her as he hovered over her mouth.

"Oaf."

And his hand claimed her jaw, and he captured her mouth with his.

Chapter Nine

ROSE

Rose kissed him back with everything she had; her iron will breaking.

Just this once.

His lips devastated hers, hot, needy, and forceful. The heat from his palm against her cheek shot straight down between her thighs, and her knees were stupidly close to buckling.

Her hand fisted in his shirt, pulling him closer. She melted into him, as everything she fantasized about in the last week had come true. A warm, sinful wave of pleasure and wanting washed over her as he wrapped his arms tight around her.

She craved more. Would kill for more.

He opened her mouth with his, taking more of what he wanted. And that possessiveness went straight to her pussy.

His tongue licked her bottom lip as he sucked it in his

mouth. Rose raked her teeth along his lip, biting down. Her hands gripped his shirt like a lifeline, needing more and more and more of him.

He released a low moan, and her stomach flipped. He kissed her as if she was his next breath.

Gray ripped his mouth from hers, and his hands found her waist. Her feet left the ground as he sat her on the counter. He stepped between her legs, driving them apart, and he yanked her hips toward him. His jeans brushed against the crotch of her leggings, and she thought she might melt from the pleasure of the friction. He gripped her hip, fingers digging into her ass.

"What are you doing?" she panted, her hands still fisted in his shirt.

His hand wound into the back of her hair, and yanked her head back to stare into his eyes.

"When I make mistakes, I'm pretty fucking thorough about it."

His mouth was on hers again, and his other hand gripped her ass possessively. He pulled her head back and exposed her neck, pressing hot kisses along the column of her throat. His five o'clock shadow sent waves of burning pleasure through her, and she let him take more of what he wanted. His hand held the back of her head, holding her in place as his mouth sucked on a fucking perfect spot on her neck.

He pressed into her, and she wound her arms around his neck, angling her hips so she caught even more friction from his jeans.

Her tongue warred with his, twining with hers. He

punished her with his kisses, each more intense and bruising than the last.

She fucking loved it.

Her body needed a few more seconds of caramelizing bliss as their mouths fought to take more pleasure. Rose pressed him closer as she felt a release from somewhere deep inside; she moaned directly into his mouth at how delicious it all felt.

He lifted his head from the kiss, his eyes searching hers. He looked as surprised as she felt, and their chests rose and fell as they caught their breath.

What had come over her? She'd been so lost in the moment. That never happened. She was calm, collected, and in charge.

Always.

When she dated, she'd had polite, impersonal sex with guys who didn't care about her. It was better that way.

No one to lose if you never had them in the first place.

A wide smile spread on his face, and his hands squeezed her ass. "So you *do* want me." He wiggled his eyebrows at her victoriously.

She shoved at his chest, and he stepped back to give her space to hop down. She glanced down at his crotch and saw he wasn't impartial to her either.

As goose bumps spread on her arms, she picked up her mental armor and gathered her wits. She stepped back, straightened her clothes, pulled her hair into a ponytail he'd mussed up and squared her shoulders.

"That was..." Her mind failed for words. Delicious? Electric? "...an accident. But it's strictly business from here on out. Deal?"

A slow smile spread on Gray's face. "I'll make you a deal: forty thousand dollars, ten percent, and all my expertise for free. I know how to time the flower orders so you can prep them, but not so long that they go bad. What delivery dates to shoot for to get the best of the season."

She scoffed at him as she grabbed her purse and coat from behind the register. She started walking to the back door, and he followed her.

"You're smart, Rose. Scary smart, but you'll still need help. And I bet you'd create something amazing here." He paused and peered up at her with kind eyes. "I bet on smart people with good hearts."

Rose's stomach dropped. Damnit, there was that flutter again. "Quoting my dad doesn't win you points, Roberts," she lied.

Gray's eyes held hers. "Look, I'm handy. I basically rebuilt my house. You're gonna need a shit ton of manual labor to turn this place into something special."

Rose hated he was right. Hated that the more she heard, the more sense it made. This man simultaneously drove her nuts and fanned her sex drive until it was on fire.

Going into business together would be a recipe for disaster.

"Let me help. I owe Frank that much."

Rose thought for a moment. "If you owe him, why not take five percent instead?"

Gray threw his head back and scowled at the ceiling as if it would give him his sanity back. "You are killing me." His eyes scorched her with a wanton heat she'd expect to find in a bedroom, not a business deal. "Ten percent, Rose."

She opened the back door, and they walked out into the parking lot. She considered his offer as she locked the door.

Free help, more money than she thought she'd get, and all she had to do was avoid entangling herself with Gray? Sounded like a good deal to her.

She stopped in front of him. "Five. It's unfortunate you couldn't meet the original asking price."

"Why? This is a better deal." He took a sip of the latte he'd carried out.

Rose leaned in to whisper in his ear as she walked by. "Because I won't have sex with a business partner."

He sputtered into his coffee as she sailed to her car, a slow curling smile on her lips. She loved catching him off guard, even if she still throbbed from his kiss.

He called after her. "You gonna spell that out in the contract, princess?"

"If you agree to five percent, then I happily will." She paused with the car door open, standing outside of it.

"You'll need to specify then, for the contract." He walked toward her. His voice rumbled low. His eyes danced with laughter and heat.

She licked her lips, tasting him on her. *Stop finding him so fucking sexy, Rose. This is not. Helpful.*

He stopped in front of her, arm resting beside her on the car roof, neatly boxing her in one more time. "Does that mean I can't go down on you, princess?"

Holy. Fuck. That throbbing started again.

He leaned in, whispering in her ear. "Bend you over

a table and tease you with my fingers until you scream my name?" His eyes locked with hers, and she couldn't form a coherent thought beyond the picture he was painting.

She should breathe. Breathing would be good right about now.

He hovered over her lips, voice barely a whisper. "Play with those perfect tits and have you sobbing, begging me to be inside you?"

Rose's mouth went dry, and her mind went blank. All she wanted was her mouth on his.

Gray angled his head, his lips a whisper's distance from hers. She licked her lips, and as she moved to him, he pressed off the car, walking backward. A mischievous smile grew on his face.

"Five it is, princess. Can't wait to see that contract."

This was the worst idea she'd ever had.

TWO WEEKS LATER, Rose walked outside Bloom, hefting a stack of record books. She'd spent the morning trying to understand her father's haphazard system for vendors, but she couldn't make sense of his shorthand. She wanted to re-use the existing vendor relationships to keep bookkeeping simple. They needed to get the business up and running in the next few weeks.

She wrenched open the antique brass door handle and walked into the work-in-progress showroom. It was overwhelming how different it looked already. Lily, Vi, Gray, and even Nash and Aaron had been busy the last few weeks renovating the space.

The store smelled fresh and happy. They'd cleaned every inch within its life and burned candles when they were there. It was on its way to having that herby smell a flower shop should have.

White subway tiles now accented the old store walls. Fresh coats of paint were painstakingly put on day after day to cover up the old green paint. The high, tin ceilings now shone, and the store seemed twice as big since they'd painted the plaster walls a bright white. The dark teal panels, old dark wood floors, and copper accents made it feel like they were in a gorgeous coastal industrial space.

When they weren't painting, caulking, or ordering new furniture, Rose ordered supplies for their opening weekend.

She walked through the space and ignored the hulking man that made chills run down her arms. She'd successfully avoided spending any alone time with Gray since their accidental make-out session. Rose had done everything in her power to put distance between them, going so far as to require Lily or Vi be with her at all times when he was there.

Focus on the store. Just ignore that perfectly sculpted back ranging over his toolbox.

She turned her attention to Lily, who blasted early 2000s punk rock through the store. She was clad in overalls, her hair tied up in a scarf, and looked like a Rosie the Riveter poster. Lily was up high on a tall ladder, putting in a floor-to-ceiling wall full of fake plants where they'd hang their new store's logo. Having a show-stopping space where people would post selfies could only help their cause for the better.

"Looking good, kid," she yelled at Lily over a My Chemical Romance classic.

"It's coming together, but this ivy is a little bitch." Lily wrestled with a twenty-foot strand, weaving it in and out of the grid she'd made.

Rose wanted the shop to feel like a trend-setting shopping experience, not a fussy flower shop. They had splurged on a neon sign in bright pink for the new logo Lily had designed. Her vision was fresh and modern, and Rose loved it.

Violet was crouched in front of her easy-to-care-for houseplant display. She spoke sweetly to a small philodendron in a terracotta pot. "Don't mind the loud music, Gilbert. You need to keep Philomena company while I'm not here. And I know you're very tough, but asking for help is okay."

"Violet, what the hell are you doing?" Rose said from behind her.

Violet waved her away. "It's scientifically proven if you talk to plants, they'll be healthier, and I just feel like they might need some comforting after listening to Lily's music."

"Tell your plants to stop being such pussies," Lily yelled.

Violet put her hands over the plants and gasped. "Language. It's been scientifically proven that—"

"I know, I know." Lily waved her hands around. "Sorry, plants."

"That's right. They're going to pay our bills." Violet straightened her shirt with self-righteousness.

Rose loved her weird little sister, who preferred plants to people. Well, both her weird little sisters, she realized as she saw Lily holding fake plants between her teeth as she wrestled with them into the grid.

"Any luck with the notebooks?" Violet asked.

"Hardly." Rose hefted them on her hip. "Did you ever look through these with Dad?"

Violet layered bits of eggshells into her soil as she spoke. "Honestly, he hardly ever wanted me to deal with the business. It's like he..." Violet shook her head. "...like he wanted me to do more. You know, he never really had a choice about the flower shop."

"Yeah, I know." Rose sat the notebooks down. They'd gotten heavier in her arms. "Grandma always made him promise that he'd never lose it—"

"On her death bed," Violet interrupted. "If you remember. Maybe Gray can help you with those." Violet jutted her chin to the record books.

"I can handle this on my own, thank you."

Violet picked up pots to carry into the prep room. "Your loss. He looks *pret-ty dreamy* with his tool belt over there."

Rose had to admit the powerful combination of Gray's permanent stubble, tool belt, and a black t-shirt that highlighted his large biceps had her mouth-watering. His arms ranged up, holding up the long shelf he was installing.

Rose was mesmerized by his drill going in and out as he screwed in a shelf. His shirt lifted at the bottom, showing a glimpse of taunt skin across his stomach. What would it taste like if she licked him right there?

Get yourself together, girl. She shook her head to clear the X-rated pictures forming in it.

"Hey, Gray," Violet called over the blare of the music.

"When you're fixing the shelves in the cooler, could you look at the door? It keeps accidentally locking."

"Sure thing." Gray grabbed his toolbox and headed to the back room.

"Oh, and Rose needs your help," Violet called. Rose followed him to the back room and stuck her tongue out at Violet. *Sisters are the worst.*

Gray sent a smug smile over his shoulder as he walked to the back. "You needed me?" His curved lips and green eyes sent sparks shooting straight down into her belly.

Nothing will happen. Lily and Violet are here. We can handle a simple conversation.

Rose rolled her eyes and tossed her hair. "I can't believe I'm saying this, but yes. I need your help decoding my dad's old vendor books."

"Ooo, so you don't know everything." Gray smiled, enjoying his moment of victory. He walked into the plant cooler in the back, and Rose had to tell herself to focus. The cooler was barely large enough for two people, so Rose put as much distance between them as possible.

Yes, he has on a sexy tool belt. Yes, he smells amazing. Yes, his shirt hugs his chest perfectly, but we don't care about those things because he's our business partner, you absolute horn dog.

"It's these vendor names. My dad put everything in initials, and I'm not sure what they mean. Do you recognize them?" Rose shoved a book toward him.

"Frank wasn't much of an organizer, but he did have a system." Gray sidled up beside her and leaned over, closer than she thought was wise. He peered over her shoulder and pointed to the first one.

"H.F., that one's probably Hadley Farms. They sell daisies and lavender. Looks like he got deliveries of both."

That was...shockingly helpful. "Ah, that's great. Could you write down the names of the ones you recognize? I need to see what they can deliver in two weeks."

"Eh." Gray stepped back and started unscrewing the wobbly shelf in the cooler on the adjoining wall. "It'd be easier if I called the farms. I already have relationships with most of these guys. Plus, they like me and will give me a better deal." He held a pencil between his teeth as he yanked out the screws and let the old wire rickety shelf fall to the ground.

"Excuse me." Rose crossed her arms and stepped toward him, catching his eye. "Why on earth would I let you be the face of our business? You're a minority shareholder."

He tucked the pencil behind his ear. Goddamn him for doing something so innocuous and making it so sexy.

"I don't know, Rose. Maybe because people like *me*."

"I'm likable," she screeched. She heard the shrillness and hated herself for it.

Gray gave her a side-eye glare. "You haven't exactly rolled out the welcome mat for anybody since you've been here."

"I'm busy. I don't have time to talk to everybody on the sidewalk like you do."

"Rose, I run my own business, talk to everyone on the sidewalk, and I'm still here fixing this fucking shelf."

She hated that it got under her skin whenever he made her feel incompetent. She already felt like a giant imposter running a business for the first time after she'd preached how easily it was done on her podcast. She'd barely slept the last week with the stress of it all.

She loved ordering new furnishings, imagining the space, and contacting potential consignment vendors for soaps and lotions, but the flower business still felt foreign to her.

Gray stood up and stretched, his black shirt tight over his chest. "I'm just saying: You want a successful business, and you'll leave soon, so why don't you let me handle it? Or do you not trust me?"

"I trust you." Rose could feel her face scrunching in a frown at him, and she tried to fix it.

"Yeah, with what?" He stepped closer to her, heat in his tone.

"With that screwdriver and the," she pointed, "gun thingy."

"The power drill?" His eyebrows raised in surprise. "Did you hang any shelves in the last fifteen years of your life, princess?" Annoyance laced his voice.

Rose gathered the books, done with this conversation. "I have people for that. And I'll be handling the vendor discussions. End of story." As she turned to leave the cooler, the door slammed shut in her face.

Locking them in.

Fuuuuuck.

Chapter Ten

GRAY

Gray rubbed his tired eyes. He'd lose his goddamn mind if he was trapped in a cooler with Rose.

Rose jiggled the door handle and then pressed her whole weight against it, apparently feeling the same panic he felt.

"Violet!" Rose let out a screeching yell.

"Okay, okay." Gray put a hand over her mouth. "She can't hear us, and I can very *much* hear you." The cooler was tucked back far in the workroom, and Lily still had her music blasting.

Rose wheeled around and fumed at him. "Weren't you supposed to fix the door?"

"Listen, princess; it's not my fault the door closed before I could fix it. *Someone* was bothering me. Maybe you're the problem around here."

Gray leaned one hand against the locked door and

towered over her. He loved riling her up and catching her off guard. She was wearing kitten heels today, and he enjoyed the way she had to lean back to maintain her furious eye contact.

"I am not the problem." Rose shoved his chest and walked around him to the other side of the cooler, three feet away. "If you hadn't chit-chatted with that redhead all morning, you'd be done by now, and I wouldn't be trapped in here with you. Maybe next time, you can charm your girlfriends outside working hours."

"Jessica and I aren't dating." Gray wiped a hand on his face. God, he didn't have time for this today.

"No? She just happens to bring you coffee and doughnuts out of the goodness of her little ol' heart wearing a skintight body con dress?"

Gray bit back a smile as it registered that Rose sounded *jealous*. "She has a crush, but I've tried to make it clear I'm not interested in anything."

"Why not? She's pretty." A biting tone filtered in through Rose's words.

Oh lord. He paced the short length of the cooler. He didn't love where this was headed. "Jessica *is* pretty, but I haven't dated in a while."

"I can name ten women who'd give their left hand to lock you down for some ungodly reason. Or are you too good for Fairwick Falls, Mr. Popular?"

Gray stewed at the towering, simmering perfection in front of him and thought about the words he was about to utter. He could lie, but that wasn't who he was.

Anymore.

Gray chewed his cheek, debating how to say it. If Rose went ape shit when he told her about his past, he was trapped in this fucking cooler with her.

"I haven't dated because I didn't want to jump into a relationship." *Better just be blunt.* "While I was newly sober."

He leveled a gaze at her, and her mouth gaped open.

Beat after beat after beat of silence hung between them. Her face shifted to the one Gray was so familiar with: wariness. He hated this shit. Hated thinking about his past and how differently they saw him now.

A familiar dull ache started in his stomach; the ball of emptiness that weighed on him was back. Made him feel like a piece of shit.

"But you knew," Rose said. "You knew about my past, about my mom. And you didn't say anything." Her anger rose with every word.

A 5x4 cooler was a bad choice for this conversation.

"I'm not your mom, Rose. I've been happily sober for four years."

"But I'd never—"

"Never what? Trust an addict?" he interrupted. "I've successfully built my business from nothing since then. I didn't owe you an explanation when I signed that contract."

She stewed at him. "I haven't had luck trusting addicts. They always let you down."

"Have I missed anything yet?" he railed back at her. "I'm keeping my business *and* yours on track."

"What are you keeping it on track with? Your little tool belt?" She shoved the tool belt on the shelf he'd just installed, causing it to tumble back down.

"Ha," she laughed. "See?"

"So, you think because one screw is stripped, in a shelf that I wasn't done installing, by the way, that I'm going to start using again? You're accusing me of being anything less than perfectly trustworthy?" Anger seethed through him, and blew hot breaths against his neck. "You have no reason to think I'd fuck this up for you, or your sisters, or for Frank."

"My father is dead," Rose spat at him with venom.

"I know! Why don't you give more of a shit that he's not here?" he yelled back.

"Why don't you keep your nose out of my fucking business?" she seethed at him.

His nose was a millimeter from hers, and he was so mad he couldn't see straight. He wanted to take her mouth and punish it with his. He wanted to throw them both against that wall and forget everything they were saying about one another, all the hateful comments.

Gray's mouth ran before his brain could stop it. His voice was low, and his hand cupped her chin. "Listen, princess," his whispers landed on her lips only a breath away from him. "We are done. My five percent has been paid for with my blood and sweat. You will not see me again. You get no help from me *ever* again. Do you hear that? I'm done."

He saw the fire spit back in her eyes, but she stood still. He felt the brush of her breasts heaving up and down against him.

He pressed closer to her, angling to her ear. "Even in the middle of the night, when you picture me making your eyes roll in the back of your head as you rock against me in your dreams, you won't get a single thing."

The door yanked open beside them.

"Gray, there's... Oh!" Violet's owlish eyes went wide behind her round glasses. Their heads whipped to the door, and Rose shoved Gray a foot away.

Violet cocked her head at them in confusion. "I told you the door locks. You should be more careful." She grabbed the door stop and propped it back open.

"My 'little tool belt,'" Gray grabbed his tools, "and I are getting the hell out of here. Violet, good luck. Your sister is a hellcat."

Gray thundered out of the back door of Bloom, hoping he'd never have to see Rose Parker again.

An hour later, the scent of newly turned earth ran like cool water over Gray, calming him. He felt his frustration and anger melt away from his fight with Rose as he worked in the soft dirt. His shovel seamlessly slid into the soft pile again and again. He'd then chuck the dirt over to the plastic planters he'd take to the Longhorn Nursery.

Duke sauntered up to him, a ball in his mouth, and Gray leaned down to scratch his ears. "Hey, buddy. You trust me, right?" Duke leaned against Gray's knees, sensing his puppy love was needed. He looked up into Gray's face, and his sneaky tongue caught Gray on the mouth.

"Blech, c'mon man." Gray laughed and wiped his mouth, scratching Duke's ears. He picked up the ball Duke had dropped and flung it down the hill.

It was a fresh spring afternoon, but the days were

starting to get warmer as they barreled toward April. Gray took a second to wipe his brow and surveyed the azalea bushes with pride. He was proud that they'd be planted in someone's yard and be a part of their life for years.

He tamped the dirt down around the young branches and started hauling them onto a cart. He had a fuck ton to do, but at least he had the fresh air and breeze surrounding him. Alex would be here in a few weeks, and he had to get ahead of schedule so they could spend a few days with just the two of them.

He still felt terrible he'd skipped his visit to Montreal a few weeks ago. Maybe that's why he was so irritated today. He was trying to balance it all, and it felt like he was drowning. He always felt like he was failing, being a long-distance dad. He'd tried to make the best of his visits, but nothing was better than holding Alex in his footie pajamas after he'd just woken up. It had been too many weeks since he'd seen him.

And to think I used to get paid to drink on a beach. He laughed at himself. He was voluntarily shoveling dirt and pig manure, dreaming about holding his son. He wasn't sure when the transition had happened from LA party boy to farmer dad, but he was glad it happened.

The muscles in his neck and back unwound from the stress of the morning as he lifted the planters. He loved working in the dirt almost as much as he'd loved photography. It had the same quick satisfaction of a job well done.

He'd loved photography, but it had been too stressful. There had been no room for error. At least he was only fighting the elements in farming rather than temperamental models, executives, and impossible standards.

Impossible standards. Rose and her never-ending to-do list shot through his mind.

She always had her shit together, but he'd seen her let her guard down. The *real* Rose slipped through sometimes, the passionate, messy person she kept locked away so everyone else was at arm's length. It was the mask, the cool demeanor she put on that irritated him. She wasn't a robot, but she sure as hell liked to pretend.

Shame echoed in his head as he remembered how he snapped at her. He'd had a long night at the greenhouse last night, an early morning, and to top it off, he'd had another nightmare about Casey. Rose wasn't the reason he was on edge, but she didn't know that. Unlike him, she probably knew very little of what the bottom of the barrel looked like.

Duke howled beside him as a luxury car pulled into his driveway.

What was Nash doing here?

Gray hefted his cart toward the driveway as Nash got out, holding two large coffee cups.

Gray sat the shovel down and dusted off his hands. "One of those better be for me." He grabbed the large cup from Fox & Forrest that he knew would have a fantastic latte in it.

Nash leaned down to scratch Duke, who sat patiently in front of him. "I was going to go through the expansion financials with you and thought you could use a pick me up." Nash calmly sipped his coffee in his impeccable three-piece suit. He couldn't look less at home on a farm if he tried.

Nash cleared his throat as they walked to the house. "How are you doing? I know today is probably hard."

Gray gulped the hot coffee, and it burned down his

throat as he realized what day it was. Maybe that's why he felt like tearing his hair out today. *Seeing your best friend OD in front of you seems like something you'd remember.* That day five years ago was when Gray decided to get sober for good. He'd booked a plane ticket to Pennsylvania and checked himself into rehab within a week.

"No, I'm good," Gray lied. *Change the subject so you don't unravel. Distract.* "The new stuff will go over there," Gray pointed to where he'd use the new equipment he was getting the loan for.

"If you were good, then maybe I wouldn't get one thousand annoyed texts from Rose about how she wants to strangle you because you're overworked."

Damn, Nash saw through the distraction.

He *was* overworked and running on empty. Whatever less than empty was. A black hole of empty.

"I'm fine. She's the one who has too much on her plate. But thanks for the coffee." Gray sent him a charming smile.

Nash's eyes narrowed as if measuring him. "I've got to run, but text me if you're up for losing this week. I'm in the mood for some basketball." Nash jingled his keys in his pockets as he walked back to the sleek, black car.

"Prick," Gray called out companionably.

"Asshat," Nash called back, smiling, as he slid into his car.

Maybe I am tired. He'd been working non-stop and had maybe, okay shit, *probably* been a dick to Rose. As Gray walked back to his plants, an idea sparked on how to make it up to her.

ROSE

As Violet and her best friend Aaron sat giggling into their wine at Fox & Forrest, Rose stabbed at her salad, picturing Gray's face under her fork.

Aaron reached over and put a hand on Rose's arm. "Hon, that lettuce is already dead."

"Sorry," Rose sent him an apologetic smile.

Aaron had practically lived with them in high school, and Rose considered him a fully-fledged member of the Parker family. He co-owned and ran the shockingly trendy café and bistro with his husband, Nick. Low lights flickered on the table between them, illuminating Aaron's brown skin and curious smile.

Aaron settled back in his chair. "Problems with the business?"

"Oh, you know. Just the usual. Yelling at my business partner and him swearing he'll never set foot in the store again. Normal adult stuff." She smiled at Aaron with the look of long-time friendship.

Aaron chuckled with a knowing grin. "I can't count the number of times Nick and I fought before we opened this place."

Nick walked to their table with a vegan tortellini to-go order Vi would take home to Lily. "Yeah, and if you're not careful, you'll end up marrying your business partner like I did." Nick smiled down at Aaron and kissed him squarely on the mouth.

Rose loved how happy they both were. She wanted that type of confident love but knew it would never be in the cards for her. Aaron and Nick were adorable and perfectly suited for each other. She, on the other hand, was a stressed-out, bossy, short-tempered hellcat, apparently.

Who could stand to love her?

"I think I'm safe. I'd honestly rather punch him than kiss him."

"It was bad. They yelled so loud I could hear them from *inside* the cooler," Violet grimaced.

Aaron sent her the same look back and sipped his wine glass. "Shocker."

"What do you mean 'shocker'?" Rose nudged his foot under the table and sent him a scowl. "I'm a goddamn delight."

"You are lovely dear, but you also have a particular way of doing things, and so does Gray. He's a nice dude, but it's his way or the highway."

"I wish he would take the highway away from me." Rose reached over to squeeze Aaron's hand. "This was delicious, as always. You are a magician and a saint, and I'm very glad you put up with us."

"Want a cookie for the road?"

"No, I'm stuffed." Rose patted her stomach. "I had three already today."

"We appreciate your business." Aaron stood up and gave them both a hug.

"I think we would be emaciated skeletons if your food wasn't so delicious and only two doors down from us." Rose gave him a smacking kiss on his cheek.

"You can repay me by taking a photo the next time Gray bends over." He sent Rose a cheeky wink.

After saying goodbye, Violet and Rose walked arm in arm to the store. She wasn't sure if it was the two glasses of wine at dinner or the twinkle lights strung through the trees along the sidewalk, but something felt so comforting about walking along the streets she knew so well.

"I need to do a little bit more before I go home. Go ahead. I can walk." It was only a four-block walk back to Violet's cottage, and Rose wanted time alone to process the day.

"You sure?" Violet unlocked the door and held it open for Rose.

"I can handle the mean streets of Fairwick Falls, Vi." Rose ran a hand over her sister's mass of curly hair. They were in their 30s, but Rose still felt a fierce need to protect her. "I'll be home in a little bit."

Violet had been pulling double duty, working a full-time landscaping design job, and putting in every extra hour at Bloom to get it ready. Dark purple circles were underneath her eyes, and Rose wanted to protect her as much as possible. Violet sent her a sleepy wave and headed to her car.

Rose examined the chaotic but happy store. *It's coming together.* Boxes lay everywhere beside half-finished projects, but Lily was almost done with the floral wall. Plus, it no longer smelled or looked like a Russian prison.

Maybe they'd pull this whole thing off yet.

Rose pushed the argument with Gray out of her head and focused on the positive. They were on track, they were on budget, and she pulled out her GTFOOFF To-Do List, with only a few more things left to close out the estate.

Rose walked to the back room to start clearing space for the new coolers being delivered tomorrow. She worked off the stress of the day, doing whatever came next on her list.

Before she knew it, hours passed, and all the other shop lights on the town square had turned dark.

As Rose walked to the register, the shop phone rang, and Rose grabbed it without thinking.

"Bloom, Rose speaking."

Silence hit the line, and the hair raised on Rose's neck.

"Put Violet Parker on the line now." A raspy voice growled from the phone.

Rose's heart thudded against her chest. "Who is this?"

"None of your fuckin' business." The oily voice sent chills down Rose's spine. "Violet owes money, and I intend to get it. She's a criminal. I could have her thrown in jail, ya know." A hacking cough cut him off from adding anything else.

Rose used her most authoritative, yes-I-am-in-fact-a-bitch-so-deal-with-it voice. "I don't know who you *think* you're talking to, but we're done."

"I don't make the rules lady, the IRS does. And when they get pissed, they hire me to make you pay. You know I could be in the shop right now, ready to take over. Would love to see that tight skirt up close and personal."

The line went dead as Rose whipped her head to the window. No one was there.

Rose's heart felt like it leapt out of her chest and landed somewhere on the floor. She laid the phone down on the cool marble counter with shaking hands.

How stupid. It was only an empty threat. But her eyes darted to the loft above the store and up the darkened staircase to the third floor. There was a winding basement below her, too.

Fuck. If somebody wanted to hide here, they could, and she'd never be the wiser. She thought about the dark parking lot outside the back door. Why hadn't she fixed the broken light bulb out there? The town square was lit with fairy lights and gave the illusion of safety, but no one was out now. It was past ten; everyone was safely in bed in Fairwick Falls.

I just need to think straight, not be intimidated by some asshole, and calm down.

She could call Lily or Violet, but she didn't want to put them in harm's way or worry them.

Rose punched Nash's name on her phone. He picked up, and the loud background noise made it immediately obvious he wasn't in Fairwick Falls.

"Are you at a rager?" she asked, laughing, getting some of her nerves back.

"Hey, I'm out with a college buddy listening to a band in Erie."

Shit. Two hours away. "Sorry, just a butt dial. Have fun."

Fuck, she was still on her own. She didn't have Aaron's number, plus he'd just tell Vi.

Who else could she ask for help? Could come help her scope out the building without making it a whole thing?

She groaned as she realized the answer.

ROSE

Rose sighed and punched the familiar name, wishing she could punch his actual face when she did it.

Gray picked up in one ring.

"Miss me already, princess?" The familiar, warm voice sent annoying goose bumps down her arms.

"Can you do me a big favor?" Her voice came out shaky, and she sucked in a breath, cursing her nerves.

"What's wrong?" Came the fast response on the other end, and Rose could cry at his genuine concern. "You okay?"

"It's just, I..." She blew out a breath and ran her fingers through her hair, trying to calm her body down. "The guy who sent Violet threatening letters just called and said somebody might be in the building, and I'm just...I don't want to worry Lily or Vi—"

"I'll be there in five," Gray bit out. "Stay right where you are. I'm going to stay on the line until I'm there, okay?" His voice was curt and serious, and Rose hated how thankful she felt.

"Fine."

"Did you see anybody come in? Hear anything?"

"I can't hear anything with you chattering in my ear." She enjoyed the distraction of his incessant questions instead of thinking of somebody sneaking up behind her.

"Tell me word for word what he said."

Rose relayed the conversation, focusing on the facts. Her eyes scanned the front windows and hallway for any additional movement. She saw Gray's SUV slam into park in front of Bloom. He ripped open the door, and Rose let out a breath of silent gratitude.

Her aggravating, pig-headed knight was here to save her.

"Thanks. I feel so stupid," Rose admitted. He walked confidently through the showroom, winding through the boxes and tables that littered the floor.

"You're just being safe."

"I know. It's just—"

"Scary," he said. "Stay here. I'm gonna do a quick once over." His brows drew together in concern. "And then I'll walk you to your car."

"Are you going to defeat them with your penis powers? I'll come with you." She marched toward the back door. "Two is better than one, even if one of them happens to have a vagina."

"I'll have you know I'm quite adept in hand-to-hand combat." He threw open the supply doors as she did the same to the office.

"Yeah? You come across a lot of thieves in flower farming?" She opened the cooler they'd been trapped in earlier that day.

Gray opened the door down to the basement. It was still probably haunted by the souls of a thousand demons. At least, that's what she thought as a child when she'd have to stay here late into the night with her father.

He took two steps down, shining his flashlight on his phone through the dark and dusty corners of the basement. "You don't know everything about me."

"Please spare me the details of the saga of Gray Roberts." They walked up the staircase to the third-floor apartment. That door made her most nervous, though she probably would have heard somebody walking around.

"I've been in more than my share of fistfights, thank you very much." He opened the door and craned his neck, shining a light around. "I think we're safe."

They walked back down the staircase and stood at the bottom, not meeting each other's eyes in embarrassment.

She tried to bite out a genuine thank you. "Thanks for coming."

As his eyes caught hers, an overwhelming sense of dread gripped her. Her heart started pounding again. A wave of nausea rolled through her, and Rose felt like she was dying.

Excellent. Just a perfectly well-timed panic attack. She loved it when they popped up out of fucking nowhere.

"Rose, you okay?"

Rose did what she normally did to make a panic attack pass faster. She dropped down into a ball, placed her palms on the ground, and tried to push the thoughts away.

You're dying.

You can't breathe.

No one will care that you're dead.

She tried to suck in air, but her lungs stayed still.

"Rose, what's wrong?" Gray knelt beside her, his hand resting on her back. "Did you see something?"

Maybe this was it; maybe she was actually dying this time. Her dad had died of a heart attack. Maybe she would die even younger.

Rose's head swam as she looked down, her vision blurring as she focused on her hands. *Just count what you see. One finger, two fingers, three fingers...*

"Rose, honey, you gotta talk to me."

Ragged breaths clawed through her as she fought for each one, but that *one word* rang in her ear like a lifeline.

"Rose, look at me." Gray's voice turned commanding, and he snapped his fingers at her. "Look at me."

"Don't—" she gasped through clenched teeth "snap—" she gasped "at me." God, he could be such an asshole, even when her world was crumbling apart.

"That's it. Get mad. Name three things you can see that make you mad."

Rose lifted her face, only too happy to name them. "Your stupid hair," she said through a shaking voice. "How it falls," she gasped for a breath, "in your face." *How she wanted to run her hands through it. It fucking taunted her every day.*

"How you never shave." His jaw, with its shadow of artful stubble that contrasted against his olive skin, made her crazy.

Her heart rate fell from near-dying to just-finished-a-run. She took in a full breath. "The trite, 'artistic'," she used a hand to give air quotes, "tattoos." That was a lie. She thought those tattoos were the hottest thing about him.

"Everyone had these in 2016." His lips wrapped into a sardonic smile.

She sucked in a full breath and sat back on her heels. Looks like it wasn't her day to die today, just a typical panic attack. But he knew that, of course. He'd effortlessly coached her through it.

"See?" he snapped at her again. "I knew I could fix it."

She snatched his hand frozen in the air, and locked eyes with him.

"Do not snap at me," she threatened, even as a sizzle of heat passed between them where they both crouched. A strand of hair hung in her face as she panted, still getting her breathing back to normal. His other hand tucked it behind her ear, his eyes softening as he glanced at her mouth.

She needed to put distance between them. She dropped her hand from his, and a glimmer of a smile passed through his lips. They both stood, and Rose stepped back.

"Thank you for," Rose bit her lip and met his eyes, "well, several things, I guess."

Gray nodded and stared at the floor. "Welcome."

Say it, Rose. Woman up and apologize.

"I'm sorry—"

"I shouldn't have—"

They both stopped and laughed nervously.

Rose bit the inside of her cheek. "I'm sorry, Gray. I am. Partners?"

Gray headed toward the front door as he locked eyes with her. "I'm sorry too. Partners. C'mon. I'll give you a lift."

Rose grabbed her bag and double-checked the back door was locked. "Gray, I can walk."

"The hell you can. I have a one-time per night policy on rescuing prin—" he cleared his throat, catching himself, "business partners."

Rose sent him a bow of her head in recognition of her rightful title. "Thank you. And I've been meaning to ask," Rose chose her words carefully, "if you'd like to meet with a real estate agent with me. To get Dad's house settled for the estate."

Gray opened the door for her as she walked through. "Look at you, little miss Pilates-pants. Collaborating with a partner and everything. You should have more panic attacks."

Rose locked the door and sent a prayer up to whatever god was listening to protect her little store from the asshole debt collector. They'd get it sorted and profitable soon. She just needed time.

"It's only four blocks. I can walk home."

"And I can haul you over my shoulder back to my car. Get in." He opened the door for her.

A secret part of her desperately wanted that, but she'd never admit it to anyone, especially not him.

A FEW DAYS LATER, Rose sat like a coward in her car outside her childhood home. She planned to do a walk-through before the real estate agent arrived. She'd almost made it out of the car twice to go in by herself, but she just couldn't do it.

Rose shuddered. She'd always hated the house. Memories of her mom dying, the dingy smell that always wafted because her dad hated cleaning, of being the "smelly" girl in elementary school. She'd made sure to rent the brightest, cleanest, most modern apartment in Santa Monica when she got her first big paycheck. She'd prove everyone, including herself, wrong.

Fairwick Falls had five real estate agents; she'd picked the highest-rated one for a meet and greet. Rose checked her phone; the agent would be here in a few minutes.

A large box truck pulled in beside her with the R&D flower farms logo on it.

Rose wordlessly got out of her car and walked toward the back door as Gray hopped out of the cab. At least she wouldn't be alone now.

"No 'hello'? No 'I missed you'?" he called.

"It's because I didn't miss you, and I don't wish you were here," Rose yelled over her shoulder. She waited on the steps for him with a smile, though, betraying her words.

He swaggered up to her. "Then how come you weren't inside already?"

"Just being polite, something I'd recommend googling if you're unfamiliar."

"You're a riot, Parker." Gray wore his R&D company polo shirt underneath his omnipresent leather jacket, and she kind of loved this buttoned-up version of him.

"Ready to head in?" He started walking toward the door.

"Hold on," Rose stalled. "How's the new greenhouse?"

They made the deal official a week ago, signing over the rights to the extended property around her father's house and the greenhouse that sat between his land and Gray's. Gray wiped a hand over his tired face, rubbing the bridge of his nose.

"Good, been busy. Got an order for a fuck ton of roses. So I'll need to seal the greenhouse properly so it stays warm for the three thousand plants I need to deliver."

"Three thousand, geez…" Rose muttered. "Are you doing this all yourself?" Now she was distracted. How did one man plant three thousand roses on top of everything else he was doing? Maybe she'd been depending on him too much in the store. This was the first time she hadn't seen him without a coffee cup in his hand.

"I have a part-timer, but I—"

"Prefer to do it all yourself, yes. I've met you, Gray. You know, you're reaching a point where it's costing you more money to do everything yourself than it would be to hire someone full-time."

"It's costing me money not to pay somebody else?" Gray crossed his arms and frowned at her.

The wind whipped around her, and she fought her teeth from chattering. Anything to stay out of the house for a little bit longer. "I mean, think of your income-to-hour ratio. If you hire an entry-level full-time employee you can trust, they can run with projects without your oversight, that'll give you time to start marketing to bigger regional partners." She felt comfortable here, chit-chatting about strategy. It was her safe zone, non-personal and only tactical.

Gray's eyebrows raised. "I've considered it, but finding somebody to trust is hard. But I appreciate your advice." His eyes measured her. Was that admiration she saw?

“Maybe you should come on the podcast,” Rose offered. “You’re an entrepreneur. I’m sure my audience would love to look at,” *Damnit, Rose. Did you say ‘look at’ like a lecherous old man?* “Erhm, learn from you.” *Excellent recovery, Rose.* “Maybe we can even do a shop launch thing. We talk about my small business, your small business.”

“Who even listens to podcasts?”

Rose pulled a face at him. “Everyone under the age of eighty-seven.”

Gray scratched the back of his neck. “Look, I just don’t want to listen to people talk about what they ate for lunch that day.”

“I promise you; I do not mention my lunch.” Her teeth chattered as she spoke. She stuck her hands in her coat pockets and wrapped it tightly around her.

“You’re freezing out here. Come on.” One of his absurdly hulking arms wrapped around her shoulders and gently guided her toward the door.

Rose checked her phone; the realtor was five minutes late. Ugh, she hated that.

She swung open the door, and it was like stepping through a curtain of time back into her childhood.

Gray let out a slow whistle behind her. “I loved Frank, but cleanliness was not one of his virtues.” He turned around, looking at the scores of cobwebs and piles of papers tucked here and there around the kitchen.

“Welcome to my childhood.” Rose strode through the kitchen, taking stock of everything. It was much the same as when she’d last left it ten years ago. Vi and Lily had started in the closet and bedrooms, making a dent in the mess but hadn't gotten to the kitchen yet.

"Is arson an option?" Gray peeked around the corner into the living room.

"I wish. We need to get top dollar. I hope to send a big check to the IRS in about a month. Maybe then that dick debt collector will lay off."

Gray whipped his head around, and his hackles raised. "Did he call again? Threaten you? Violet?"

"I can handle it." She didn't want him to think that she needed him.

Again.

"I know you can handle it, but sometimes it takes two people to handle it. Why won't you let anyone help you, Rose?"

"Why won't you let anybody help you, Gray?" Rose pointed her finger at his chest. He snatched her hand and held it, a gaze sizzling between them.

She felt that same magnetic draw to him again. *Escape. Escape, now. You can't get tangled up with him, and you keep getting too close dummy.*

Chapter Twelve

GRAY

Rose jerked her hand out of his grasp, and Gray felt his heart thud into his chest. They were playing a dangerous game with just the two of them there.

"Let's look around." She shoved at her hair, a nervous tick he'd noticed when she was flustered.

"This is where you grew up?" He tried to create some distance between what his dick wanted to do and his duty: to close out Frank's estate.

"Until I high-tailed it out at eighteen and didn't look back," Rose said as she wandered through the family living room and opened closets.

"The house is bigger than I thought. I never met him here. Frank always came over to mine." He peeked around a tiny office with an old rolling chair. Stacks of yellowed paper covered a scratched-up wooden desk.

Rose opened the door to an old childhood bedroom that

was practically a museum. Posters of boy bands and female role models hung up on the walls. The bedding was covered with a thin layer of dust. "This was mine." She looked like a woman confronted with every single one of her demons at once.

Distract her. Make her laugh. Rile her up. Anything to get rid of that haunted look in her eyes.

"So, this was Princess Parker's lair."

She threw a dusty stuffed animal at him, and he caught it easily, laughing. A spark was back in her eyes. *Good.*

His eyes searched the room for clues about who she was and what made her tick. There was something he couldn't shake about the combination of her brains and her sharp edges that hid a secret gooey middle she rarely showed. She was like a riddle he couldn't stop trying to solve.

"Didn't peg you for a boy band fan. I thought you'd prefer listening to dictators' speeches for inspiration." He toyed with the pencils on her childhood desk.

"I had crushes just like anybody else."

"Probably on the hall monitors." He closed the door behind them as they walked out into the hallway.

Neither of them peeked into the bedroom where Frank had passed in his sleep. Rose kept gaining momentum as she walked faster and faster through the house to the back door. He found her wheezing as she stood outside.

"Hey." He put a hand on her back. "Just breathe, okay?"

She leaned over her hands on her knees.

"Don't barf on me, Parker."

She laughed and gained her breath back. "I'm just... It's a lot, you know?" She stood up and shoved her hair, rubbing her breastbone. "Let's walk around the yard. Being there brought back all the old memories. I hated going near that bathroom."

"Is that where your mom..." He couldn't imagine witnessing that at such a young age.

She nodded her head. "And then with Dad's bedroom right there...it's a lot." She crossed her arms over her chest and marched toward the driveway. She started walking faster and faster, her gasps back. Jesus, this woman was a walking disaster.

"Rose. Rose!" He jogged and caught her as she walked beside his truck. He grabbed each shoulder, forcing her to look him in the eye. "Just give it a minute. Talk to me."

She rubbed her chest, her eyes looking every which way other than at him. "This was all theoretical until..." She tried to catch her breath. "Having to put everything, all of my past, to rest." She bit her lip and kept her eyes narrowed to avoid tears spilling.

He pulled her in for a hug. She was stiff at first, and her arms hung at her sides.

"...Are you *hugging* me?" she said with disbelief.

"I know it's a new feeling for both of us trying to be on the same side; just hear me out." He tightened his grip around her, and her head landed on his shoulder. "You don't have to be on top of it all the time, Rose. That's why I'm here." Her arms snaked around his waist and pulled him close. The burst of happiness that landed somewhere in his chest was probably coincidental.

"Oh god." She pulled back suddenly, with her arms still

wrapped around his waist. "Is that why you're here? Because my dad didn't think I could handle it by myself?"

"Rose." He laughed, shaking his head at her. "When will you learn? Help doesn't mean weakness."

"Says the guy who doesn't want any help on his farm."

Ouch. Point for Parker.

His arms were still wrapped tight around her, and he hoped she wouldn't let go. "I think he knew we'd both need somebody to irritate the hell out of us to distract us from missing him. And just maybe, so superhuman Rose Parker didn't have to carry the load alone."

Her chestnut hair blew in the spring morning breeze. It was a dull, overcast day, and her cheeks had turned pink from the chill. He was like a madman, coming back to the torturous fountain for more.

His hand found its way to her cheek, his thumb brushing the edge of her jaw. "All I'm saying is that maybe he knew we'd make a good team." He'd craved the feel of her velvet skin since the first taste of her. She leaned into his hand and stared at his lips, and he fought the urge they'd agreed was off-limits.

Why did she have to look so perfect standing here in the drizzly spring day?

His thumb caressed its way from her jaw to her cheekbone as his hand wound up into her hair. Her breaths grew ragged, and though they'd said anything physical was off-limits, he could see she considered it.

"Gray?" she whispered.

"Yeah?" His eyes never left her lips.

"Just one more time." She pulled his shirt to bring him

down to her.

As Gray's smile went wide, her mouth was on his, hot and sweet.

He kissed her as if his life depended on it. His tongue met hers as she pulled him even closer. The satin press of her cheek against his filled an aching void he didn't know he had. He sucked in the scent and taste of her.

His kisses became hungrier, possessive. As if he was drowning and she was the answer to his prayers.

He needed, needed, needed more.

His hands fisted in her hair, pulling her head back so he could deepen the kiss. She tasted like cinnamon, and he wanted to bury himself in it. His tongue licked at her lips, wanting to memorize the taste and the feel of her. It was like she was made to fit right fucking here in his arms, and this could be the last taste he got of her.

He nuzzled his way down to her throat, taking what he wanted. She raked her fingers through his hair, and he moved to her earlobe. She sucked in her breath and shuddered under him.

His cock went hard as he thought of hearing her moan again. It had almost destroyed him the first time at the shop. He wanted to feel every inch of her and hear her sob his name.

The feel of her tits pressed against him was almost too much for him to take. He went back to her mouth, sucking in her full, pouting bottom lip, and ran his tongue across it. She melted against him as their tongues met.

This was madness, and he never wanted to stop.

His hands moved down her waist and reached under her,

lifting her up. She wrapped her legs around him, and he spun her around, pinning her between himself and his truck.

He ground his cock against her, pushing into the truck, and he heard that perfect little moan again.

"That's it, honey. Moan for me," he whispered into her ear. "I've been thinking of how good you'd look on my cock."

She rolled her hips toward him and let out a moan, molding as much of her body onto his as she could. His hands squeezed the ass he'd fantasized about the last two weeks and rocked her against him. His cock ground into her, and she moaned again against his mouth, never taking her lips from him.

He broke their kiss, foreheads touching and breaths heaving. Her long nails raked through his hair, and he was so fucking close to taking everything he wanted right here on the gravel.

Don't be an animal. She deserves better.

They considered each other a silent moment, chests heaving.

Rose bit her lip. "You better put me down."

But I'd rather throw you in my truck and fuck you senseless.

Gray complied but kept her close, still between himself and the truck. He leaned down to brush his lips along her jawline. "You know," his mouth found a delicious spot on her neck, "I have a very comfortable bed three acres away."

Dangerous game, Roberts. Dangerous game.

She shivered under him as he nuzzled her neck. Her hands brought his head up and framed his face. Gray felt that clutch in his heart as he gazed back into those caramel eyes.

No, you son of a bitch. Do not fall for the woman who hates the town you love. She can't wait to get the hell out of here and has declared publicly, many times, she doesn't like you.

Why did it have to be her?

"Gray, I—"

They heard the crunch of wheels on the gravel and pulled back, still dazed. The agent was here.

Gray turned away to hide his aching cock. *Think of all the shit you have to do today. Get it under control.*

Rose turned over her shoulder and put on her game face. "Hey, Amber."

Oh fuck. Amber Edgemore. The real estate broker that had hounded him for months, if not years, for a date. That took care of his hard-on.

"Hey, handsome," Amber shouted across the yard as she sauntered toward them.

Amber came up to Gray and gave him a peck on the cheek. "It's nice to see you. You haven't called me back yet."

Fuck. Fuck. Fuck. "Yep, and busy working with Rose to get her dad's estate all wrapped up."

"Hey, Rose. I'm so sorry about your dad. Frank was the best." She gave Rose a half-hearted hug. "I can't count the number of times that he bought popcorn from my son for Boy Scouts. Ready to get started?"

"Why don't I have Gray show you around since you two seem to know each other." Rose's eyes danced with laughter even as she sent him a placid smile.

Oh, hell no. He didn't have time to deal with a woman made of super glue and clingier than a baby monkey.

Gray extricated himself from Amber's arm, which had already wound through his. "Rose, I'm gonna go take your advice. I need to finish these deliveries and start writing a job description."

Rose narrowed her eyes even as she bit back a smile. "Gray Roberts," Rose said under her breath. "After you made the biggest fuss to be involved in estate decisions."

He sent her a smile he hoped would melt her defenses.

Rose turned to the agent. "Amber, can you start the walk-through? The main bedrooms are in the back."

"Sure thing. Bye, handsome." Amber waggled her fingers, and a grating noise clanged from all the bangles on her wrists.

"You think you're so sneaky." Rose tried not to smile.

"You have no idea what I just saved myself from," Gray chuckled. "Hey, why don't you come to the farm later this week? You can see how everything works, given you're in the flower business now."

"I don't know, Gray," Her eyes stuck on the gravel under their feet, not meeting his gaze.

She was avoiding him. Oh god, was *he* the Amber in this situation?

"We won't..." he pointed at the truck where he had just taken her mouth and half his sanity. "This is just so you can learn the business."

You crafty motherfucker. Was it possible to lie to both Rose and himself?

She considered him. "I'll see if I can pencil it in our schedules." Her lips were still bee-stung from where his lips had taken them, and he would give everything he owned to haul her fireman-style into his truck and finish what he'd started.

But instead, he sent her a wave and headed to his truck. Being responsible was pretty fucking stupid.

An hour later, Gray unloaded his usual Tuesday delivery in the back of Cooperstown Florals.

"Hey, Gray," Allison, the owner, popped her head around the corner. "Everything ready to go?"

"Yep, your usual delivery is loaded in. And I threw in an extra potted plant on the house since you liked them last week." He sent her a friendly smile. He needed to keep his customers happy, and Frank had taught him that people loved free shit that showed he cared.

"Thanks. You're the best. Hey, Gray?'

"Yeah?" He paused, going out the door. He had about seventeen million more stops today but always had time for customers.

"I heard things were going well at Frank's place."

"Yeah, we're excited about the redesign. We open in a few weeks."

Allison smiled. "I've always thought Fairwick Falls could use a bigger flower presence. I'm glad his girls are doing something with the shop."

Gray knew he should probe a little. Allison ran a great floral business. It was tasteful; elegant. Just the kind of thing Rose would love. "You should come by and check it out."

"I wouldn't want to intrude. Make it seem like I'm checking competition or anything." Allison leaned over the counter and sent him a flirty, sparkly smile.

Gray weighed on how to position it. "Rose mentioned she'd love to collaborate with another flower shop in the area. Maybe work together on bigger projects someday."

There. That should plant the seed.

"I might do that." She glanced down, hesitating for a moment and worrying her lip. "Do you want to grab dinner with me? Some time?"

Gray blinked a few times, completely blindsided.

"Um, I'm sorry. I'm..." Gray searched for the words. Dry humping my business partner semi-regularly? "...not dating at the moment. But thanks for the offer."

Allison smiled sheepishly, blushing. "You can't blame a girl for trying. Let me know if anything changes." She sent him another mega-watt smile.

He waved as he walked through the backdoor out to his truck.

Allison was an objectively beautiful woman. She had long legs, pretty long blonde hair, a great rack, and was smart and easy to talk to.

And I couldn't care less. Maybe he'd been waiting this whole time for someone who could challenge him. Could drive him crazy with her demands and drive him wild with her touch.

Gray stopped in his tracks on his way back to his truck. *Goddamnit.* He slammed the door as he climbed back into the cab. He let out a rage-filled yell and hit the steering wheel.

Rose Fucking Parker had ruined him for other women, and she wasn't even his.

Yet.

Chapter Thirteen

ROSE

"What the hell?"

Rose frowned at her phone's navigation and glanced at the enormous house and rolling farm before her. She knew her jaw hung open, but she couldn't close it.

Gray's place was gorgeous.

The hell?

"He built this?" Rose muttered to herself. Several stories loomed over the driveway. A worker in the flower fields carted soil and plants from the large pristine greenhouse to a new barn. Rose scratched her head, her entire image of Gray shifting under her feet.

She threw the car in park and opened the door as the floppy-eared hound dog she'd seen in Gray's backpack ran toward her. He gave her a tiny "awoo," and her heart melted.

"Hi, buddy." She kneeled down to scratch his ears. Floppy ears and a sweet face tugged at her heartstrings. Dogs had always been her soft spot. She'd been too busy since... well, forever for a dog.

"Careful," Gray yelled from around the corner as Rose leaned down to get up face-to-face with the handsome pup in front of her.

Before she knew it, her face was coated with pupper kisses, and a laugh bubbled out of her. "Oh, man." Rose wiped her face and gave the dog endless ear scratches. "You certainly are a handsome fella. I'm declaring you my new boyfriend."

Gray jogged up to her and sent her an arched eyebrow. "Your new boyfriend's name is Duke. The 'D' in R & D Flower Farms, and employee number one. His primary responsibilities include being our morale officer."

Duke grabbed a ratty tennis ball and threw it at Gray's feet. Gray picked it up and chucked it for him so he could run down the hillside toward the fields.

"Welcome," Gray said, sticking his hands in his back pocket. His face was easy and relaxed, and he looked mouth-wateringly sexy in a tight black work shirt with his sleeves pushed up, exposing the ropes of muscles around his forearms. Delicate black ink tattoos dotted his hands and wrists, and black line art ran the length of his arms. What would it feel like to trace them with her fingers? Shit. She was leering at him like a class-A creep.

She stood up and dusted off her knees. "Your place is amazing, Gray," Rose admitted, dazzled by it all. "Are you some sort of secret millionaire, and I wasn't aware?"

Gray let out a sly smile. “Nope. Sorry to ruin your dream. I inherited my grandparent’s farm, but easy to forget how far it’s come, I guess. Come on, I’ll show you the greenhouses first.” Gray’s shirt strained across his broad chest, and Rose had to stop staring to keep her mind focused on the task at hand.

Don't think about what it would be like to rip his clothes off. Don't think about how good his stubble looks. Ignore the tattoos that you can see. Ignore how adorable his home is that he's made and just get down to business. “So, tell me how it works.”

“You possess many virtues, but patience isn’t one of them.” He elbowed her as they walked down the sloping hill to the greenhouse. “Over here, we’re planting fields full of lilies to harvest in the fall. And we have peonies in the greenhouse right now.”

A little buzz hit her heart. “Those were always my favorite.”

He snorted.

“What? I can’t have a favorite flower?” She asked. They strolled down the hill together, and the smile he sent her was downright distracting.

“No, it’s just...fitting that peonies are your favorite. A temperamental flower that only shows its bloom for a little bit and is the most gorgeous one out there sounds...well, exactly like you.”

His eyes flitted to hers before looking away and swallowing a smile.

She cleared her throat and ignored how much she wanted to melt at his words. “This is all quite impressive.”

"Aw, Parker. You're going all soft on me."

"I just didn't think you had such a big operation. When you said my father mentored you, I assumed your business would end like his."

"Frank knew exactly what to do. He just preferred to hang out instead."

Gray opened the greenhouse door, and the scent of fresh spring flowers wafted around Rose.

Rows and rows of pinks and purples sprawled out before her. Early buds of peonies, daffodils, and tulips sat in small planters along the large tables. Small bushes of blooming hyacinths with fluttery blue and purple flowers lined the walls. Hanging baskets wove a tapestry from the ceiling with greenery and new buds springing out.

Wow. He'd built all this by himself. It was so much more than she'd ever made.

"This is our biggest greenhouse, but we still need to keep expanding to meet upcoming orders." Gray busied himself with picking out some leaves as he talked. Rose was distracted by seeing an entirely new side of him. He looked like a proud father, lovingly caring for each plant. Where was the sarcastic, motorcycle-riding tattooed hunk who hated her?

His arms ranged over the plants, checking each container's moisture level. "We have to watch out for clearwing moth larvae. If they infest the plants, it'll destroy all these peony buds."

"You love this, don't you?" Rose's head cocked to one side.

He sent her a shy smile. "Of course I do; I'm making something from nothing."

That phrase rang in her ears.

"I like to think about how my products will be used. How they'll be sold, how they'll be part of the best parts of people's lives. Maybe if they're lucky, they might see a wedding or a baby shower, or be with a proposal, or just show somebody they're important."

Rose started coughing to cover the sudden wave of emotion that hit as he spoke. Did she fall into some parallel universe upside-down time loop as she crossed onto his driveway? She cleared her throat. "That sounds magical."

"Let's get you some iced tea." He opened the greenhouse door. "We can go up to the house."

"That's not necessary," Rose waved her hand. "I should go anyway."

Duke bounded toward them.

"You don't want to feed Duke some treats?" Gray asked. "He'll be disappointed."

Damn him. Feeding Duke treats sounded fucking amazing. She gazed into soulful hound dog eyes that blinked up at her. "Are you using your dog to keep me here?"

Duke ran beside her as they walked to the house. She tugged the ball out from his mouth and threw it. He let out a *yip* and excitedly chased it up the hill toward the house.

"I would never stoop so low as to use my best friend to keep a woman here."

"Keep your business partner here," Rose corrected, shoving his arm.

"I believe you're both." His eyes landed on every curve of her body before meeting hers.

She sucked in her cheeks and bit them to keep an idiotic giggle from spilling out.

They walked into the house, and Rose took in the gleaming kitchen countertops on top of expensive cabinets. The copper accents sparkled in the minimally decorated yet modern kitchen. "Your kitchen is beautiful. Who was your designer?"

"I guess I was. I'm still working through the rest of the house. This used to be my grandparents' cattle barn. I've converted it over the past five years."

Duke gobbled up treats from Rose's hand, and she sipped the iced tea Gray had poured for her and peered up at the exposed ceiling beams. "So those are real?"

"Yep. Real, load-bearing, old ass beams."

The early evening sun glinted off the windows and reflected in, bathing the kitchen in orange light.

Who was this guy? She'd worked alongside him for weeks, but apparently, she barely knew him. "Have you been a farmer since school?"

Gray smiled. "Not exactly. Follow me." He led Rose into the living room, and she glanced around the open space. The walls were snowy white but gave way to a dark wood ceiling. A stone chimney ran the length of the two-story wall, with a fireplace big enough to stand in. The floors were a warm, beautiful old wood. Brass fixtures complemented the warm, earthy furniture.

The large photo above the mantle caught her attention. A

portrait of a young zebra gazed directly into the camera with a near-human expression of longing. Family surrounded it but chose to look directly into the photographer's lens.

"This is exquisite. Where did you get it?"

"I shot it while on assignment."

Rose turned around and considered him, confused. "You shot...you're a photographer?"

"Was. Some freelance magazine assignments here and there, like that one," he said, gesturing to the print.

Rose turned back around to the picture and gaped. Turned back to him, started to speak, then turned back to the photo.

She was definitely in an upside-down time loop.

"How do you go from National Geographic quality photos to being a flower farmer in Fairwick Falls, Pennsylvania?"

"Well," he crossed his arms, and a frown ghosted over his face. "You make it big with some agents and models by being a hotshot photog who thinks he's God's gift, and then party too hard for too long. Hard enough to land in rehab, where they recommend changing your friends and scenery. I came back to lick my wounds and get my head on straight, away from LA."

Rose bit her lower lip, uncomfortable at how real things had gotten. She wasn't sure what to say.

"Converting the farm to florals gave me something to work on while I sorted myself out. I still have a few pigs from my grandparents' farm. Turns out the secret to great flowers is pig manure." He blushed and scratched the back of his neck, then opened the patio door to his deck.

Oh god, why was he being adorable? She was this close to asking him to be an asshole again. "I've never seen a pig up close. Do they have names?" They walked out onto the deck.

"Oh sure, Patsy Swine and Sir Francis Bacon. My grandma loved a pun. They are loyal members of the Roberts' empire," he said, laughing with her. "Want to see them?"

Rose's face changed to one of trepidation. "I'm not dressed for a barn," she pointed to her wedge heels.

Gray held a hand out to help her down the deck stairs to the grass. "C'mon, I can at least show you where they live."

Rose looked at his outstretched hand. *Nothing unprofessional about an offered hand.* She took it and allowed him to lead her down the steps. At the bottom, his fingers interlaced through hers, and she felt her heart plummet into her stomach. It felt so much more intimate than either of their make-out sessions. So much more intentional.

She met his eyes with a question but noticed a car pulling into the driveway. "Expecting company?"

His face lit up with recognition as two tall, beautiful women and a little boy got out of the car and spoke in rapid French, one woman stretching, apparently arriving after a long car ride.

"Papa!" the little boy yelled, running toward Gray.

"*C'est qui, ce p'tit bonhomme-là?*" Gray yelled, crouching down with a giant surprised smile on his face.

Rose stared down in astonishment.

Gray was a dad? Who spoke French?

Am I having a stroke right now?

Gray enveloped the little boy in a giant bear hug,

swinging him in a circle. One of the women slowly walked up the drive to meet them.

"I missed you!" Gray planted noisy kisses on his cheeks, causing a raucous round of giggling. "*Salut, ça va*?" he yelled and waved to the woman walking up.

"*Papa, c'est qui ça?*"

"In English, Alex." Gray smiled, looking at the boy.

The small boy drew his brows together in concentration, making his face a carbon copy of Gray's.

"Who?" Alex said finally, pointing to Rose.

"This is my friend Rose. Rose, this is Alex, my son, and his mom Giselle." He gestured with his head toward the six-foot tan goddess standing before Rose.

"Bonjour. Nice to meet you," she said in a husky, delicate French accent, her hand extended.

Rose felt like a ton of bricks had fallen on her. How had Gray not mentioned any of this? He was so intertwined with her life, business, and even her father. She was apparently just an afterthought in his life if he hadn't decided to mention any of this.

"Hi, it's nice to meet you too," Rose said hesitantly, trying to get her bearings. She took the woman's delicate, golden hand with designer jewelry on it.

"Giselle, this is Rose, who I told you about."

Giselle's face brightened. "Ah. So you're the one who has stolen our Gray's heart."

"G, I told you—" Gray shot her a warning look.

Giselle smiled warmly. "I'm only teasing, but it has been ages since he told us about someone special." She gave Rose a conspiratorial wink.

Someone special. Is that what she was to Gray? Rose saw the second woman open the back door slowly, looking green.

"Is she okay?" Rose asked.

Giselle spoke in rapid French, and the woman waved and went back inside.

"Morning sickness," Giselle beamed.

Gray's face burst into a grin. "That's amazing! Congratulations!" He enveloped Giselle in a hug and kissed each cheek. "Giselle's wife, Andi has been going through IVF for a while."

"Oh. Congratulations! That's so exciting." Relief flooded Rose's system for some reason. *Am I jealous of Gray's ex*? *Impossible*. She unclenched her jaw and breathed out a sigh.

"Giselle and I had been long-time friends when I was a photographer, and we had a short fling before I got sober. She got pregnant, our amazing Alex was born," he swooped Alex around, causing another round of giggles, "and we've been a long-distance family ever since."

Alex reached down to Duke, who'd trotted up, and Gray let him down to play.

Giselle smiled as Alex ran around. "We live in Montreal and come down for visits since Alex is young. Someday he'll get to spend all summer at the farm," she said sweetly to Alex, who beamed up at her. "I'm sorry we didn't call, Gray. I know we're a few days early. Andi was feeling so sick. She wanted a quiet place to rest before we did more driving."

"It's no problem. I was about to show Rose the pigs."

Alex piped up, "Piggies!" He tugged on his dad's hand, attempting to drag him to the barn.

Get the heck out of here before you learn seven more adorable things about Gray. Rose wrapped her arms around herself. "Let's reschedule, Gray. We can do this whenever."

Gray swooped down and tickled Alex's belly, then threw him over his shoulder so Alex was upside down, causing even more laughter. "You don't want to visit *les cochons* with Alex and me?" A hopeful smile beamed on his face.

Better not get more emotionally tangled than she already was. She was only a business partner who would leave soon.

"Business can wait. Family comes first," Rose said with a half-hearted smile.

Gray's face fell a fraction but turned around so Alex was facing Rose. "What do we say to Rose if she's leaving, *ma puce*?" Gray asked.

Alex was giggling but managed to get out a delicate, accented "Later al-e-gator!" as Gray threw a hand up and waved as he walked toward the barn, Alex bouncing over his shoulder.

Rose was completely thrown. This was one hell of an upside-down time loop. How many layers could one person have?

"So Gray tells me you are partners. In business," Giselle added with a quiet smile.

Rose turned to her. "Yes, he owns a part of my business. We're a flower and gift shop in town."

Giselle turned to lean against the patio wall, all French elegance. "How lovely. Gray is a good man." She smiled as Gray chased Alex to the barn. "He's a good papa, despite the distance."

"It was so nice to meet you, but I should go. Enjoy your visit." Rose walked back to the patio door.

Giselle sent her a quiet wave.

Rose grabbed her keys in the kitchen with lightning speed. *Keep it professional and simple. He has a full life and doesn't need anyone else in it, especially not you.* She hustled out to the car, sparing one more head pat for Duke before she hopped in and drove back home.

ROSE

Today's To-Don't List

#1: Don't forget to plug the opening on the podcast; must hype up business so we see online sales.

#2: Don't be weird that Gray didn't mention he has a son, or that he speaks French, or that he was a photographer. Don't be weird, Rose. Don't be weird.

#3: Definitely do not, do not, DO. NOT. kiss Gray Roberts ever again.

Rose opened the backdoor of the Bloom workroom, already late. Well, late for her, which meant only an hour early before her podcast with Gray started. They'd agreed that he would talk about his expanding farm and the Bloom launch. She mentally cataloged everything she had to do in the next hour: podcast recording set up, check the Wi-Fi...

Rose stopped dead in her tracks as the smell hit her.

It smelled like an honest to god flower shop.

Chills ran down her spine as she took in the workroom full of flowers. The last time she remembered it smelling like this, she was six, her mom was still alive, and the business was thriving.

She closed her eyes, transported by the fresh, herby, spring smell of greenery and the chill that only came when you had coolers full of precious flowers ready to sell. She caught notes of chrysanthemums, roses (of course), some lilies, and the ever-stalwart carnation. She opened her eyes, and it hit her: it smelled like their future.

They were really doing this. They were reopening a flower shop and making it better than the town had ever seen. They had two more days left before the opening on Saturday.

Rose shifted the things in her arms as she clicked around to the main showroom in her heels. She hefted her computer bag, microphone, and headphones through the back room of the shop and heard Lily's off-key caterwauling.

Lily stood at the counter behind the register, finishing a few arrangements for opening day. Piles of fragrant eucalyptus branches and sweet pea blossoms sat beside her as she scrunched her face in concentration, finishing the floral sculptures.

Rose pitched her voice over the music. "Hey, I think the sign was supposed to come today."

"Already on it, partner." Gray's booming voice sounded around the corner, followed by a power drill. He was on a ladder, marking a spot for their neon sign that had finally arrived.

Lily had finished the focal point in their large showroom with a fake plant backdrop, lots of Violet's potted house-plants, and a cute chair with floral pillows. Rose imagined friends taking cute selfies in front of it. It was part of her grand plan to make the space not just a simple hometown flower shop but a full experience.

"A little farther up!" Rose called out from where Gray was marking the spot for the sign. It would light up in a bold pink handwritten font, mimicking their official logo.

"You're welcome!" he called out over his shoulder.

Rose's mouth watered shamelessly when she spotted Gray's low-slung tool belt. His tight black t-shirt hugged toned muscles and biceps and went loose around his middle. There was something about that damn tool belt that made him irritatingly attractive.

Heat pulled in her middle, and she tried to drag her eyes away from him.

Lily cleared her throat loudly, and Rose snapped out of her trance. She wiggled her eyebrows at Rose. "See anything you like?"

Rose stuck her tongue out at Lily, giving her a shut-the-hell-up grimace. The sound of the power drill died down. Gray plugged in the neon sign with the bright pink logo on the greenery, and it popped to life.

Rose felt pride blossom inside her. They had made this from nearly nothing. And maybe, just maybe, they might pay off the tax debt, help Violet, and make something special here.

A bittersweet shadow hovered in the back of her head, knowing they'd have to sell the shop they made. *But I can't stay here. What would I do, run a flower shop in Fairwick Falls? I'd lose my mind. I'm meant for bigger in my life.*

"It looks great. Thank you." She sent Gray a warm smile, and their eyes connected.

"Hey, Lily, can I grab one of those Bloom shirts?" Gray ambled over to the stack they'd have for their opening day. "I forgot to bring a change of clothes with me."

"I bet Rose's podcast would break a record if you went shirtless." Lily sent Rose a wink as she handed Gray a shirt.

Gray let out a booming laugh as he grabbed it from her.

She hated that he fit so easily into their tiny sisters-only family. But soon, she wouldn't have to see him quite so often. The store would be up and running, things were almost wrapped up with the rest of the estate, and he'd be out of her hair for good.

She could finally go back to LA and not think about how his mouth felt against hers or how she craved his smell. She even went so far as clandestinely smelling men's shampoos in the grocery store to see if she could figure out how to replicate his smell like a complete and utter weirdo. Leaving him would get easier in time.

"I need to get set up." Rose cleared off part of a display table and dragged back two chairs so the new Bloom sign was in the background. They'd have to sit close and share a mic. She shot a subconscious glance over to where Gray had been standing with his toolbox and couldn't find him. "Where'd he go?"

"He's right here." Gray poked his head out from around the backroom corner, shirtless.

Gray brought the rest of his body around the corner as he grasped one of the pink Bloom shirts over his head, stretching it to put it on. They got a show of his sculpted chest dotted with tattoos and firm abs tapering down into a solid, trim waist for a split second before he tugged the rest of the shirt down.

Lily tucked her phone in her arm and started applauding. She leaned over and whispered to Rose. "If you don't get that, you're a dummy."

Rose felt her cheeks flush like a goddamn nun. Absolutely ridiculous. She'd seen plenty of sculpted half-naked men running up and down Santa Monica Beach; he was nothing special. *Except he's right in front of you, and you know exactly what he tastes like. He holds your head when he kisses you, and growls dirty talk in your ear that makes you weak in the knees.*

Rose shoved Lily, changing the subject before she expired from a frustrated sex drive. "Go away. We have to record a podcast so people will think I know things." Lily wandered to the back.

Gray strolled over to the chairs and leaned on one. An awkward silence landed between them, and Rose busied her hands by clearing items off the table for more space.

"How was your visit?" Rose tried to keep the hurt out of her voice that he'd never mentioned he had a whole other life she knew nothing about. *Don't be weird.*

Gray moved items off the table to help. "Short, unfortunately. They're already on their way to Hershey." His voice had turned melancholy, and the light left his eyes.

They stacked boxes in silence for a minute, and Rose could feel the tension between them rise. She had to say something. Who sprung all that information on a person in one day? "I didn't know you had a kid." There was a flinty edge to her tone that she hated.

He straightened and bit his lower lip, considering her. His eyes were full of sadness that she didn't understand. "We're just business partners, right? Did you need it for the contract?"

A knife twisting in Rose's stomach would have felt more pleasant. Her face fell and she reached for that shield she'd forgotten about for a while. Of course, she was just a partner. How many times did she remind him of that? He didn't owe her anything.

But it still fucking hurt.

"No. I just..." A reminder went off on Rose's phone, and she squared her shoulders, back to business. Where she belonged.

"Almost time." She gestured for him to sit in front of her laptop. "Our part of the podcast will just be us chatting. It should feel conversational and easy. Just us shooting the shit."

"I have never, and will never, see Rose Parker shoot the shit. I will see her walk through a meticulously curated *list* of strategic talking points." He snarled at his least favorite word.

"Well then, get ready to be surprised." She opened her recording software. "Hey, Angela."

"So this is the hot farmer you talked about," Angela sent Gray a wave from the video screen.

"I did not call him hot."

Gray snorted with laughter, and Rose clenched her teeth together. *Thanks, Ang, for the worst timing ever.*

"Mmm..." Angela waved her head back and forth in thought. "You definitely used the word mouth-watering."

"You've told her about me?" Gray sent Rose a smile that went straight to her gut.

"Ready when you are." Angela hit the record button.

It was almost time, and several listeners were in the waiting room. "Showtime." Rose scooted her laptop camera so she was centered below the Bloom sign to kick off the podcast.

GRAY

GRAY ZONED out as Rose and her co-host opened the podcast. He kept replaying the picture of Alex's little hand waving up at him from his car seat in the back window as they drove away that morning.

Emotion clutched at Gray's throat. It never got easier to say goodbye to Alex when he left with his mom. Gray knew they were so lucky in their happy family dynamic, but he wished he could see them more. He'd driven to Bloom right afterward, eager to take his mind off missing Alex and, hell, Giselle and Andi too. Gray smiled over the memory of last night's vicious game of Chutes and Ladders. They made one heck of a modern family unit.

He fucking hated the feeling of having all that love ripped from him. His gaze drifted to Rose as he thought about how perfect she had looked standing in the sunset in his kitchen. In his life.

But she was going to leave too. He didn't know if he could take having that ripped away if he let himself get too close. She'd drawn a clear line between them when he went to the barn with Alex. She didn't want to involve herself in his complicated life. Just business partners.

She was talking animatedly at the screen, fielding responses from the hundreds of listeners and brainstorming on the fly with her co-host. She was fucking magnificent, quick, and kind to her listeners. He loved that she was ambitious and went for what she wanted.

Rose glanced over her shoulder as his part was nearing, and he sent her a sad smile, reminding himself he would lose her soon.

"I'm so happy to introduce my business partner: local entrepreneur and flower farmer Gray Roberts." Rose moved her laptop camera so that they were both framed in front of the Bloom backdrop.

Gray sent the camera a wave. He'd never been comfortable in front of one, and there was no way he could keep up with Rose in her element.

Rose smiled at him. "This is a podcast, Gray. You have to talk."

"Hi, everyone." His cheeks flushed, a little embarrassed with himself. Text boxes popped up on screen from listeners.

> Attagirl87: Is he like her 'partner' partner or just her partner, because hiiii.

> GetThisShipDone_4: Uh, where is this business located??? Because I need to check out this new shop. 👀 For uh... business reasons...

Rose jumped in, swallowing a smile. "So, Gray, tell us about yourself."

Keep it brief. If you don't say much, you can't fuck it up. He cleared his throat. "I'm just a farmer in Fairwick Falls," he shrugged, "and a tiny co-owner of Bloom, as Rose likes to remind me." He pointed to the sign behind him.

"That's not true." Rose smiled at him playfully.

Oh, now they were friends?

"His farm is huge, and he's expanding like crazy. He just signed with a new regional distributor."

He caught her eyes and shrugged. "I mean, I have a few acres. We're just getting started, really." The silence in the room was deafening.

She was trying to make him into something more than he was. And he was just fine being himself. It was okay to be new at something. To be terrified it was all going to go south.

"He's being very humble." Rose smiled at the camera with her mega-watt grin that he'd kill to have directed his way for once. "As I mentioned, my sisters and I are launching a refresh of our family's one-hundred-and-twenty-year-old flower shop in gorgeous Fairwick Falls. We hope to have a community-level impact with our products."

Gray snorted, thinking about how much she couldn't wait to leave this "gorgeous" community. She sent him a quick glare.

"Gray, can you talk about your process in helping launch the store?" Angela asked.

He was done with this. "I'm just the handyman," Gray said, waving a hand. He crossed his arms, waiting out the rest of the podcast. Angela and Rose quickly filled the rest of the time, answering follow-up questions from their listeners.

As they signed off, Rose slammed the laptop down. "What is wrong with you?" She threw off her headphones and glared at him.

He shook his head, biting his lip. "I'm just tired of people leaving."

"Who's leaving? I'm right here."

"You'll be out that door as soon as someone hands you three hundred thousand dollars."

"So I can save my little sister."

"But what happens after she's saved?"

"Look, as my business partner, you knew—"

"No, Rose. We're not business partners. We're friends. You are," his breath hitched, "a gigantic pain in the ass sometimes, but you're still my friend. Yeah?"

Her eyes blinked suddenly. "Yeah."

"And yet, you can't wait to leave the store, your sisters, me, as soon as you can." He knew he was caught up in his feelings, but goddamnit, he didn't have the energy to be cheerful today. Couldn't shove it down any further.

"Just because I have to leave doesn't mean I don't care."

"Why do you have to leave?" Gray's voice was ragged at the edges. He couldn't claw the hurt back from his voice. "So you can live a life full of anonymous faces? So you can reach higher heights and have no one to share it with? No sisters around, no friends dropping in on you?"

This woman meant more to him by the day, and he was losing his grasp on why she wasn't already in his arms. In his bed. In his kitchen the next morning, with her hair tousled, talking about her plans for small business domination.

"I'm used to a solitary life. I..." She took a gulp, a tear threatening at her eyelash. "I've always preferred it that way."

Message re-fucking-ceived. She wasn't interested? Great. She could leave like all the important people in his life. Casey. Frank. Alex and Giselle, and now her.

He grabbed his work shirt and headed for the door. "Then I'll leave you alone the way you prefer. But Rose?"

"Yeah?"

He turned to see her framed against the store they'd built together.

He bit his lip to keep it from wobbling. "I wish you preferred it with me." He shoved open the door and left her to her solitude.

Chapter Fifteen

ROSE

Fifteen minutes before the start of opening day, Rose zoomed around the store, adjusting displays as Lily put the final touches on a new arrangement.

Violet flipped on the fairy lights wound artfully through the store, and lit a few candles. "I meant to sweep one more time. Do you think it's worth it?" she asked with growing panic.

Lily glared at the arrangement she was finishing. "Relax. No one is coming to eat off our floors. They just need to buy flowers."

"How are you calm?" Violet puffed as she power-walked through the store, perfecting the display of hand cremes.

Lily blew a stray curl out of her face. "You've got to manifest the perfect day, Vi. Just repeat, 'I'm one with the flowers.' 'People will come in and buy our shit.'" Lily said with a solemn, trance-like tone. Her hippie vibe was on full display today, with a cute peasant-style off-the-shoulder shirt and long flowing pants.

Violet shook her head as she placed the opening day cookies she'd baked on the register as a thank you to their customers. She was wearing her signature bright floral blouse, which Rose assumed was a nod to their dad's omnipresent Hawaiian shirts.

Rose took a deep breath. She was more nervous than she was letting on. *It's just a small-town store. If this doesn't work, we'll try something else.*

But deep down, it was the first real thing she'd made in a long time. This wasn't a spin on a client's idea or a PowerPoint presentation for someone else's business. It was hers.

Theirs.

The ghosts of their childhood played in Rose's eyes as she surveyed the store. Lily playing in the cast-off flower petals as a little girl, and now her arrangements were living sculptures, looking like a cottage garden come to life. Little Violet saving dying plants, and now her houseplants were sprinkled throughout the store, creating a thriving jungle of ferns and vines along the walls.

Rose had molded the business to what she'd always wanted. A bright, friendly store full of nice things to give to someone you loved.

Heaps of beautiful flowers sat in woven baskets like a flower market in Covent Garden. Early peonies, roses, lilacs, daisies, and baby's breath created a meta-arrangement, overflowing and lush.

Rose's eyes went misty. They'd done it. In a few short

weeks, they'd turned an eyesore into something bright and magical.

"Hey," she said to them. "Come here." She held out her hands.

Violet and Lily glanced at each other skeptically.

"Yeeeees..?" Lily said slowly.

"Look at what we've made." Rose scanned the room to take it all in.

"If I wasn't so tired, I think I might burst into tears," Lily said in a watery voice.

"He'd be so proud of you," Rose said quietly.

"Of us." Violet squeezed her.

"Of us," Rose conceded. She wiped a tear from her eye, careful not to smudge her eyeliner. She glanced at the clock. "It's time."

Violet danced in place. "This was your idea. Flip the sign."

Rose smiled back as she walked over, took a breath, and flipped the heavy chalk sign to 'open.' She peered out the glass door and spun around. "No customers coming our way yet."

The clock ticked to 9:01.

"It's okay, it's barely nine a.m.," Rose said to calm her nerves more than anything. "Looks like we have time to sweep."

She hurried to the back room and grabbed a broom as the door jingled with their first customer.

Gray walked in wearing a slate gray shirt, dark tie, and dress pants. "Hey, partners," he said quietly. His eyes locked with hers. "This looks breathtaking."

God, it felt so awkward. His words had run through her mind at least once an hour since she saw him two days ago. *I wish you preferred it with me.* What did that even mean? He teased her non-stop about how bossy she was, but her hand itched from where he'd interlaced his fingers with hers.

"Hey, Gray. Are you hanging out with us this morning?" Lily said brightly.

Gray snapped out of his trance and glanced at Lily. "Nope, sorry. I have a few appointments today, but I wanted to be the first customer. I need to buy some flowers."

"Ooh!" Lily smiled with a sparkle. "Is it for me? You know how I love roses."

Gray laughed. "Noted, but no." He walked over to the coolers and surveyed them. "Wow, Lily, these are amazing. How could I choose?"

Violet grabbed the broom from Rose's hand and walked past Gray. "Our resident taste expert is the oldest sister." Lily put on music that hummed out of the store's speakers and went back to work on the next arrangement.

Gray stared expectantly at Rose, and she finally walked to him. "Depends on what the occasion is."

"Which is your favorite?" He peered down at her. His aftershave gave Rose goosebumps again, but she tried to put it out of her mind. She couldn't get more tangled up than she already was, living in the murky middle between *let's make out when my defenses are down* and *business partner I want to strangle sometimes.*

"I love this one." She pointed to a sculptural arrangement featuring bright white tulips, likely his, accented with soft yellow flowers and spunky pieces of grass intertwined.

Gray's eyes flitted across her face, briefly staring at her mouth, and then opened the cooler and took the arrangement out. He walked to the counter.

"You can't pay for that," Lily scoffed. "Take the first one on the house. I mean, those are your flowers."

Gray smiled. "Let me be your first customer. For Frank."

He still paid tribute to the man who stood by him when no one else would. Rose felt a clutch in her throat and blinked rapidly to get rid of a mist that caught her by surprise. God, was the whole day going to be like this? She wasn't used to all these feelings.

"Do you have any arrangement cards?" Gray asked.

Lily handed him a small notecard. "I gave you the friends, family, and owner discount."

He put the card in a small envelope and put it in the arrangement. "Thanks. The place does look seriously amazing."

Lily's wide grin sparkled at him as she walked around the counter. "We couldn't have done it without our free labor. You made all this happen." She threw her arms around him for a quick hug.

Gray grabbed the flowers from her and stopped in front of Rose. "Rose, I'm sorry for screwing up your thing." He handed the flowers to her. "Happy opening day." His hand came up to her arm as he placed a gentle, slow kiss on her cheek. His stubble grazed her cheek, and she felt him linger before stepping back.

She pulled toward him with wanting, and goose bumps ran down her arms. She tried to regain her footing. "You don't have to—"

"I wanted to," he said quietly with a shy grin and eyes that searched hers for a moment. His hand fell from her arm. "I need to get going. Have a good first day, partners. Text me if you need anything."

Violet gazed out the window to the street. "Hopefully, you won't be our only customer."

Gray walked toward the front door, a bounce in his step. "Oh, I don't think that'll be the case." He turned around with a cheerful look. "I bet you'll be surprised how many people need flowers today." He sent Rose a wink and walked out into the fresh April morning.

Violet and Lily watched Gray walk out the door and spun to look at Rose as the door clicked shut.

Lily's mouth gaped. "Shut. Up! Holy shit, that was so sexy. He bought you flowers from your store and then stood there all sexy with his little tie."

Rose set the flowers on the register and stashed the card in her pocket. "Don't be silly; he was just apologizing," Rose shook her head and willed the stupid grin off her face.

The doorbell jingled, and two customers walked in.

"Welcome." Lily walked over to greet them.

A thrill ran through Rose. She allowed herself to hope for a good day of business. No sooner had the two women walked in than a few more came in behind them. That kicked off a busy morning of helping customers, putting in orders for events, funerals, and even Mother's Day arrangements.

Mrs. Maroo walked in at lunchtime with her pickleball teammates. "This can't be the same store. It just can't be!" Her eyes took in the store with wonder, and her face split with a smile. "Oh Rosie, I bet your dad is busting his

Hawaiian buttons with pride in heaven." She gathered her in a fierce hug.

Rose smiled with embarrassment and muttered a quick thanks while Mrs. Maroo squeezed the life out of her.

She finally let Rose go and turned around, looking at the store. "This place is gosh darn beautiful. I might have to come here just to be near all these pretty fresh things."

"You're welcome any time. We can always use the company," Rose said with warmth, and realized she meant it. She really did want her favorite people to pop by to say hello in her store. It sounded idyllic.

"Oh!" Mrs. Maroo fished in her oversized purse and pulled out three envelopes. "I found these in a folder that was misplaced. They should have been with the rest of your dad's things, but they got misfiled."

She handed the three letters to Rose, each sealed with a name on it. Rose's heart pounded as she looked at the familiar handwriting on the envelope.

"You know half the town is coming here out of pure nosiness, but I hope you make them all repeat customers! These flowers are gorgeous! Marge, did you see these chocolates?" Mrs. Maroo power-walked through the store to catch up with her friends.

Rose glanced through the store for Lily and Violet. They were both busy with customers, enjoying the hustle and bustle of the busy crowd.

She looked down at the envelopes with her dad's chicken scratch handwriting. *We'll talk about this later.*

Throughout the day, it felt like the entire town stopped by to grab flowers. Pop got away from the diner for a few minutes, and Aaron and Nick came by and brought them "happy opening day" coffee and donuts.

They had a steady stream of customers all day, and Rose realized no one was leaving without purchasing a flower, which seemed statistically impossible. Around three, she started to panic they were getting low on stock.

"Violet, do you have any potted plants? Any additional things we could sell?" Rose started looking in the back, but they'd put everything on the floor for their grand opening.

Violet stared back with an equal amount of panic. "Everything I have is for my landscaping customers. I never expected it to be this busy."

Rose thought about Gray's comment. "I bet Gray put people up to this, so we'd have a good first day." She marched out to the floor and found Nash browsing the arrangements.

"Hey, Rose," He greeted her with a friendly hug. "Great opening. Things are looking busy."

"Did anyone tell you to buy something today?"

"Don't you want me to buy something?" He loved the chance to needle her when he could.

Rose playfully punched his arm. "Answer me."

"Fine..." He laughed, rubbing his arm. "Gray *suggested* that I make it a point to stop by the store and pay my respects. Plus, it's my mom's birthday this week. So two birds, you know?" He turned back to the cooler. "She'll know somehow if I don't get the most expensive one, so you're welcome." He pulled out a stunning arrangement of white roses and a small bouquet of daylilies.

They walked to the counter. "Would Gray have told other

people the same thing?" she asked, looking around at who was in the store.

"Maybe. He's a friendly guy who loves to chat with folks."

"Hey, Nash, nice choice." Lily rang him up at the register as she locked eyes with him.

"Hey, Lilypad, haven't seen you in a while." They gazed at each other quietly, and Rose was picking up a vibe. *He didn't know she existed, my ass.*

"Well, I've gotta go," Nash said suddenly. "Good luck with the rest of your opening day, Rose. Bye, Lily," he said quietly.

Rose smiled at Lily with a shit-eating grin.

Lily stuck her tongue out at her. "We're gonna need more flowers tomorrow. Figure something out with that MBA brain." She stepped away to greet more customers.

Shit, right. They needed at least one more day of stock until their next order was delivered on Monday morning.

Luckily, she knew a guy.

She texted Gray asking if he could spare some flowers for tomorrow and thought about thanking him for the flowers again but decided against it. It was already too confusing. Her hand rubbed her cheek where his stubble had grazed her. Her phone dinged with a response that he'd drop more flowers off that evening.

A steady buzz of customers lasted another hour until Violet walked up to Rose when they finally had a lull. Her brows quirked with confusion. "Don't you think it's weird everyone bought at least one flower today? Even Pop did. I love flowers as much as anybody, but...that's weird."

Lily rubbed her temples. "Don't look too closely at a horse's teeth," she thought for a second, "or whatever the saying is. Lord, I'm so tired." She leaned on the counter, and the door jingled again.

"I've got this," Rose went to greet the next customer.

By the end of the day, they'd sold every last flower in the place. The last customer walked out at 5:01 p.m. with the last batch of baby's breath.

Rose surveyed the destruction. Lily lay on the counter with her head in her arms. And Violet sat on the prep counter, stretching her arm muscles.

They completely sold out, and the impact of what they'd just done hit Rose like a ton of bricks. "Guys, look."

"What now?" Lily whined.

"Look. Look at this."

"I know," Lily yawned. "It's a complete mess. We'll have to come in extra early and prep the stuff Gray's bringing over."

Rose shook Lily off the counter. "Lilybug, this was a goddamn smashing success! People literally cleaned us out!" Rose danced in place, gaining more energy.

Lily started laughing, and Violet joined in. "Ok, okay. I get your point."

"We should celebrate. Let's go to the new Italian place across town," Violet said.

"God, yes." Lily grabbed her bag. "And I will have three glasses of wine and collapse into a heap at home."

Rose turned off the register. "Ok, but I have to be back here in a few hours for the flower delivery from Gray."

A chorus of *oooo's* rang out, and Rose rolled her eyes and

smiled. “You’re both the worst.” They stumbled to Rose’s car and fell in, happy to be off their feet.

Rose drove through town as she and Violet talked about the best parts of the day. “I wonder what Dad would have thought of us running out of flowers. I don’t think he ever had two customers at once.”

Violet peered out the car window, her head leaning against it. “I think he would have liked today. He’d have been out front the whole time.”

“Chatting with everyone and getting underfoot.” Rose smiled, but her eyes went misty.

“Rose,” Lily called from the backseat, “pull over.”

Rose glanced in the rearview mirror. “What? Why?”

Lily pointed across the road to an all-too-familiar cemetery. “Look.”

Rose slowed to a stop and peered over the rolling hills of modest gravestones, only to see a brightly colored mound she hadn’t seen before.

The mound was at the terrible spot they’d been at three months ago.

A flutter landed in Rose’s heart. She wasn’t sure what she was looking at, but she turned into the cemetery anyway. It would be the first time they’d visited since the funeral.

As she drove nearer, Rose’s heart leaped into her throat. She drove the winding roads with watery eyes. She parked, and they slowly got out in awe.

Rose couldn’t believe her eyes.

In front of her were heaps and heaps of flowers. Hundreds, no thousands of brightly colored flowers piled this way and that, creating a voluminous floral quilt that flowed out into a wave of color.

Every single one of the flowers they'd sold that day all piled lovingly on top of their father's grave.

A few handwritten notes fluttered in the breeze and stood with the flowers that blanketed the dirt that hadn't yet grown grass on it. White daisy petals fluttered in the breeze, pressed next to chrysanthemums, bouquets of irises, and roses, all lovingly placed side by side.

Violet and Lily wrapped their arms around Rose, who stared in wonder. Violet had tears running down her face while Lily was already sobbing.

"They did this," Lily hiccuped, "for him."

All their customers, all the kind words they'd had that day. It was a big love note to their father from the town he'd loved so much.

Rose felt tears run down her face, and she knew in her bones this was no accident. Her heart cracked open as she realized who would do this lovely thing without ever admitting to it. A single name rang in her head. *Gray*.

Lily crouched down and felt the flowers she had so lovingly prepared a few days before. Her fingers ran over a daylily bouquet like the one Nash had bought. She stood up, pulled out a single rose, lily, and violet, and placed it on the headstone.

"So we'll be with him." Her voice wobbled as she walked back.

Rose held out her hand to Lily. "We're always with him when we're in the store, bug."

"I hope he's proud of us," Violet whispered. Her lips quivered and made her look like the little girl Rose remembered.

An errant strong breeze whipped their hair about them in the spring evening.

Rose squeezed them. "It's safe to say that was a 'yes,'" She let out a watery laugh and remembered the three letters in her purse. "I have something for you." She turned back to the car, grabbed the letters, and held them out. "Mrs. Maroo dropped these off." They looked down in wonder, and Lily let out a small sob.

Rose gathered them both in a hug. They'd read their letters privately when the time was right. It was all still too raw.

They took a long look at the grave. The flowers shone orange in the sunset that peeked through the trees. The bright spring florals reminded Rose of her dad's brightly colored shirts and sunny attitude.

This was a perfect spring day he would have loved. *Gray probably knew that.*

They stood for what felt like an eternity as they watched the sunset on the horizon, yet it still felt too soon to leave.

As the last slip of orange disappeared from the headstone, Rose took a big breath. "Ready?" She squeezed them, and they walked back to the car.

She turned around once more before she got in. The flowers snuggly blanketed the grave, providing cheery companionship and making her smile. He never wrote this in his final wishes, but it would have made him sing with joy to see such a lovely sight.

There wasn't a more loving tribute for the man who befriended an entire town.

ROSE

Two hours later, having dropped a tipsy Violet and Lily off at home, Rose drove to Bloom to meet Gray.

She was exhausted but already filled with a mixture of happiness and nerves for the upcoming few weeks. They'd need to prove themselves so potential buyers would be interested in the business.

As Rose parked in front of the shop, she remembered Gray's card in her pocket. She opened the small envelope and smiled at his loopy handwriting.

Rose - these pale in comparison to you, but I hope you'll forgive me anyway. Yours, Gray

Rose tried to swallow the smile that burst onto her face.

Yours, she repeated to herself. Not *your partner*, not *your friend.*

Hers.

Don't catch feelings, Rose. She felt her heart tug as she ran a finger over the card. She stashed it safely back in her pocket.

Rose wandered through the decimated store. Most shelves were empty, and every piece of greenery was gone. As she waited for Gray, she restocked the soaps and chocolates. Finally, she jumped when a loud pounding came from the back door.

"Who's there?" she called as she walked back.

"Who the hell else would it be?" Gray yelled, apparently tired from his day as well. Probably not the right time to ask him about her dad's grave.

She flipped the lock and opened the solid metal door. Gray was in the back of his dark box truck, grabbing buckets of flowers. Rose walked to the end of the truck and reached out her hands to take them.

"No, these are covered in dirt. Let me handle it," Gray said.

"Suit yourself." Rose walked back inside, leaned on the worktable, and waited for him to bring them inside.

She flipped open her permanent to-do list, starting a new draft for tomorrow. *Restock flowers, create grab n' go arrangements, ask Vi to bring in more plants from her greenhouse*, and as Gray walked through the back door, all the thoughts in Rose's head fell away.

He was wearing a worn flannel shirt with a tight black t-shirt underneath. He'd rolled the flannel sleeves up to his elbows, showing the multitude of delicate tattoos she had an insane urge to trace with her tongue. His hair was a mess, as usual, falling into his face, but the thing that caught Rose's breath was the black-rimmed glasses on his face.

She didn't even know she had this fantasy until it appeared in front of her. A bad boy on a motorcycle was her catnip, but a bad boy wearing glasses?

A shudder ran through her. *Yes fucking please.*

He picked up buckets of flowers from his truck, biceps flexing from their weight. "I hope hyacinths, tulips, and daffodils are okay. That's all I had ready." His face was carved into a scowl, and he looked distracted.

Rose stepped back so he could haul the buckets to the storage coolers. "Of course. I appreciate whatever you can spare. I'll get a full order again on Monday." She tried not to stare like a horndog as he efficiently carried the huge buckets, his chest and arms flexing from the work.

"Long day?" Rose put away her phone, ready to see what would make Mr. Popular so gruff.

"I don't wanna talk about it." Gray shoved buckets full of tulips into the cooler. He jogged back out to the truck and came back with another armload. She silently watched him walk away and enjoy the view as he brought in another armful of flowers.

Gray unloaded the last few buckets into the coolers and looked at Rose with concern as he brushed off his hands. "That's all I had ready. Sorry."

"Sure you don't want to talk about it?" Rose leaned back on the prep table. "Don't friends talk about bad days?"

Gray huffed out a laugh. He rubbed his fingers on the

bridge of his nose. "Things just piled up one after the other, plus my eyes are so tired I had to take my contacts out. My meeting this morning ran late, and planting the dahlias took a lot longer than I had planned. The new full-time guy was late today, which put us behind schedule. I'm already fucking behind schedule."

"You hired someone full-time?"

He sent her a half smile and nod. "Marco Polizzi. Today was a one-off. He's been great otherwise. Just the worst timing with everything today."

He'd taken her advice. She'd practically drooled when he walked in, but taking her advice was the sexiest fucking thing he'd ever done.

"And you had to rescue your business partners, er, friends after all that. Thank you again."

"It's just...these days—" Gray stopped and shook his head, holding something back.

"What?" Rose leaned against the table and faced him.

"I just feel pushed to my brink, you know?" He wiped his hand across his mouth. "With the store opening, the farm expansion, pushing my trip to see Alex, plus my business partner being a pain in my ass all the time and about to leave any fucking minute...." He sent her a hollow, sad smile. "Drugs were the easy way out to take the edge off, that's all. I'll just have to punish myself at the gym tonight."

"There's a gym in Fairwick Falls?"

"Well, my homemade gym." He shoved at his hair.

"Bags of soil you duct-taped together, farmer?" Her mouth quirked as she teased him. It had been too long.

"You offering to help take the edge off instead, princess?"

He walked closer to her, his expression had turned playful, but Rose saw the heat behind it.

She loved it when he crowded her. When he took charge in the dance they did around their attraction. "So I'm a princess again." She bit her lip, and his eyes darted to it.

"When you're a pain in the ass, you are. Also," he trailed a finger lightly down her arm that sent goose bumps trembling down her body, "I didn't hear a no."

Rose felt the breath leave her body and could only whisper a response. "I would never."

He leaned toward her, his eyes on her lips, whispering. "You're too good for a quick bang?"

His hair casually fell over his forehead, needing both a haircut and her hands run through it. Her gaze lingered on his square jaw, and her fingers needed to graze the dark stubble on it. Feel it against her cheeks, against her breasts and thighs.

Goddamnit, she wanted him so badly.

"I guess if it'll help you out," she whispered, grabbing his shirt to bring his mouth down to hers.

Gray wrapped his hands around her waist in an instant. His hands were in her hair and on her back, bringing her closer.

God, she loved the taste of him. His stubble grazed her cheek as he opened her mouth with his tongue. It shot an arrow of need directly down to her core and ignited the fire he'd left smoldering there weeks before. She grazed her teeth against his bottom lip, taking as much as he'd give her.

Silky, thick hair brushed her hands as they wound

through his hair. It was smooth and thick. Perfect for pulling him closer to her.

Gray's hands worked their magic, one stroking the side of her breast. Her breath hitched, and she felt desire curl into her. She leaned into him, desperate for his hand on her nipple. Her hands ran down his biceps, grasping his muscles in the way she'd imagined for weeks. The scent of him—cedar and his aftershave—surrounded her, igniting more and more need until she clawed at him.

He planted kisses along her jawline and down to her neck. She could feel the desire practically dripping off him as he nuzzled her neck. She heard herself gasp.

"Rose," Gray purred her name slowly between kisses.

"Shh, don't stop." She dragged his head back to her mouth.

"Rose," he said firmly and pulled back. His thumb stroked her cheek. "Rose, we need to talk about...this." His chin gestured to the small space between them.

"What 'this'?" Rose asked, genuinely confused. She felt drunk with lust.

Gray walked away in frustration. "We're business partners. And any time I see you, I..." He wiped his face in frustration. "I want more than a stolen kiss every few weeks. That we never talk about after it happens."

He came back to her and placed his hands on her hips. His head angled down to hers, and his eyes ensnared her. "I want you. In every way imaginable."

Run, Rose. You're getting too close to the edge of everything you've ever wanted.

"Things would get messy," she said slowly.

"Promise?" He sent her a wicked grin.

She poked his ribs, and he grabbed her hand. "You know what I mean."

He brought her wrist to his mouth and placed a long, slow kiss on the inside, and goose bumps showered down her arms.

His gaze locked with hers. "Every time we're alone, I'm fighting this urge. Tell me you feel it too." His breaths grew shallow as his lips came back to her wrist, working his way slowly down her arm.

Didn't she deserve a moment of happiness? Even if it was fleeting?

The wet press of his mouth against the sensitive skin of her arm drew her in. "I guess we're only temporary business partners. But we can't date." Rose managed to get out as her breaths came in shallow gasps. He kissed the inside of her upper arm, and his other hand grasped her ass.

If he didn't keep going, she'd kill him.

"I'm leaving. Soon," she said through gritted teeth. He'd jumped to her neck, and she was having a hard time not rolling her eyes to the back of her head as he placed open-mouthed kisses along her shoulder.

"No dating then. Just consider this another accident." He moved her hair out of the way and nuzzled into the curve of her neck, his stubble grazing against her.

Her knees almost fucking buckled. God, was she that starved for him?

He moved to her earlobe and nipped at it. Heat gathered like a waterfall in her core. He whispered into her ear. "How do you feel about being fucked repeatedly until you scream? About coming on my face like a good girl?"

Ah fuck. He'd just named her secret fantasy out loud.

"Yes," she sobbed, not even trying to play it cool.

He pulled back, and his hand grasped the back of her neck, his mouth close to hers. "You want me to fuck you, princess?"

Rose nodded, all coherent thought having left her. "Just sex. Get it out of our systems," she gasped. God, why wasn't his mouth on hers yet?

His hands moved to her waist, framing it with the span of each hand. "I should warn you..." He sent a lethal smile at her as his eyes danced with dark delight. "I prefer to be in control."

A thrill ran through Rose. Despite appearances, she wanted someone else to be in charge in bed. Give her all the attention to detail she gave other people, and show her how much he wanted her.

"Deal."

His hand moved from her waist and cupped her breast, his mouth still hovering over her. "You'll tell me to stop when you want to stop."

She nodded, entranced as his hand squeezed her breast, and she leaned into him. "Don't stop."

Gray placed a feather-light kiss on her lips, and Rose leaned in for more, needing more like it was her next breath.

Gray's other hand came up to her other breast as he pulled away from her lips. His insistent hard grip on her breasts became feather-light strokes along her nipples, already hard from his attention. Her blouse was thin, and he played with each nipple, dragging both index fingers around and around and around. A throb started somewhere deep inside her.

His stormy eyes held hers, and with each stroke on her hard nipples, she lost a little more of her will to not throw him down on the table and ride him. Her hands grabbed for his waist. She'd wanted to run her hands up and down his body for weeks, maybe months. It had felt like a lifetime. She pulled at his shirt like a mad woman, wanting to feel him.

"Ah," he stopped her with one word. "Focus is on you, princess. Hands on the table behind you."

He came up to kiss her jaw and pulled each side of her blouse down over her shoulders. She'd worn a wide v-neck blouse, and he yanked it halfway down her upper arms, pinning her arms to her sides. A thrill ran through her at how he'd taken control.

"I said I was in charge," he whispered into her ear. He gently, slowly slid each bra strap off her shoulders. Her blouse and bra barely covered her breasts.

His fingers traced the swells of her breasts, up around each bra cup peeking out from the neckline. He dipped his fingers underneath her bra and squeezed hard.

"You're so fucking gorgeous." He captured her mouth again, kissing her with everything he had.

She grasped at the tails of his flannel, bringing him closer. His mouth punished hers, and she opened greedily for him, needing more.

His hands came to her skirt, and he slowly rolled down the zipper. "I didn't bring a condom," he said in a low voice. "And I'm guessing the ice princess didn't pack one either."

"Fuck you," she spit out with little heat, enjoying their game.

"Oh, I intend to, princess. Later. But tonight, we'll get creative." A smile curled on his lips as he kneeled and tugged her zipper.

Rose felt the skirt fall to the floor, pooling around her heels. *I would have worn sexier underwear if I'd known this was in the cards.*

Gray let out a low whistle. His hands settled on her hips, the heat of his hands sending an electric shock through her. She had on a dark pink thong, which didn't cover much. He placed hot, slow kisses along her belly, hips, and the tops of her thighs.

"Is there a reason you still have me trussed up like a prize pig?" She wanted to be a brat for him and loved that spurred the fire in his eyes.

He stood, and his hand grasped one side of her ass in a punishing grip. "Feeling sassy, are you, princess? For that smart mouth, you'll do the next part." He left a lingering kiss on her mouth. He leaned to whisper into her ear. "Looks like you're already wet for me."

Her panties were soaked.

He pulled back and kissed the side of her mouth. She thought her heart might jump out of her chest.

"Since you know every damn thing," he said. "Show me. Take that manicured hand, put it in those wet panties, and show me how you come."

Holy hell.

"So you're lazy now, too?" she said with a curved smile. He gave her ass a smack that stung just a hair.

Yes. Exactly what she'd wanted.

"Do not test me, Rose." He growled in her ear, and her body throbbed from those words.

His body was flush against her side, and he met her eyes with fire that would consume her. "Show me."

She bit her lip, locked eyes with him, and moved her hand to her panties.

She dipped below the soft fabric. A low rumble sounded at her side as Gray's eyes were now laser-focused on her hand sliding down.

She was practically dripping. He'd barely even touched her, but she could *hear* how wet she was.

Her fingers found her throbbing clit, and she circled it once and bit back a cry. Gray's hand had come up to her right nipple, dipping under her bra to play with it.

"Show me how you like it," he whispered into her ear.

"Fuck," she sobbed. She moved her fingers around her swollen clit faster and faster until he grabbed her wrist, seizing it in place. Her eyes locked with his.

With a slow movement, he lifted her hand out of her panties into the air and took her fingers into his mouth, sucking on them as his eyes closed in pleasure.

Rose pulsed with need as his hot mouth locked around her fingers.

He opened his eyes and smiled like he'd won the lottery.

In that moment, Rose was fully and completely fucking ruined for another man. She took his mouth, tasting herself on him, but he pulled away.

"We're not done."

"But I want you." She grabbed at his shirt, needing more of him.

"That was just the appetizer. You're the next course." He spun her around and pressed a hand to her back, bending her over the prep table.

Rose watched from the corner of her eye as Gray knelt behind her. He guided her foot up and out of the skirt pooled around her ankles.

"Spread your legs, princess. I want to see you."

Fuck.

His hand pulled her leg to the side, and she spread her legs wide for him, still bent over the table.

"Good girl," he purred.

Why did that make her so wet?

The cool air kissed her ass as she bent over the table. She felt so exposed, and as his breath came up to her pussy, she clenched, wishing he was already inside her. He moved her panties to the side, and the heat from his breath made her shiver.

"God, you're perfect." His hands wrapped around the outside of her thighs, bracketing her in place. Her blouse still dug into the sides of her shoulders. She wanted to wiggle against him, hump the table, anything to end the pressure aching in her pussy.

He placed kisses along the back of her thigh, licking as he went. "I'm going to eat this pretty little pussy, princess. Unless you don't need my help?"

"No," Rose mewled, not even embarrassed at how she was begging. "Don't stop."

His arms wrapped around her legs, pulling them even

wider as a hot, firm stroke of Gray's tongue hit her clit. Rose screamed with pleasure. He licked in long, firm strokes, teasing her clit as he buried his face into her.

Rose felt the buildup of an orgasm overtake her, shooting through her system and making every nerve-ending sizzle.

His tongue dove into her, thrusting and licking. She could cry from the pleasure. She moaned and pressed her hips back into him shamelessly. He pulled her thighs back into his face, and the scrape of stubble against her clit, her thighs, was almost too much.

"Yes, yes," she panted as he sucked her clit and slid a finger inside her. As another orgasm built in her, Gray ripped himself away from her. Rose whipped her head around as he stood up and heard herself whimper.

He pulled her up from the table to stand in front of him. She grabbed for his belt, and he didn't bat her hands away this time.

His cock bulged against his jeans, and Rose ran a hand down it as she unzipped them as fast as she could.

He stepped away from her one more time.

"You are the fucking worst," she huffed, smiling at him.

He sent her a wolfish grin back.

"Wait until you see what's for dessert."

Chapter Seventeen

ROSE

Rose watched Gray saunter to a chair, his jeans unzipped and hard cock visible through his boxer briefs.

She stood against the table in heels, a thong, and a blouse.

He sat down and patted his leg for her to come sit.

She walked across the room to him, and his eyes raked her up and down, taking in every inch of her legs and hips. She loved when he watched her. When he stared at her like she was his.

She stood in front of him, and he placed hot kisses on her stomach, each hand twining around her thighs.

His fingers dug into either side of her panties, and he pulled them down until they were on the floor. He helped her step out of them and picked them up, laying them on his lap.

His hands guided her, so she straddled his thigh, and he started to pull her down so she'd ride his leg.

She was too wet. "Gray, I'll ruin your jeans."

He yanked her down so her pussy landed hard against the worn denim.

"I want you to ruin them. Ruin me." His eyes met hers with ferocity, and it was all she could do to hold herself back from rocking on him right now.

He yanked down her blouse and bra, freeing her breasts. His mouth came down to claim a nipple, sucking hard, and Rose rocked against him. Needing friction.

His hand stilled her hip. "No."

"Gray," a steel glint in her voice.

"Am I in charge, Rose?" His eyes narrowed, hand digging in and curving along her ass.

"You are when your tongue is on my pussy," she shot back, hovering over his lips.

A smack with a sting on her ass gave her exactly what she wanted, and she couldn't hide a smile. He kissed her hard and quick, a dark delight in his eyes.

"For that, princess, you'll be punished." He pulled down his boxer briefs and gripped his cock. Rose's mouth salivated at the throbbing hard length that already had beads of moisture on the end.

He stroked his cock twice, never breaking eye contact. "You have to sit perfectly still as I tell you all the ways you've driven me mad."

His other hand brought her close as he whispered in her ear. "The first time you made me come was after I saw you on the road." His hand pulsed up and down on his cock, and

Rose ached inside at the shock of how much he wanted her. "I had to go behind a tree, like a fucking animal, and stroke my cock, picturing you on it."

Holy hell, that was so hot. She tried to press against his leg, shamelessly taking her pleasure, but his hand held her in place.

"After you left the greenhouse in the rain, I stayed," he kissed the underside of her jaw. "I pictured you on your knees with that smart mouth wrapped around my cock."

Rose sobbed with pleasure as his grip loosened, and he rocked her against his leg, moving her hip so she could rub her clit against him. *Yes, yes.*

"And after I kissed you? Do you know what happened?"

She dug her heels in, needing more friction, needing more of him as she ground against his leg. She kissed the side of his cheek as he buried his face in her neck. His jeans were completely soaked with her.

His hand was stroking hard against his cock, and Rose desperately wanted to touch it, but her arms were trapped against her sides.

"Rose, answer me," he rocked her harder.

"What did you do?" she whispered, climbing higher and higher as she ground against him.

"I couldn't sleep a fucking wink knowing I'd never be inside you. I came into my hand more times than I can count that night, imagining your tits in my hands, what you'd taste like. You have been torturing me, Rose. Killing me."

His hand slid along her ass as she rocked, taking more and more. She moaned against him as she fucked his leg. His grip was punishing, and she loved it.

"Come on me, Rose. End my misery of not knowing what you look like when I make my good girl come."

He rocked her harder and faster against him and grabbed her panties from his lap, wrapping them around his cock as he beat it. The sight of it sent a blinding white shock of climax through her, unfurling from her center through every ending of her body. She screamed into his mouth, and he came into his hand, a loud groan grinding out of him.

Gray pulled her to him, kissing her as she finished rocking against him.

She lifted her lips from his, panting.

A breath held between them as she considered how big of a mistake she'd just made.

She was ruined for him. She wanted that again and again.

He pulled her head down to his shoulder, and she nuzzled in. He fixed her shirt so her arms could move, and she wrapped them around his waist.

His heart was beating like a hummingbird, like hers.

He placed a kiss on her forehead.

Rose stared at the floor. What happened next?

She inhaled his scent and took a minute to feel okay. This is what safety feels like, she thought, chagrined at how foreign it felt to her. His arms held her close, and she couldn't help but nuzzle in for a split second. She felt the hard planes of his chest and stroked a thumb along his back to soothe herself.

Her fingers traced the lines on his forearms that had haunted her for so long, noticing a few were floral vines.

"Is it out of your system yet?" Gray asked as he wrapped his arms around her.

His tone was light, but Rose felt the weight behind it. *Was* this a one-and-done thing?

It had to be. It didn't matter how much she already craved his fingers gripping her ass again. His presence kindled something in her even when she felt like crumbling. She'd never had this kind of chemistry with anyone else. She couldn't get used to someone giving her everything she wanted if she was leaving soon.

Why did it have to be him?

A warmth of something Rose couldn't name bloomed in her chest. *Danger, Rose Parker. You are in danger of letting someone have too much of you.* And when in doubt, Rose got tactical when she started to feel herself slipping.

She lifted herself off him, enjoying the ache between her thighs as she stood up to grab her skirt.

She'd just ignore his question. "Guess we should start scoping out potential buyers. Maybe you can introduce me to the major players." She zipped her skirt and ignored the eyes she knew were staring into the back of her head.

She glanced up to see he was zipping his jeans. Her panties still lay on his lap.

"Sure," he cleared his throat. "Saturday?"

Rose checked her calendar, avoiding his eyes. "Sure."

"It's a date." Gray stood up and put himself in front of her so she had to look up at him.

"It's not a date."

"A work date."

"It's not a date, Gray."

He held up her wet panties and made a show of putting them in his pocket. "Maybe it's not a date, but these are mine now."

There was that throb again.

"C'mon, I'll walk you to your car." He headed toward the front door.

"Don't be silly. I'm parked right outside." But he kept walking, and she rolled her eyes as she followed him. He held the door open for her and flipped off the light.

Rose locked the door and turned to see him leaning against her car.

"Hell of an opening day, partner." His arms were crossed as he held eyes with a double meaning.

Indeed.

"Gray," she started but paused. Should she even ask? "Did you have anything to do with the flowers on my dad's grave?"

Gray rolled his lips together as he considered whether that was a bad thing or not. "He was special, Rose. He deserved something on the big reopening day. I hope," he paused, looking for the right words. "I hope that's okay. I know you didn't get along, but..." Gray met her eyes. "What?"

Rose took in the kind, frustrating, sexy as fuck man before her.

"You're a good man, Gray Roberts. He would have loved it." Her heart thudded against her chest again.

This man had done unspeakable things to her five minutes ago, but that admission felt like she'd just bared her soul to him.

His face turned suddenly serious, and his hand came to her jaw as he kissed her deeply, making Rose feel like the most precious thing in the world. Their tongues fought and danced, but after a long slow kiss, Gray pulled back, leaving her dazed.

His thumb lingered on her chin. "For the record, you're not out of my system."

Rose's breath caught in her throat as she stepped back. She couldn't get entangled for long. Gray turned around and walked to his truck.

This had to be a fling. She had her real life to get back to soon.

But she still felt the heat of his hand on her face, and her hand went to it.

Rose got in her car and sat, her heart still slamming against her chest. *You can't catch feelings. You're leaving soon.*

Whether you like it or not.

"WHAT THE HELL do you think you're doing?" Rose yelled at the greasy-looking man backing up to the driveway and attempting to hook Violet's car to his tow truck.

Rose had barely slept last night, replaying the opening day and her sexy session with Gray over and over in her head. At five a.m., she'd heard the beeping of a truck in their driveway. She'd thrown on a robe in record time and sprinted down the stairs of Violet's cottage.

The pot-bellied man turned around with sweat stains all

over his white shirt and an open button-down shirt with a name patch that said "Lenny."

"I just tow 'em when I'm told, lady."

Rose wrapped her robe around her tighter and marched down the front steps.

"Rose, what's going on?" Lily called out from behind her. She was in her sleep shorts and tank top, hair mussed from sleep.

"I'll handle it. Go back inside."

"Does she think we're still, like, seven years old?" Lily said to Violet, who appeared beside her in oversized striped pajamas.

"Hey, that's my car!" Violet padded out in her giant fuzzy slippers behind Rose.

Rose got in his face. "Why are you towing my sister's twenty-year-old paid-for car from her own house?"

"Look," the guy said through the cigarette between his lips, "you don't pay your taxes, I take your shit. Simple."

Rose plucked a piece of paper sandwiched between the windshield wipers on Violet's car and Rose's rental. It looked eerily like the mail that Violet had gotten for the past few months, and she realized his voice sounded familiar.

Lily stormed at him. "You're the asshole that keeps hounding us even though we're trying to pay the tax debt of our *dead father*?"

"I mean, that's what you say, but it still ain't paid, so my job is to put some pressure on ya." He lit a cigarette and blew it into their faces.

"You can't do this. This isn't legal." Rose walked to the

back of Violet's car and planted herself between it and the tow truck.

"You think standing there with your little twig body is gonna stop this tow truck?"

"Look." Rose shoved a hand through her hair, causing her robe to rise higher. A leer crossed the pale, greasy face in front of her, making Rose shudder. "We've already sent in forty thousand dollars. We just had our store opening. My dad's house was just listed for sale. We will happily send all that money when it comes into our bank account at the end of the month." Rose spoke in short, clear sentences so the Neanderthal in front of her could follow.

"All I know is the big guys don't got their money." He shrugged at her. "Maybe your fancy boyfriend can help you out."

"Boyfriend?" Violet turned to Rose with surprise. "Do you—"

"No!" Rose glared at him. "I don't—we don't have boyfriends."

He threw the cigarette down onto a flower patch and stomped it out with his foot, crushing the blooming hyacinths.

Violet lunged at him. "You monster."

Lily, despite being half Violet's size and height, caught her. "He's not worth it, Vi."

Rose planted her feet and sent him her steeliest stare. "I promise you I will send a deposit in two weeks. Just leave us the hell alone, and do not move this car."

The oil stain in front of her took a long look at her. "Two weeks, but only cause I got such a good show when you was walkin' out this morning." He ogled her breasts, and she clutched her robe closer around her.

Violet huffed out a growl. "This calls for pancakes." She marched back inside.

Rose stayed put until he drove his tow truck off the driveway and gave them the middle finger salute as he left. She returned it with an equal amount of maturity.

"Your finger sure showed him." Lily shuffled back into the house.

Fuck. This was not in the plan.

They walked back into the kitchen, and Violet had already made coffee and vegan pancakes.

"So while that guy is a complete asshat, he's not wrong. We still don't have the money to the IRS. Even after yesterday's opening day and the house and greenhouse sale, we'll barely have a third of what we need. I am taking all ideas." Rose grabbed a soul-sustaining cup of coffee.

"Hmm, a couple of weeks." Lily tapped her finger against the counter, thinking. "What could we do in a couple of weeks? God, that would be early May already."

"It's almost Mom's birthday. I always put flowers on her gravestone. You guys want to come with me this weekend?" Violet said quietly, ladling batter on the griddle.

Unfortunately, their mother's birthday was always near Mother's Day, which caused a double edge stabbing sensation in Rose's heart. She was grateful it only happened once a year. She could wallow and then move on.

An idea percolated on the edge of her brain. "Mothers..." *Shit, that's it. Mothers.* "What about a mother-daughter event?"

If she was going to experience pain, Rose preferred to monetize it.

"Oh, like a fancy mother/daughter lunch?" Violet asked.

Rose stood up, her vision flowing now. "A fun, luxurious one. Nothing stuffy. Maybe people could buy a package for themselves and their mom? Mimosas, massages, make a special bouquet together?"

Lily clapped her hands together. "Ohmygosh, I love it!"

"But Mother's Day is only in two weeks. Is that enough time?" Violet handed Rose a plate of fluffy heaven covered in syrup.

Rose speared a bite of pancakes. "It's got to be. I can get started on the pricing and invites if you can start on the social posts, Lil."

Lily was inhaling a stack of pancakes, so she sent Rose a thumbs up.

"Maybe Nick could help?" Violet suggested. Rose had forgotten that Aaron's husband was originally a massage therapist.

"Yes, perfect!" Rose whipped out her phone and started taking notes. She pulled up the Notes app and saw her "GTFOOFF" list. She swiped it away and started a new draft.

Rose furiously sent texts and emails to get the ball rolling on the event. They would only have a few weeks to put something together and sell tickets. Hopefully, the event could get both their finances and Rose's plan to leave back on track.

"I think we should start getting ready. We have an early morning." Rose yawned and rubbed her hand over her face.

"Think Pop will sell us two-gallon buckets of to-go coffee? I barely slept."

"Somebody came in late last night." Violet wiggled her shoulders at Rose.

Rose took a massive bite of pancakes to avoid answering her.

"Hmmm. Did it take *that long* to unload flowers from Gray's truck?" Lily put on a fake-innocent smile.

Heat grew on Rose's face. Shit. She should've known these nosy buttfaces would figure out something happened. She gulped her mouthful of pancakes and closed her eyes, waiting for what she knew would come. "Gray and I kissed again—"

Lily and Violet screamed, clapping their hands.

There it was.

She was *not* going to tell them what else they'd done last night.

"And it was the last time, but that is technically none of your business, and we don't need to talk about it." Rose ran upstairs to get ready, like a coward.

"Oh, don't you dare." Lily chased up after her. "We get way more details than that."

"It's nothing serious," Rose called out as she walked to her room. "Just think of him as a six-foot-three release valve."

"Lily, you owe me twenty bucks," Violet called, coming up the stairs.

"For the record, I thought you'd bone way sooner." Lily air high-fived Violet over Rose's head. They each stood in the doorway of their bedrooms.

"We didn't bone," Rose spit back, sipping her coffee. *Okay*, technically, *we didn't bone.*

"So, are you and Gray dating? Fuck buddies?" Lily put Rose back in the hot seat.

"I'd call us," Rose paused for effect. "None of your business." Rose took a breath, all business again. "We'll focus on selling the store now, so I probably won't see him as much. He knows it's nothing serious because I'll be gone soon. Once the shop sells."

All the fun was sucked out of the room at that moment.

Lily's face fell, and she started to close the door to her bedroom. "We know, we know, Rose. You'll be gone soon."

Rose didn't miss the sad look on Violet's face as she also closed her door.

Rose bit her lip. It was what was best for all of them.

Right?

Chapter Eighteen

GRAY

A perfect sexy daydream of Rose riding him was interrupted when Gray saw the worst fucking view in front of him: his parents pulling into his driveway.

Maybe if he ignored them, they'd go away. He carried his load of manure from the barn to the west greenhouse compost pile. Gray stalled as long as possible in the greenhouse and finally ambled out as they walked to him.

"Hi, stranger." His mom waved with one hand and held a Tupperware full of snacks in the other. He was still mad as hell at his dad for screwing with his deal, but he felt a shadow of shame crawl up his neck from ignoring their calls the last few weeks.

"Hi, Mom. You'd better stand back. I smell like pigs today."

"Don't be silly. I grew up with pig manure." She kissed him on the cheek.

"Your roof looks like it's about to cave in." His dad pointed up at the apex of the older greenhouse.

Missed you, too, Dad.

"It's fine." Gray tugged off a glove and ran a hand through his hair in frustration.

"We just wanted to make sure everything was okay." His mom rubbed a hand on his arm.

"I'm fine, Mom. Just busy."

"Bill said he decided to give you a shot." His dad's eyebrows raised expectantly, waiting for a thank you.

Gray bit his tongue so he didn't say something he'd regret.

His mom took his arm as they walked to the house. "What have you been up to?"

"Been really busy. I own part of the flower shop in town, and we had our grand re-opening a few days ago." Gray left out his tenuous fuck-buddy relationship with Rose that haunted his every waking hour.

"That's small potatoes, son. You should focus on bigger investments. A shop like that won't turn much of a profit."

Gray finally broke. "What the hell do you know about it? You're a mayor for twenty years and suddenly know everything about flower shops with built-in revenue from a small town without any other competition?"

"Now, Gray." His mom patted his arm.

"Mom, I'm done. I'm done with you both not respecting what I do."

His dad pulled out a check. "We think you can do lots of things, son. But we don't think you should have to do it by yourself. Now, I know you've taken out several loans that we're not sure you can repay," Gray threw his head back and tried not to scream. "Take this check and consider it a peace offering." The paper flapped in the breeze as his dad held it out.

Gray tugged the check from his hands and ripped it into tiny pieces without looking at the amount. "I do not need your help. I'm doing perfectly fine."

"But you look so tired." His mom ran a hand down his hair, and her eyes were full of concern.

He was pretty fucking tired. Tired of not spending every night with a woman he wanted to bed. Tired of missing his best little buddy and not having time to fly and see him. He was tired of doing everything himself and getting no thanks for it.

"Giselle mentioned you postponed your next trip to Montreal." There was a disappointed tone in his mother's voice.

"You know this is the busiest season."

"For farmers," his dad interjected.

"Yes, Dad. For farmers. Because that's what I fucking am. I'll see Alex soon. We FaceTime all the time."

His mother clicked her tongue. "They aren't young forever, Gray. You've already missed so much with him."

"Did you both come here for a reason or just to make me feel like shit?"

"We just want you to be the best dad you can be," his father said.

"Like you?" Gray laughed through his frustration.

"At least I was there for you. I wasn't a thousand miles away."

"First of all, I dropped everything when Giselle surprised me a few weeks ago. Alex got every second of my attention for the few days they were here. But when I was a kid?" Gray got in his dad's face, anger spilling over. "You never saw anything I did. You didn't *know* me. You didn't *see* me. Or maybe you didn't like what you saw." He waved a hand at the land behind him. "I have a thriving business. I'm sober. I'm actually happy. But you see none of that. You just see what I'm not." He turned on his heels. He was done.

His parents called after him to come back, but he jogged to the greenhouse.

He was literally running away from his problems, he knew, but he had shit to do today, and being treated like trash wasn't on his agenda. He needed to make time so he could see Rose tomorrow on their non-date date.

Her voice, her words, rang in his ears. *You're a good man, Gray Roberts.*

Fuck. It was like she just saw him. All those flaws, and maybe all the good things, too.

ROSE

Rose glanced out the window of Violet's cottage for the tenth time, trying not to draw attention from Lily. She couldn't let Lily know how much she looked forward to her non-date with Gray, or she'd never hear the end of it.

Today was just a recon trip, but if they got lucky, Rose would make connections with people interested in purchasing Bloom. A twinge landed in Rose's heart as she thought about selling the business they'd *just* launched a week ago.

"Ready for your date?" Lily said, and Rose jumped as she was caught peering out the window again.

"It is very specifically *not* a date. We're touring farms and shops together."

"Hmm." Lily peered at her through narrowed eyes. "Then why do you have your date look on?" She waggled a finger at Rose's jewelry and face.

"I always look nice, goober."

"Mmm, not like this." Lily chuckled behind her mug of tea.

Rose heard a low rumble and saw Gray pull into the driveway. Goose bumps ran down her spine seeing him on that fucking bike.

Lily started upstairs. "You can lie all you want to me, Rose. Just don't lie to yourself." Rose sent her a mental middle finger as she grabbed her coat and walked out to Gray straddling his bike.

"We are not going on that." She stopped on the cottage stoop, hand on her hip.

"You afraid?" He sent her a challenging smile.

Yes. "Of course not."

"I bet you've never been on a bike."

She stomped down the stoop stairs in her sleek leather boots. "I'll have you know I've driven one myself before." Sure, it was a moped, and she'd been terrified the whole time, but he didn't need to know that. "We cannot meet potential buyers riding a motorcycle. We have to project a certain image."

He shrugged. "My image includes a motorcycle."

Gray threw a thumb at the boxy, 1990s rental monstrosity she still hadn't returned to the airport. "Does that project the image you want?"

"God, fine." She took the helmet he gave her and wrestled with it to get it on.

He sent her a mischievous smile. "I have a feeling you're gonna like the bike in a few hours."

"Hey," she paused before she hopped on. "Just so we're clear, this is not a date."

He sent her a teasing look. "Who said anything about a date? As if an ice princess would spend time away from building her empire of world domination to spend time with someone she," he gasped for effect, "*liked*."

Rose hated that she wished this was a date. She wanted him to sweep her off her feet into a vacuum of time where there were no consequences to their actions and just have fucking fun for once in her life.

But no, this wasn't a date.

"Har har. Point taken." She straddled the bike and wished she'd opted for pants today.

His leather jacket strained across his large chest and biceps, and his hair was completely tousled by the wind. Looking at his arms bulging through the jacket sent tingles all down her body.

This was going to be a long day.

Gray revved the motorcycle engine as he started it, and

Rose jumped in her seat. She felt the rumbling vibrating between her legs and realized this whole thing was a bad idea.

"Put your arms around me!" he yelled over his shoulder.

She knew this was coming; she'd seen people do this.

She tentatively placed her hands on his sides. As he took off into the street, panic rose in Rose's throat, and she gripped him like a lifeline. His back shook as if he was laughing. *Jerk.*

It was a warm day in April, but Rose felt chills as the wind whipped around them, driving through Fairwick Falls. He made a slow meandering pass through the cute historic cottage neighborhood where Violet lived and rounded the corner through the town square.

"Aren't we going the other way?" she yelled up at him as they paused at a stop sign.

"Pop bet me apple pie pancakes I couldn't get you on the bike, and I had to show him proof." He revved his engine twice and took off around the town square, going by Canon's Diner.

Rose traced her teeth with her tongue and shook her head. *This guy.* She saw heads poke out the diner door, and one of the servers waved at them. "Oh my god," she said under her breath. Rose's cheeks were flaming red under the helmet.

He turned over his shoulder as they stopped at the single stop light in town, waiting for it to turn green. "Don't worry. I'll share them with you." Rose poked him in his very firm abs, and he chuckled as he took off.

After she got used to the shock of being out in the open

(how was this even legal?), she realized she *liked* the feeling of wind whipping around her. She liked molding herself to Gray and forgetting everything that lay on the other side of the ride. The landscape of the countryside flew past, and Rose felt like she was seeing it for the first time.

The heat from the bike and his body throbbed through her as they drove down the country lanes to their first stop. *This is like riding an oversized vibrator.*

Rose was thankful when Gray pulled into a gravel driveway because she'd lose her mind if they'd kept going.

Gray cut the bike's engine, and silence rang out over the acres of flowers. Their first stop was at the Jeffries Family Farm, which was doing a booming online business.

They pulled off their helmets, and Rose hopped off the bike.

"How was your first ride?" Gray sent her a knowing smile as he swung his leg over the bike.

"I told you I'd ridden before."

"Your panicked death grip told me otherwise."

"You're such a baby." She combed her hair back into place with her fingers.

Gray patted his torso. "I'm only now getting blood back into my organs."

She shoved his arm as she smiled at him. "You drive like a madman, but it wasn't scary in the least." *I am such an excellent liar.*

"Just thought it was maybe time for you to let loose and enjoy the ride rather than only focusing on the destination."

Their feet crunched on the rocky gravel surrounding the farm. Customers wandered the fields picking out brightly colored tulips and enjoying the spring day. Rose was overwhelmed by the shades of crimson, bright lemon yellow, and green in the hilly acres surrounding her.

"Wow." She let out a quiet breath.

"Great, right?" His face was peaceful as he gazed over the fields. "Andre," Gray called suddenly, sending a hand up. "I met the owner at a poker game your dad hosted, but I've never been here." A tall, black man with horn-rimmed glasses and a baseball cap sent him a wave and meandered over.

"Roberts. Here to pay me that fifty bucks you lost last game?" He smiled as he walked over, grabbing Gray's hand in a firm shake and doing that bro-hug thing that men did.

"Didn't you see my Venmo?" Gray responded, smiling.

"The one that said, 'This is' followed by a horse and shit emojis?" Andre laughed with Gray.

Seemed like Gray was friends with everyone. How did he do that?

"Andre, this is my friend, Rose."

"Business partner," Rose corrected, putting her game face on. Andre's eyebrows shot up.

"Frank's daughter," Gray said suddenly.

"Oh shit. Man, your dad was the best. I'm sorry for your loss." He grasped Rose's hand with both of his.

Rose knew that was coming, but it still always surprised her. *Deflect.* "Thanks. Your tulips are gorgeous."

A swell of pride had Andre smiling. "This year is a good crop. Gray said you guys wanted to talk business?"

"If you're interested in purchasing a storefront," Rose

took over with confidence. "We just reopened my dad's shop."

Andre crossed his arms and considered it. "I bet Frank would have loved to see what you've done with the place. I'm not planning on opening a brick-and-mortar, honestly. I've thought about it in passing, but it's not a priority right now."

Rose's hopes fell. *It's okay. This is just our first stop.*

"Of course," she said. "You have a lot to handle. I'd love to look around, though." She wanted to give him an out so they could keep a friendly relationship for the future.

"Sure. I'll be around if you need anything. We can talk terms if you want to purchase anything for the shop."

"Thanks, man," Gray waved as they wandered to the tulip fields. Gray's leather jacket and heavy work boots stuck out like a sore thumb among the young families and girls doing influencer-style photo shoots.

"Is there anybody my dad didn't know?" Rose asked.

"He made people a priority, Rose. I don't know what to tell you."

"Are you insinuating I don't?"

"Local places run differently. It's about how well you know your customers and your commitment to the community, not just 'Is your product good.' People support small businesses that support the community."

It stupidly sounded like such a foreign concept to her, but she'd lived in big cities her entire adult life. Getting things done as quickly as possible and conquering the next meant success, not relationships. "Does that mean you'll get a better price with Andre if you negotiate?"

"Oh my god," he laughed, bending over. "How are you so smart and yet miss the point entirely?"

"I get it, I get it." She waved her hand in the air as if pushing away the reminder. "Relationships blah, blah, blah."

"Is that how you won the hearts of all the men in Los Angeles? Relationships, blah, blah, blah?"

"Surprisingly, kind of." Silence settled through them as they wandered between rows of red and white tulips. "On to the next place?" Rose pulled out her phone.

The wind picked up. "Hold on, Speedy. Close your eyes and smell that."

"I don't have time for this."

"Come on. Just close your eyes and smell it."

"Fine." Rose let out a big breath, tired of receiving life lessons today. She closed her eyes.

The wind whipped around her, and she noticed the smell of sweet ambrosia and apple blossoms. It smelled like the embodiment of spring and sunshine. The sun warmed her face, and the breeze drifting by felt like a hand caressing her. She let out a breath and felt a coil deep within her relax.

She blinked her eyes open and studied Gray's smiling face. His lopsided grin was a new one, a hidden arsenal in his charm offensive against every single person who liked men.

His hair blinked in the bright sunlight, shining off the long, dark strands. Their eyes locked, and an understanding hit her: oh god, she really liked him.

Like, *really* liked him.

This was so unfair.

Chapter Nineteen

GRAY

Gray saw Rose's face turn from absolute bliss to stone in a blink of an eye. "Thank you for the educational experience. I am ready to go," she said.

Gray could see the blocks of her shield falling into place. He'd seen beyond it as she opened her eyes. A blissful, happy moment, and then something cold came down.

She turned to leave and opened her phone, checking that fucking to-do list. "Do you want to go to Allison's store next or Friendly Florals?"

Goddamnit. He thought they had a moment, but he lost her. He jogged up behind her, his hand coming around her waist.

"Rose, stop. We have plenty of time. We can just enjoy the day." She moved in front of him so his arm fell. He was determined to win her over; break down the ice shield she felt she had to put up.

"We have a lot to go over today, and I told Violet I'd help with the favors this evening for next week's event." She walked backward as she spoke, and her heel slipped into a gopher hole.

She yelped, falling backward, and Gray grabbed her waist, pulling her toward him. He caught her in a dip, clutching her close as her hands grasped his jacket, eyes wide.

He sent her an arched eyebrow. "If you wanted romance, Parker, you just had to tell me." He pulled her up to standing, keeping her close. His traitorous eyes glanced at her bright red lips, and he wanted to capture her mouth again. Practically ached with it.

She rolled her eyes, and he let her go. She shoved at her hair, embarrassed. "Thanks for saving my outfit from the mud, I guess."

A few minutes later, Gray wound the bike through the country roads to Friendly Farms. They talked with the owner, and he wasn't planning to expand his shop footprint anytime soon, but they had a good conversation to plant the idea in case things changed.

Gray had higher hopes for their visit to Allison's store in Cooperstown. He'd told Rose that Allison was thinking about expanding, given her success.

His stomach sank as he crossed into his hometown. He hated being back here, near his old dealer that had gotten him started in high school and near his father's reputation as the longest-running mayor the town had ever had.

They drove through Cooperstown, and before he parked in front of Allison's store, he scanned the area for signs of his father. George Roberts loved being the Cooperstown mayor and felt it was his right to stick his nose every damn where.

No sign of him, so Gray parked, and they walked to the front of Allison's store.

Rose took it in with an approving smile. "This is charming."

Allison's shop had a classic Americana feel with a striped overhang, wrought iron benches with lush planters, and a painted buttercream front.

They walked up the few short steps to Allison's store and into the bustling flower and gift shop.

Rose looked around the space with a smile. "I like the style. A little more rustic than my preference, but it's similar enough to Bloom." Rose ran her hand along a gift table filled with candles and knick-knacks next to a table of house plants.

"You supply here?" She pointed toward the arrangements in the cooler.

Why did it make him so happy that she recognized his stuff? "Yep. Allison's been one of my customers since day one."

"Hey, Gray," a sultry voice said quietly behind him. "I'm so glad you stopped by today."

"Allison, hi." Gray gave her a brief hug. "Thanks for chatting with us. I know today's busy."

"It's my pleasure. You must be Rose." Allison held out her hand to Rose.

"Your store is lovely."

"I stopped by Bloom on opening day," Allison said. "I didn't want to interrupt, but it was honestly such a breath of fresh air to see what you've done with the place."

"Gray made sure we had an excellent opening day." Rose patted him on the back. "Though we're only re-opening the business to get it re-established for acquisition. My real life is in LA. I'm only here for a few more weeks until we can get that underway."

Gray's stomach dropped. *Weeks?* He thought he might get at least a few more months with her.

Allison's eyes lit up at the mention of acquisition. "I've thought about expanding into Fairwick Falls, given Frank was a lovely guy, but didn't love the floral business, I don't think. If you don't mind my saying so," Allison chuckled.

"Yes, I met my father. Flowers were not his passion." Rose laughed along with her.

"I'd love to keep talking, and please let me know if you have any offers that come through. I don't want to miss out."

Rose sent her a happy smile. "Here's my card. If anything comes up or if you have any questions, stop by or call the shop."

"Will do. It was nice to see you, Gray." Allison sent him a sparkling smile that did absolutely nothing for him.

They wandered out of the flower shop. Dark clouds had gathered on the horizon, and the spring day threatened to turn into rain.

"She's pretty," Rose said casually, as if he and Rose were buddies, not...whatever it is they were.

"You my wingman now, princess?"

"I'm just saying. She obviously likes you. You should ask

her out. You know, when I'm gone. Or now," she added quickly. "I'm not the boss of you."

Why did she always have to remind him she was leaving? He had a feeling his heart was already spoken for, even though it shouldn't be.

"Just stop talking about it," Gray snapped.

He felt like he was being pushed to the brink, having the perfect package in front of him, knowing it would be snatched away at any moment. "You're here now." His eyes laser-focused on hers as her large light brown eyes widened. "That's all we need to talk about. Don't mention it again."

Rose opened her mouth to respond and closed it, brow furrowed.

They put on their helmets in silence, and Gray started the bike. It was too loud to talk, thankfully. Riding in silence, they headed back to Fairwick Falls.

His temper thundered through him. It was rare that it came out unprovoked. Maybe it was the growing storm in the sky, but he wanted to rage against the world for tempting him with someone so perfect for him and not letting him enjoy it.

The black clouds rolling through the sky meant it would be a heavy spring storm. Gray thought he could make it to his house in time, but raindrops splattered his helmet as he drove the bike down the highway near his house. He turned into a greenhouse on the far edge of his property. They could wait out the heaviest part of the storm there.

By the time he pulled into the greenhouse driveway, rain came down in thick, heavy drops, flying at them in sheets.

They both ran to the greenhouse, her unstable on the

gravel in her high heels. He loved that she wore those fucking heels all the time, so impractical, but so her, perfect and powerful. They ran into the building, gasping, and tore off their helmets.

"Oh my god, I'm soaked!" Rose wiped the sheets of rain off her arms. She glanced up, and her jaw dropped.

He had to admit, this was one of his more spectacular spaces. This greenhouse was stocked full of plants ready to go out to stores. Baskets hung from the ceiling, and nearly every inch was covered in greenery.

Lilacs, daffodils, and poppies mingled on top of one another, creating a colorful mosaic throughout the open space. The sweet scent of florals tickled his nose, and the windows at the top of the building let in ambient light as a thundering soundtrack of rain hit the roof. It felt damn near enchanting.

"This is mine," he said. "We're on the edge of my property."

"Wow," Rose let out a long breath. "I mean, I knew you had a big operation, but...wow."

"These are some of my favorites." He tried to casually play it off as if every word she said didn't stroke the deepest part of his ego. Even as water dripped off her, her hand came down to the head of a daffodil, and she ran a manicured thumb around the edge. Gray walked to the back to find some towels.

"So pretty," she murmured. "It's stuffed in here."

"Yeah. It's prom season, so we're full of supplies to make corsages."

Rose let out a small huff and a half smile as she wiped the

water from her sleeves. "Right, corsages." She shook her head as if remembering they existed. "I never went to prom."

He called back to her, rummaging through a pile of semi-clean towels. "How's that possible? I figured you were the high school heartbreaker."

Rose wandered through the greenhouse, her hand grazing over the petals. She bent down to sniff a carnation. "I was...Smelly Rose. In grade school," she clarified quickly. "My dad hated doing laundry, and I didn't know how to wash clothes when I was little. Taught myself in fourth grade, though. The nickname stuck, and it's a small town, so I was Smelly Rose well into high school."

Tears pricked at Gray's eyes as he grabbed a towel, thinking of a fourth grader teaching themselves how to do laundry. He loved Frank but damn. That was hard.

"It did not help," she smiled back at Gray, "that I was also *kind* of overly competitive and made sure to win every award to stick it in their smug little faces."

Gray snorted with laughter as he walked back. That sounded more like the Rose he knew. "Good. Sounds like they deserved it." She chuckled along with him.

He took her coat off and rubbed a towel up and down her legs.

"I can get it, Gray."

He stood up. "But then I don't have an excuse to touch you," he whispered in her ear. He grabbed the hair from underneath her neck and wrapped it in a towel, squeezing out the rest of the water. With her hair lifted, he placed a long kiss on the back of her neck. The tension between them ratcheted up.

"How do you like the bike?" he murmured behind her ear, his hand sliding around her waist.

Rose rolled her eyes at him even as she sighed at his touch, her hand covering his. "You think you're so clever."

Thank you, motorcycles.

"I am clever." He placed a kiss under her ear. "Did it do what I wanted?"

"You mean, have I been vibrating between my legs for two hours?" She raised an eyebrow as she turned to face him, staying close.

"Exactly."

Concern drew her brows together. "Last week was a one-time thing, Gray."

"So, I'm completely out of your system?" He placed a kiss on her cheek, and she leaned into him.

"Yes," she whispered. She pulled on his jacket, drawing him closer, molding herself to him.

His hand came up to her throat, and he felt her pulse quicken under his touch. Rubbing his thumb back and forth, her breath hitched, and she focused on his lips like she wanted to devour them.

They both knew she was a liar.

She caught his mouth in a deep kiss, practically climbing him. She ravaged his mouth, and he melted at her teeth against his lip. He deepened the kiss, wrapping his arms around her and taking exactly what he wanted. Her hands moved to his hair, and he felt the familiar tug of her pushing him to kiss her harder, faster.

He inhaled her scent as he tasted her, the unique blend of apple blossoms and her amber scent that grabbed him by the balls. His tongue met hers, and his cock went hard. He'd throw himself at her feet before he let her go.

Rose wrapped her arms around him and pressed her body to his. "I missed this," she said between kisses.

Gray's hands roamed her body and had already made their way under her blouse. "Missed isn't the right word," Gray said as he made his way down her neck. "Craved." His hands ran along her silky skin, around her ribs, and up to her breasts. Gray desperately wanted everything from her. Had dreamed of being inside her for fucking weeks.

They slowly made their way across the room, their mouths never leaving each other. He was lost in her scent and the feel of her in his arms. He held her head while he teased her nipple, hearing his favorite sound in the world: Rose moaning for more.

He could spend forever riding his hands up and down her curves, lingering in the dips and valleys between her breasts, her hips, her ass.

His hands wound into her hair, taking more of her against him. Had it only been a week? It felt like an eternity since he'd tasted her.

Her hands roamed his abs, running her fingers under the inside of his belt line. His cock twitched in response. Gray growled as she started unbuttoning his pants. "You're playing with fire."

"I want you," she panted, tugging on his belt. He'd give her anything she asked for at that moment.

"But you remember Rose," her name sounding like honey on his lips, "our deal. I'm in charge." His teeth caught her earlobe, and she leaned against him, wanting more.

"Yes," she huffed out.

"Are you going to listen this time?" He fucking adored that she loved it when he took what he wanted.

Even more when she decided to be a brat first.

She smiled into his neck. "Maybe if you fuck me properly this time, Roberts."

God yes. His hand moved to her breast and found her nipple, pinching it lightly and pulling on it. She moaned against his mouth as she kissed him. He squeezed even harder. "Now, will you listen?"

"Yes," she gasped.

He threw a towel down on the ground, and his hand reached her jaw. She'd worn a bright shade of lipstick that had him staring at her mouth all fucking day. Every time she smiled, spoke, and thought, those pouting red lips danced.

"I've been dreaming of those red lips wrapped around my cock for hours. Weeks." He kissed the side of her mouth, hand still toying with her nipple. "Kneel."

Her eyes flashed up to him, and her bottom lip caught between her teeth as a smile played on them. Lord, she'd be his undoing.

She knelt in front of him, big brown eyes staring up at him, and he sucked in a breath of pure lust. She unzipped his jeans, rolled down the zipper, slowly pulled down his boxer briefs, and grabbed his cock. *Fuck yes.* He was hard as steel and hoped like hell he could last longer than five seconds.

Her hand grabbed his shaft, stroking it, and he nearly lost it right there. It was like she'd reached into his soul. She ran her velvet tongue along his length, and Gray grasped for the table. His knees might actually fucking fold at the sight of her staring up with those smirking red lips and his cock in her hands.

Pleasure ran through him, but he held himself back. She brushed his tip between her plush lips and took him in, sucking hard. He wanted to fuck her mouth so badly, but it would all end right there. He wanted this to last as long as possible.

"Play with your pussy for me," he ground out.

The smacking wet sounds of her mouth almost sent him over the edge, and he barely held it together as she lifted her skirt to slide her fingers under her panties.

He held her head, thumb stroking her velvet cheek. She took in more and more of him into her mouth, bobbing her head until he was almost completely sheathed in her mouth. Those wet red lips stretched around the base of his cock, and her eyes closed as she rubbed her clit so he could see it.

Jesus Christ. Rose Parker did nothing second-rate.

He ran his hand along the back of her head as she moved his cock in and out, her smart mouth stretched around him. "Look how well you take me, Rose." She moaned in pleasure at his words, smiling around him.

She sucked on him hard, playing with him on her tongue as she stroked him. Need curled at the base of his spine, he could so easily come right down her pretty throat.

He had to stop this before he came right here. He slowly pulled out of her mouth and tugged her up to stand. He kissed her and grabbed her hips, walking her backward until they hit a counter with a clear surface.

His hands moved her to sit on the table. "Spread your

legs, honey. I want to see you." He rucked up her skirt and spread her legs even wider.

Her panties were dark, already so wet. "Hands on the shelf behind you." She lifted her arms above her head, grasping the front of the shelf.

He pulled her panties to the side and found her hot clit. "You're so wet for me, aren't you, Rose?"

His thumb traced a circle around her. She'd closed her eyes and moaned, pressing her hips against his fingers.

He ran a finger along her pussy, playing with the ridges with feather-light teases. Her hips jerked, and her legs clenched. He wanted her in a moaning mess before he fucked her, he wanted this to be her best time ever.

His other hand lifted her blouse, and he was happy to find she'd worn a strapless bra that day. He flipped the cups down and squeezed one of her perfect breasts, it spilling out of his hand. Her tits had haunted his memory, and he placed a licking kiss over each one, desperately needing it in his mouth.

"Want you," she panted, "in me."

He stilled, his mouth hovering over hers. "Am I in charge, Rose?"

"Then you should know to fuck me," she said with fire in her eyes.

He pinched her clit, and her eyes rolled to the back of her head, biting her lip between her teeth in pleasure.

His hand left her breast and came up to her neck, wrapping around the delicate column. He held her face close to his. "I want you too much to make you beg, honey. This time." His mouth claimed hers.

He grabbed the condom in his pocket and ripped it open, sheathing himself in it. He'd almost left his phone at home, but he'd remembered that fucking condom.

His eyes bore into her, panting, spread, and waiting for him. Her dusky pink nipples puckered, and she grasped the shelf above her still, her full breasts exposed. God, she was his dream girl. Gorgeous, confident, sexy as hell.

He guided his cock to her entrance and rested his forehead on hers, hand covering hers on the shelf.

He slowly, agonizingly slowly, pressed into her as they both watched him enter her. He squeezed his eyes shut to keep himself from finishing right there.

"You're so perfect, Rose. So tight when you grip me."

She squeezed around him and kissed him, and as he opened his eyes, a gossamer moment spun between them as he seated himself. Their breaths held, and neither moved.

Her eyes roamed his face, and he ran a hand through her hair, holding the back of her head. He took in her pouting lips, the mouth that ran circles around him, her doe eyes that went soft when she stared at someone she loved but now held him captive. She was fierce and gorgeous, and his.

His heartbeat clapped like thunder, rattling his lungs, and like a lightning bolt, a realization flashed in front of him.

Oh fuck.

He was in love with her.

Chapter Twenty

GRAY

Gray pulled out slowly and sheathed himself in her again. He kissed her, claiming her bottom lip between his teeth.

His arms wrapped around her, bringing her as close to him as he could. He wanted more of her. All of her.

"Wrap your legs around me," he ordered. He picked her up and sat down on the table with her on top of him.

Gray needed to worship her. Make her feel cherished.

Her hands found their way to his face, thumbs tracing his cheekbones like she'd never seen him before. Strands of her hair fell around him like a silk curtain, and the window behind him illuminated her in soft white light.

A patter of rain on the roof accompanied their heavy breathing as she slowly rolled her hips over him. His hand squeezed her ass, and he tried to take a mental picture of this moment. This perfect moment of Rose on top of him, gazing at him like he was the only man in the world.

He brought her down to his lips. He needed to shove every single thought to the back of his head so he didn't accidentally say something stupid out loud like he'd give up everything to be with her.

Like he was in love with her.

"Ride my cock like a good girl. Show me how well you take me," he whispered.

She thrust harder as he grabbed her hips, grinding against her. His thumb came to her clit, and she moaned as he punished it with hard strokes.

"Yes," she cried. Harder and harder thrusts had her putting her hands on the shelf behind them. Her breasts bounced in his face, and he captured a nipple in his mouth, sucking hard.

"Harder, Gray," she cried.

He slapped her ass playfully as he sucked even harder. The walls of her tight pussy clenched around him, and his balls tightened.

He grabbed her hips in both hands, rocking her ass up and down his cock. He thrust hard as she came around him, screaming his name. Hearing his name on her lips was the final straw, and he emptied himself into her hard.

He pulled her down and gave her the most tender kiss he could muster. When he pulled back, he saw tears form on the edges of her long black lashes.

Gray tucked Rose into his lap, pulling her legs across his and throwing his jacket over her to keep her warm. The rain pattered on the roof, and he brought her head down to rest on his shoulder.

This was the closest to cuddling he'd gotten in a long fucking time and certainly the longest Rose had ever let him hold her. For a split second, he let himself dream of the possibilities. Of the future they could have together.

His fingers traced lazy circles along her arm. A lot had changed since the last time they were in a greenhouse together. The intoxicating scent of her hair danced in his nose, and he placed a kiss on her head. He rested his head against hers and savored this one perfect moment.

Rose stared into the distance but broke the silence between them with a low, unsure voice. "The tax guy threatened us again."

Every muscle tensed as Gray held her. "Why didn't you tell me?"

"It was a few days ago, and I handled it. It's fine," she murmured, nuzzling in. She situated back into his arms. He wiped a hand down his face. He was going to murder this guy if he ever met him.

"You need to tell me this stuff, Rose," he said more forcefully.

She leaned back, a fire kindling in her eyes. "I can handle it."

"Of course, you can handle it," he spat back, his thumb tracing her bottom lip. He shook his head at her in disbelief. "You are the most capable person I know." God, he loved that about her.

It's like a spotlight hit every quality he would miss, like a part of him when she left. He admired how independent she was. She took no bullshit from anybody and was always the smartest person in the room. It was sexy how she got what she wanted, and it was flattering that she wanted him.

He tucked her head back on his shoulder and leaned his head against hers. "Of course, you can handle it," his tone softer. "But we're partners. I want to help you."

Her fingers traced the tattoos on his forearm. "It's not your battle."

"It's *our* battle." He squeezed her to him. She didn't have a smart retort for that, which he was thankful for.

"Want me to find the guy?" Gray offered.

"No, we just have to buckle down. We have the Mother's Day event coming up. We can send in a big chunk of the tax payment in another couple of weeks."

"I wish you would have told me sooner. I can help. Somehow." He wanted her to be able to talk about this kind of stuff with him. Maybe it was him? Was he the problem? "Do you trust me?" he said suddenly, his mouth getting the better of him. Fuck, what was she going to say? No?

She snuggled into his arms and glanced up, her brows drawn together. "Of course. You've saved me more times than I'd like to admit."

He nodded, not fully believing her words. He heard her voice echo in his mind from their cooler conversation. *I haven't had luck trusting addicts.*

"Why?" she asked. Her hand rubbed along his chest, and he almost chickened out.

Cards on the table, Roberts. "I'll never stop being a former addict. It'll always be a part of me."

Her fingers caressed his brow as she played with his hair.

She pushed it away from his face. "I know," she paused. "But this can't be forever. I'm lea-" She stopped herself and bit her lip.

He felt like she'd just punched him in the gut with brass knuckles. It was worse because she was wrapped so perfectly in his lap. She fit in the corner of his chest like she'd been made for it.

He tensed. He wanted to scream, *just let me prove it to you so you'll stay*, but instead, he nodded and shoved the sadness deep down. He needed to get the hell out of there right now. "It's stopped raining enough." He shifted so she would hop off his lap.

Was this it between them? Who knew how many more times he could convince her to sneak off. She seemed dead set on checking off every item on that fucking to-do list. She wanted to run away from Fairwick Falls, away from her past and anything that wasn't in the shiny, perfect new future she imagined for herself.

They walked toward the door in silence. Something had shifted between them when they'd had sex. A part of his soul was tucked somewhere in her heart, and he felt a little off-kilter, it having left him.

She turned around in the doorway, a picture that reminded him of the first time he'd seen her like that. Rain dropped against the background.

"Gray, I..." she trailed off.

If she fucking told him she was leaving again, he'd lose his mind.

"...nothing. Never mind," she said and walked out to the

bike. As her legs swished away, he tried to take a mental snapshot of what he saw, hoping it wouldn't be the last time.

ROSE

A WEEK LATER, Rose stood in a nearly empty store getting ready for the mother/daughter event the next day.

Violet took a customer's credit card at the Bloom register and bent down to the tiny pothos plant on the counter. "Oh, I'm so glad you're giving Herbert a home."

Rose saw the bemused man across from Vi at the register and mentally facepalmed. She'd *told* Vi not to be a plant mom weirdo in front of customers. Rose glanced at Nick, who was setting up his massage station. They both smiled at their beloved, quirky Violet.

"The plant has a name?" the man asked, seemingly charmed.

Violet's eyes lit up with excitement. "I like to name the ones I've raised since they were little babies. Now, he does *not* like a lot of sun and enjoys a gentle mist of water every week or so. Don't you, buddy?" Violet lovingly caressed the leaves.

"I'll...do my best. Can I come back if I have questions?" The man looked nervous to disappoint Violet.

"Oh, of course. I'm always here. Well, not always, but you know. Happy to help." She shrugged her shoulders as she handed him his receipt.

The customer gave Violet a charming smile, and Rose picked up *vibes*.

As he left, Rose elbowed Violet. "He was *into* you, Vi."

"Go get that plant daddy's name," Nick called over. "He was cute."

Violet sent them an exasperated shake of her head. "He was not *into* me. He just takes his plant parenting seriously, which I appreciate." She hustled to the house plant corner in the store and fussed over a few smaller plants. "Don't worry. Someone will want you guys too."

Seeing Violet so happy the last few weeks had made the conversation with Allison earlier today even harder. Allison was interested in the business they were building in Bloom, and they started discussing what an acquisition would look like.

Rose felt a buzz on her hip and checked her phone. "Hell yes!" Rose yelled in the thankfully empty store.

"Going to have a Gray booty call?" Violet winked at Nick as she walked back to the counter.

God, that sounded amazing right now. They hadn't seen each other since last Saturday at Gray's greenhouse. Flirty texts had been exchanged, but she'd been completely underwater throwing the event together.

"Even better. The check just posted for Dad's house sale." Rose pumped her fist up into the air. A sixty thousand dollar weight was lifted off her shoulders. Maybe this would keep the tax guy off their back for a while. Violet and Nick both whooped.

Rose tapped away on her phone. "I'm going to transfer

this to my account, and then I'll put in a wire transfer to the IRS on Monday."

Violet flipped the store's sign to Closed and started setting up stations for the event.

"You really didn't catch the vibes that guy was giving you?" Rose asked as she set up the nail art station.

Vi rolled her eyes back. "Guys don't like me, Rose."

Rose and Lily had tried to convince Vi for years that her curves tended to make men drool, but she never believed them.

"What about Justin? You liked him, right?" Nick asked.

Violet blew a stray curl out of her eyes. "Liked is a strong word. I wasn't *into* him, you know?" She put their soaps and lotions into boxes so they could reuse the display tables as seating for the event. "I'd rather hang out with Herbert's brothers."

"Let's be honest," Rose sent her an arched look. "You'd rather watch some soapy romantic drama." She'd discovered a ton of feel-good romantic soaps on Violet's DVR, and Violet was obsessed with one historical romance, *In My Heart*.

"So what? The main lead is *so* cute. I'm not ashamed of loving romance, Miss 'Love isn't Real.'" Violet teased back.

It's real, just not for me.

Romantic relationships were for other women. Women who weren't difficult, or bossy, or obsessed with succeeding. She'd had a few relationships, but to be in love meant she'd have to expose her most vulnerable places. No one would want her after seeing that.

"I hear you, Rose. I was the same way." Nick put the finishing touches on his neck massage station, complete with a bouquet of lavender and eucalyptus. "But then Aaron had to come and knock down all those walls I put up. I just wanted to open a coffee shop, and that pain in the ass made me fall in love with him." Nick's southern twang came out and made Rose chuckle.

Curiosity tugged at the back of her head. "How did you know it was love? Just for, you know, research purposes." Rose asked in what she hoped was a nonchalant voice.

Nick's eyes went dreamy. "I wanted to tell him about every type of day I'd have, the good ones. The bad ones. My heart literally skipped when I saw him. I thought I was dying, y'all." They chuckled with him. "I wanted the best parts of him that balanced the best and worst parts of me. And I was better because of knowing him."

Violet let out a romantic sigh. "Ugh, I love *love*."

The door jingled, and Gray sauntered through it with two coffee cups and a bag of pastries. A flutter landed in Rose's belly at seeing him. *Totally different than my heart skipping a beat. Not even on the same planet*, she told herself.

"To what do we owe the pleasure?" Rose smiled over at Gray, and his eyes locked with hers. His dark t-shirt hugged his biceps, and shivers ran down her spine at how good he looked.

"Saw the lights on and thought I'd bring you a pick-me-up." He sat the bag down, and Vi and Nick both reached in.

Gray walked over to her, handing her the latte, and he whispered in her ear. "I'd hoped I could whisk you off to the cooler for a quickie, but guess it'll have to wait." He pulled back, and a wicked delight danced in his eyes.

Need curled in her belly again. It had been a long, long week without him around. Rose's gaze kept flitting to his mouth. She worried her bottom lip, imagining what his mouth tasted like. That artful stubble that perfectly framed his jaw taunted her, and she barely resisted the urge to run her hand over his face.

"It's looking good in here." He glanced around. "Need any help?" His eyes landed on hers, soft and happy.

Rose sipped the latte; of course, he'd gotten her order right, damn it. No sugar, extra foam, extra hot, and cinnamon sprinkled on top.

She needed to put distance between them. She was leaving soon, right? She shouldn't turn this into more than it was. "Nah, we've got it. Thanks for the coffee, though."

"Gray, do you believe in love?" Violet asked through a large bite of chocolate chip cookie.

Rose closed her eyes with embarrassment. She was going to kill her.

Gray sent Violet a curious look. "Of course. Nothing better than the feeling of seeing that one person you've thought about all day. The person who gets you, who sees you. Your heart leaps into your throat when you lock eyes, and everything seems just a little brighter." He glanced down at the coffee, very specifically not looking at her.

Her cheeks flushed with heat, and Rose decided the top of her coffee cup was very fascinating.

"Rose doesn't think it's possible." Violet offered, hiding a smile.

She was definitely going to kill her. "Don't you have potted plants to bring out, buttface?"

Violet cackled as she and Nick walked to the prep room to grab decorations for the event.

Gray's fingers traced a pattern on the table in front of Rose. "Never been in love before, I take it?" He bit his cushy bottom lip, and she'd give every pair of heels she owned to take his mouth right now.

"I believe in the *business* of love," Rose countered as she pulled out glasses they'd fill with champagne tomorrow. "There's proof in business. A give and take."

"That's a shame." Gray sipped his coffee as he walked to the door but turned back. His dreamy face that sent shudders down her spine stared back at her with open wanting. "I bet you'd be easy to love."

He opened the door and walked out, and goddamnit, why did she feel like crying at those words? Tears tugged on the edges of her eyes. *No, Parker. Get through this. You're just tired.*

Rose rolled her shoulders and thought her turn at Nick's massage station couldn't come soon enough.

As the door clicked shut, Rose walked to Vi and poked at her ticklish sides. "Violet Renee Parker, you are so dead."

"I don't know *what* you're talking about," Violet said through raucous laughter. She scampered away from Rose, still laughing. "For someone who doesn't believe in love, you flushed awfully fast."

I believe in it, Vi. I just don't believe in it for me.

~

GRAY

"Hey, Pop." Gray hit the checkout counter with a friendly thump as he walked into the diner the next day. It was surprisingly quiet for Mother's Day afternoon, though he guessed most families were home already.

"Therrrrre's trouble," Pop called out companionably from the cash register.

"Hiya, handsome. Sit over in my section," Margie called out as the tingle of welcome bells on the door echoed in Gray's ear. She power-walked by on her orthopedic sneakers in the old-timey waitress outfit she still loved wearing every day.

"Margie, you know everything around here, right?"

"Is this how you ask for my number? Because I'm spoken for."

Gray snorted and sent her a smoldering smile. Margie was seventy-five if she was a day, and the entire town hadn't been able to convince her to retire yet. He sank into a booth in her section.

"Don't break my heart like that, Margie. One of these days, I know you'll finally go out with me."

Margie cackled and put her glossy, lacquered red nails on Gray's arm. "Such a charmer. Whaddya wanna know?"

"Roadside Towing Company; who runs that? I've searched all over the internet and can't find anything." He'd finally dragged the towing company's name out of Rose after badgering her via text all week.

"Hmm," she thought, glancing up at the ceiling as if it would give her the answer. "I think that's that Leonard guy;

was caught once or twice for thieving, possession... I don't know. Been a long time since I listened to the scanner every night."

"Do you know his last name?"

"McCauley, I think? Pop," she called over. Gray loved that Margie called him Pop even though they were siblings. "Who owns Roadside Towing? Leonard McCauley?"

Pop waddled over, wiping his hands on his apron. "Leonard..." he clicked his tongue, "... Anderson."

Fuck. "You're sure?" Gray asked.

"Sure am. He's a little SOB." The bell rang from the window, and Margie walked to grab her order.

"Sit down, Pop. Can I buy you a cup of coffee?" Gray offered as the older man levered into the booth across from Gray.

"You look like you just saw a ghost, young man. That name mean anything to you?"

"No reason," Gray lied. "Just sounds like a guy I used to know."

Gray, unfortunately, knew Lenny Anderson all too well. He was the first dealer Gray had ever bought from and the first guy he had ever dealt for. Meeting Lenny Anderson was the start of Gray's downfall.

"How's it going with that pretty firecracker?" Pop asked.

Gray was hoisted out of his thoughts. "It's not, um..." he trailed off, unsure how much Rose wanted the world to know about their just sex deal. He wasn't sure he could even say 'sex' to Pop. "We're just partners."

"Bullshit." Pop leaned back with a knowing smile on his

face. "You're a terrible liar. This is why you always lose in cards, Roberts."

"I lose because you cheat." Gray pointed a finger at him.

Margie came by with the coffee pot and a perfectly timed snort. "See? I told you somebody would finally figure it out." She elbowed Pop. He waved her away, and she walked on to the next table.

"Rosie's a very pretty girl." Pop eyed Gray with a smile as he started to get up.

Gray took a sip of coffee and considered. "She's leaving soon. And you know I'm here for good."

"Don't do what I did," he warned in his gravelly voice. "Don't sit in the shadows and wait for when she gets enough hints, when the timing is better, when your business is making more money, when the weather is nicer."

Pop leaned forward to lock eyes with Gray. "There's never a better time than right now to tell a pretty lady you wanna buy her dinner for the rest of her life."

Pop glanced at the wall above Gray. Gray followed his gaze, which landed on an ad for Mrs. Maroo's law office.

"Really? You carry a torch for Maroo?" She'd been widowed for a long time. Pop could have made a move.

Pop waved his hand at Gray. "I missed my chance when we were kids like you. Thought I wasn't good enough for her, and now," he huffed and pointed at his apron. "It's too late for me, but you're a young man. Handsome. Can get anybody you want."

"What if I want Rose?"

"Then the real question is: what are you willing to risk

for it?" Pop levered himself out of the couch, groaning with the leather as he stood up.

"Thanks," Gray sipped watered-down coffee that now tasted like home. "And Pop, it's never too late. I'll be your best man." Gray sent him a smile.

Pop chuckled as he shuffled back to the kitchen.

Margie slid a piece of apple pie with cheddar under his nose. Gray had wanted to hurl the first time somebody had suggested it, but now the taste was inextricably linked with one of his favorite places on earth. He sent her a wink as she swished away, and he toyed with the end of the gooey pie.

Could he go back and talk to the guy that ruined his life? No, Gray interrupted himself. *I am the guy who ruined my own life.* Lenny just held out the tempting plate of pills that made Gray forget every stupid thing he'd ever done, made him feel invincible, and set him on a path that derailed his life.

He thought of Rose's beaming face in the spring sun. She had his heart in her well-manicured palm, and it had only been two months since he'd first seen a crazy lady standing on top of her car.

Could he put himself out there, despite knowing it couldn't last? It pissed him off that she kept downplaying what they had. Nothing made him feel as alive as when they were together, and she challenged him, made him laugh, made him want to haul her to the nearest darkest corner. No self-medicated stupor felt as good as her smile in the sunshine surrounded by tulip fields.

Who wouldn't grab onto that with both hands if given a chance?

Urgency gripped him. She was leaving soon. *Weeks*, she'd

said to Allison. Panic clawed up his spine. She was sand slipping through his fingers.

"Goddamnit." He tossed his fork down, pulled out his billfold, and threw a ten on the table. Before he knew it, his feet took him out the door and into the warm sunshine.

Eyes locked on the pretty storefront currently full of happy ladies, he marched across the town square to do what needed to be done.

Chapter Twenty-one

ROSE

Rose admired the happy, feminine chaos in front of her. Pairs of mothers and daughters laughed and gossiped over the vibey music Lily played in the store. They'd sold every single ticket, and their first big event at Bloom was thriving.

"This is going so freaking well!" Lily whisper-screamed to Rose and Violet. Their guests, instructed to come in their cutest pajamas, were pampered with a fuzzy robe, face masks, and a mimosa or chocolate bar.

Nick gave neck massages on one side of the store while several pairs created their own Mother's Day bouquets, and still more got matching floral nail art.

Rose would have never thought that an event like this could do well in a flower shop, but she supposed they were more than that now.

"I think you're right," Rose said. "Hopefully, they'll all be repeat customers." They'd sold a truckload of arrangements before Mother's Day and would be ahead of schedule soon if business kept up.

The door to Bloom flew open, bells clattering on the antique door. Thirty-five heads whipped around at the jangling sound. Gray stalked in on a mission, and Rose's blood ran cold with anxiety.

Was something wrong? Did the debt collector do something else to Violet's house?

Conversation ceased as all eyes locked on the panting wall of man who'd invaded the event.

Gray's gaze pinned Rose as if they were the only two people there, and heads started to ping-pong back and forth between Rose on one end of the showroom and Gray at the door.

Gray snatched a large bouquet of peonies that Lily had set out for decoration.

"You wanna go on a date with me?" Gray called out over the showroom holding up the flowers, standing at the door, catching his breath. His eyes burned into hers.

His brows were drawn together, and his eyes were frantic and vulnerable, like he'd just asked for everything he'd ever wanted.

Heads whipped back to Rose, waiting for her response.

Her mouth fell open.

Flames of embarrassment flew through her. She was in the middle of their first big event, and he wanted to ask her out *now*?

She stammered, "I—but..." She let out a big sigh and shoved her hands through her hair. She crossed her arms and could feel the entire room waiting expectantly.

Of course, she wanted more with him, but it wasn't that simple. And she had fucking customers to entertain. She plastered a smile on her face for everyone's benefit. "Can I talk to you outside?"

She weaved around the tables, and with every step she took, Rose's temper grew hotter and hotter. She marched for the door, leaving a tittering crowd behind her. He opened the door for her as she stormed past.

She made it to the sidewalk before she exploded. "What the hell were you thinking?"

"I was thinking dinner sounded nice." He handed Rose the bouquet, a concerned look on his face, but a hopeful smile tugged at his lips.

She snatched it from him and managed to stop short of throwing it at his head. "How dare you embarrass me in front of our customers. You have my number. You know where I live. Why couldn't you ask me literally any other time, you boneheaded miscreant?"

He shoved at his hair and spoke fast, taking a step toward her. "I'm sorry, I didn't mean to embarrass you, I just...I didn't want to lose my chance. God, I fucked this all up. It's just, you're leaving—"

"Exactly." She swatted him with the flowers, at her wit's end. "I'm leaving." It nearly came out as a sob.

Don't cry, don't cry, don't cry. She bit her cheek as she pushed thoughts of everything she'd leave behind to get back to her real life.

He took a step closer to her, braving her temper. "But

you're here now. So let me spend as much time with you as possible."

Her eyes searched his. God, she wanted to say yes.

His voice was low, and his hand came up to her face. "Or are you saying you don't have feelings for me?"

She didn't move away from his hand, the anger quickly draining away. "Of course I have," she took a breath, "feelings for you." She was practically drowning in them. "But you know I hate surprises, and I don't need you bullying me into dating you." She poked him in the chest.

He interlaced his fingers with hers as he held her hand to him. "I think you do. I think you need someone who will break down those walls you've built up and let you live the life you want. The one you really want. I see it, Rose. I see how happy you are here and how much you want everything you think isn't for you."

"What I really want," she interrupted, "is sticking to the list. This was not on the list."

"I don't want that fucking list." He tossed her hand down. "I want you." He wrapped his arm around her waist and hauled her to him.

He brought his lips down to her in a mind-melting kiss. His stubble grazed against her face, and his lips parted hers. He took and pressed, drawing her breath out of her. A moan escaped her as she kissed him back.

Somewhere in the back of Rose's head, she knew she was in the middle of the sidewalk in broad daylight as Gray wrapped his arms around her and lifted her, but she was too busy tasting him. Need curled through her as she kissed him.

Something clicked into place when she was right here, and she didn't want to leave.

She pulled away slowly, coming up for air, and he sat her down. Why did this man have such a hold on her?

His hand came up to her chin. "Tomorrow night?"

Petals from the blooming dogwood trees above them fluttered down, and Rose tried to remember this moment so she'd have it forever.

She let out a big sigh and blew a puff of hair out of her eyes. "You are infuriating. And yes, I would love to go on a date with you tomorrow night." Her eyes narrowed at him even as butterflies danced a rumba in her chest. He couldn't know just how much she wanted this, otherwise he'd get even more ideas in his head.

Gray chuckled, bringing her close for a quick kiss.

Out of the corner of her eye, Rose noticed thirty faces pressed up against the front window of Bloom.

"So, are you going?" Lily yelled from inside.

"Son of a bitch," she muttered under her breath.

Gray tugged her closer and whispered into her ear, sending shivers down her spine. "Don't keep your customers waiting."

She huffed out a laugh as she shoved him playfully. "Yes!" she yelled back, loud enough to hear inside. A chorus of cheers broke out as the faces peeled away from the front of the store and clapped.

"I don't know how," she turned back to Gray, "but I'm totally getting you back for this in the future."

He pressed a kiss up to her temple and let her go. "As long as there's a future, Rose, it's fine by me."

The next evening, Rose quickly walked up the driveway to Gray's house for their first date. *This is just casual. One date doesn't mean forever.* Though she'd changed her outfit about fourteen times that evening.

She saw a post-it taped to the door as she walked to it.

Let yourself in.

Rose smiled. *Wonder what he's up to*?

She opened the door and heard thundering paws running toward her. "There's my handsome guy." Rose leaned down to greet a panting Duke.

She glanced around the entryway. No sign of Gray. She spotted a large, flat box on the counter with a long-stemmed red rose on top of it. She picked up the rose to smell it, curious about what was in front of her.

Rose unfolded a piece of paper on top of the box, and a zing of excitement shot through her.

Go to prom with me?

What on earth? She smiled from ear to ear.

She opened the large flat gift box, and her breath caught. In the box was a beautiful, light gold gown. Rose lifted the bodice. The sleeveless gown was a delicate filagree lace, weaving a high curved neckline out of nothing. It was backed by tulle and shimmers of beads, creating a magical, golden fairy dust effect.

He must be joking.

"Gray?" she yelled, seeing if he would show his face.

He remembered I never went to prom?

She lifted the dress out of the box to get a better look.

The tulle hung to the floor, creating a slim ball gown skirt. Rose held up the dress to herself. It was her size, give or take a few inches. She spied a bathroom off the entry hallway.

What the hell. Who didn't like playing dress-up?

Rose quickly changed and surveyed herself in the mirror. Not half bad. She'd kept her hair down that evening, which suited the romantic gown. She allowed herself a happy twirl.

Woah, when was the last time she twirled?

This has to be casual, Rose.

She walked into the living room, calling out louder than before. "Gray?"

"Up here!" he yelled. She rounded the corner and saw a beautifully carved railing leading to the second floor.

"Our date is in a bedroom?"

"Follow the sound of my voice," he called out. She walked up the stairs and down a long hallway of bedrooms in various states of construction cleanup. Streams of light poured into the hallway out of the last open door.

Rose peered through and saw a large bed with a snowy white duvet, an open floor plan with a fireplace in the corner, and double French doors leading to an extended balcony.

Rose tentatively walked through, certain this was Gray's bedroom. "I'm not sure what you did for prom, but you don't usually start in a bedroom." She tried to shake off the jitters she was feeling.

She was in a ballgown in Gray's bedroom. Weird.

Gray appeared in the doorway on the patio, and Rose's heart stopped.

He stood in a dark black suit with a long dark tie against a crisp white shirt. His hair was combed back, nearly behaving except for a few rogue strands fallen against his forehead. He held two champagne flutes, one with seltzer and one with the real stuff.

"Rose," he said in awe. "You look...amazing," he paused, staring at her. "Breathtaking."

He walked toward her with the glasses. "There's probably a better word, but half my brain just fell out looking at you."

He leaned in and placed a slow kiss on her lips. She never got over how good he tasted. She lingered there, trying to remind herself this was temporary. This needed to be the most casual of casual dates. The jeans and T-shirt of dates.

But when she pulled back, she felt the silent crack of her heart open more. "You look pretty good yourself." His tailored jacket reminded her of his previous life as a high-end photographer. "Though I can't believe you remembered my prom story."

"What's a better first date than a teenage ritual we're twenty years too old for?" he beamed at her.

"This view is stunning." Rose walked toward the large patio.

Stunning was an understatement. The patio off the bedroom was a huge balcony overlooking a valley below, rolling hills leading miles beneath them.

The early evening sky had streaks of orange and yellow,

giving way to purple edges. It was the perfect vantage point for a sunset dinner.

"This used to be the barn loft. I'd come up here as a kid and watch the sunset. And later, I'd come up with a girl sometimes and..."

"Watch the sunset?" Rose shot a look over her shoulder. He walked toward her with a smile.

"Something like that." Gray wrapped his arms around her waist. "I never got tired of seeing the view, so I figured out how to see it every night." He quickly kissed her shoulder before he walked over to the dinner table he'd set up for them.

Rose was surprised at how right that kiss felt. It was such a simple thing, but he'd done it casually without thinking.

"We're eating out here?"

"Is that okay? I have some blankets and a fire pit if you get cold."

Rose breathed in the evening air. "Perfect."

"I'm going to go grab our salads. Make yourself at home." Gray walked back into the bedroom.

She leaned against the wrought iron patio railing and gazed over the valley. The sun reflected over the sloping, green hills full of trees, with small open fields dotted with cows. The tangerine rays of the setting sun cast a glow over the valley, and a fresh breeze blew a stray hair across her face. It smelled like freshly mowed grass and the sweet scent of lilacs.

I cannot get used to this. I don't belong here. I hate small towns. Hate relationships. She took another sip of champagne and felt a shiver of possibility run through her.

Or do I?

This town felt like quicksand. The longer she was here, the harder it was to leave. Tinges of shame poked through her brain, thinking about what her colleagues had probably already said behind her back about getting fired.

She'd worked hard to be known as a shark that could deliver what her clients wanted. Her reputation had probably deteriorated already. Could she have an identity without her corporate climbing past?

Gray carried their salads to the table. "You look pretty great against that sunset, Parker. Can I take some shots? I have my camera."

"Maybe when I don't want to eat my hand from starvation. The store was so busy I couldn't take a lunch break today."

He pulled her chair out for her to sit down.

Rose raised an eyebrow. "Look who has on his fancy manners tonight."

"I always have manners when I'm on a date."

A moment of silence landed between them as he sat down.

What did you say on a date with the guy you initially hated but have banged several times and might be starting to fall for?

"How was your day?" Rose asked.

So original.

"Busy planting a million and a half rose bushes. I thought of you every time a thorn got the better of me." He sent her a wink. "And video chatted with Alex. He still hasn't gotten the hang of staying with the phone when he talks to you, but I'll take what I can get."

"Alex seems like a great kid." Rose tested the waters. They still hadn't talked about that day at the farm.

A smile formed on his face, quick and happy. "He is. The best, really. I wish I saw him more, but Giselle and I thought stability would be good until he was older."

"You surprised me that day." Rose smiled warily. "A secret photographer, a secret dad, who secretly speaks French." She speared her salad with each word and glanced up at him. "Any other secrets I should know?"

Gray peered at her mischievously, "If I told you all my secrets, how could I keep you on your toes, Parker?"

"Roberts, don't test me." She sent him a playful glare.

"No other secrets and I barely speak French." He chuckled, a spark in his eyes as he held her gaze. "I'm allergic to mustard. Does that count?"

Rose felt a small knot of tension relax. She hadn't realized she'd been holding onto that fear of more surprises. "As long as another beautiful international family doesn't pop out of the woodwork, we're good."

"You don't talk about your life in LA, either, you know. Anyone you've missed the last few months?" Gray asked.

"No," Rose said quickly. "All the people I knew were colleagues, and no one's reached out since—" Violet and Lily were the only ones who knew what happened, and it felt like ripping open a part of herself, exposing her underbelly, to admit it now.

"Since what?"

"Since I," she gulped, "since I was fired." Her eyes could barely meet his.

His eyebrows raised. "I thought you decided to leave." She noticed the lack of judgment in his tone.

"I know, I just—" She swept her hand over her face. "I feel like I have to be perfect all the time, and it could damage my reputation if it gets out. I haven't told my listeners because—"

"Because you expect them to be perfect, too?"

"No, God..." Rose put her fork down. "They should be themselves. They should make mistakes and grow and learn, try things, try their best...what?" She saw his eyebrows raise.

"That's some excellent advice. You should probably take it." He laughed as he sipped his seltzer. "People can make mistakes. I have first-hand experience in making really big ones, Rose. I don't expect you to be perfect. You don't expect them to be perfect."

"You don't think I'm perfect?" She sent a sly smile at him.

"Your ass, yes, is just...chef's kiss. But I am fully aware," he grabbed her hand, "that you, Miss Perfect Rose Parker, have made mistakes. I think you should tell your listeners."

It resonated with her. She didn't want to continue the narrative that women had to be perfect. She rolled it around her head, playing with the idea. "Men can make mistakes," she said, thinking out loud. "Why can't we fail just like them? And get up, dust ourselves off, and try again without having unfair expectations put on us?" She felt fired up for the first time in a while.

"I probably haven't told you this," he took her hand, "but it's really fucking sexy when you're passionate about something. I like it on you." He brought her hand to his mouth and placed a slow kiss on her knuckles.

Rose felt that flutter around her heart. That same movement she'd felt when she visited her dad's grave and realized who Gray might actually be—a good man who might want her just the way she was.

Gray topped off her drink and jogged downstairs to grab their main course. Rose caught a chill as she waited for him and walked into the bedroom to grab one of the cozy blankets on the bed.

The room was sparse as if it had been recently finished. The modern, dark wood king-size bedframe stood against the snowy white walls, and the industrial, high-end lighting fixture had been dimmed to nearly dark. Rose ran her hands along the rough-hewn mantle over the fireplace.

He noticed the blanket around her shoulders. "Are you cold? We can eat inside."

Rose considered the last sliver of orange on the horizon. They still had showtime left in the sky. "No, let's stay out here. You can't beat the view."

They talked about their days, his spent planting, harvesting, and potting the next big batch of flowers. Hers spent greeting customers and planning for the Lopez bridal consultation the next day.

Rose realized with a start that it felt like their tenth date, not their first.

Rose finished her steak, and a companionable silence landed between them. "Thank you. For all this," she said suddenly. "I thought we were going to have a low-key night."

Not a soul-defining, picture-perfect date. An anxiety alarm rang in the back of her head.

You're not worth this, Rose. You are bossy, and you'll disappoint him, and you're leaving.

Not. Worth it.

Gray grabbed her hand and brought it to his lips. "I don't get you long, so I wanted to make it count."

"You care, Gray. A lot. That's... unusual."

"Unusual? To care for a beautiful, smart woman?" His eyes met hers with surprise. "You must have had a talent for dating idiots in California."

Rose chuckled as she speared a piece of caramelized sweet potato. "Let's just say this is the first, first date I've enjoyed in a long time."

He smiled at her as his eyes danced. "Is this our first? You don't count all the times you'd yell at me, and then I'd kiss you senseless?"

Rose sipped her champagne, and a smile curled her lips. "I thought this was prom, Roberts? Aren't you going to ask me to dance?"

Chapter Twenty-two

ROSE

"That wasn't an answer, Rose," Gray said as he stood up and found a remote, clicking on a speaker to a lo-fi playlist. He walked over to her and offered his hand.

"I know," she said and stood up. "I'm sneaky like that."

He tucked her blanket around her shoulders and pulled her close, swaying with her under the stars.

"The one thing Pennsylvania has on LA." Rose was mesmerized by the sky. "I forgot what a clear night sky is supposed to look like. It's beautiful."

Gray pulled back to look at her. "You're beautiful, Rose. Honest to God, breathtaking." He stared at her as if she was the most precious thing in the world. As if he'd never seen her before. She couldn't look away. She was breathless but couldn't put her finger on why.

"Gray, I—" Gray's mouth stole her words. He'd pulled

her in, his hand gripping her lower back and the other holding her chin. He kissed her as if she was his next breath. She met his mouth, pulling on his lapels and needing more of him. She wound her arms around his neck, her skin hot with need. Scraping her nails through his hair, she heard a low moan escape him as he deepened the kiss. He walked them back into his room.

His hand fell from her cheek and grabbed her waist, his thumb stroking her side. She felt the thrill of her pulse quicken as she leaned into him. Her nipples hardened under his touch.

As his tongue fought with hers, Rose started to lose herself. Her head swam with need. She could only think of his hands. God, his hands felt so good. You could have sex on a casual date, right? In formal wear?

Their mouths met in a heated frenzy. Tongues clashing, warring with each other. Gray's hands slid down to grab her ass, claiming her. She shivered, and he broke away suddenly and closed the patio doors.

As he walked back to her, he tugged on the knot on his tie with hunger in his eyes. He tossed it on the bed and dove for her mouth as if he needed her for his next breath.

His hands made quick work of her zipper, and he pulled the top of her dress down. She gasped as his mouth nipped along her neck. She moaned again as his hands found her breasts, her bra having fallen off with the dress. Every nerve ending had been on a hair trigger for hours. Taking her nipples between his thumb and forefinger, he played with her, and she felt the beginning of an orgasm start through her.

"So perfect," he whispered against her lips. "Just like this. Just you."

She ripped open his shirt, needing more of him. Her hands came up to feel his chest, and she placed open-mouthed kisses on the tattoos she hadn't yet worshipped. She wanted to eat him up, never taking her mouth from his body.

Gray slid the rest of the dress past her hips, and the dress pooled on the floor.

She stood in her panties and heels, and his breath sucked in. "I'm a lucky sonofabitch," he said roughly.

His mouth went to her breast as his hand squeezed the other, and desire shot straight to her pussy. She leaned back against the dresser behind her, arching into him.

"More," she breathed, pleasure ripping through her in a torrential downpour.

His hand caressed down her abs, and he ran a finger under the panty line on her hip.

"Are you going to come on my face like a good girl?" he murmured against her breast, still laving it with his tongue and teeth.

"Yes," she panted as she captured his mouth again, needing the taste of him.

She pushed his shirt off his shoulders and started unbuckling his belt. She could feel his cock against her, but she wanted more. She craved it.

He grabbed her hands suddenly. "You have to come first, honey." His finger dipped under her panties, feeling her wet and ready. He slid his fingers in deep with his thumb pressed on her clit.

She moaned shamelessly. Her eyes were barely able to stay open but still locked with his.

Jesus Christ, I might come right here. She was about to resort to begging, promising him anything if he'd give her more.

His head moved down to her breasts, and as he placed kisses along her abs, he bent down to his knees. He shoved one leg up on the dresser as she leaned back for him.

Her bottom lip sucked between her teeth. She wanted this so badly. Would have killed for this again. She'd pictured his head between her thighs a thousand times since March.

He placed long, slow kisses along her hip, then her inner thigh. He teased her with feather-light touches against her clit, and her hips bucked, chasing the sensation.

Then suddenly, he ripped her panties to the side, and his tongue devastated her. She felt the wicked sensation of his stubble between her thighs fucking finally. He nipped her with his teeth on her clit as he peered up at her, and she threw her head back, screaming with need.

He lifted his head, blowing on the sensitive skin. "Show me how much you want it, honey."

She pushed his head down harder between her legs, gripping his hair and riding his face. He grabbed her ass for better leverage, and she felt her climax so close. "Don't stop."

He slid two fingers inside her, punishing her with his mouth, and she came against him. She felt waves of surging pleasure ripple through her as she shuddered, her hips rocking against his mouth.

She leaned back on her hands, trying to catch her breath. He placed a slow kiss against the inside of her thigh. She felt him smile. He worked his way back up to her neck.

"I will never get enough of that." He kissed her jawline as he continued to nip at her. He wrapped his arms under her and lifted her off the dresser as if she were a sack of potatoes. "The bed is more comfortable."

"Would you believe this is the first time I've been carried?" She closed her eyes again, feeling completely relaxed, "And I'm barely coherent enough to enjoy it."

He kneeled on the bed and laid her down.

"You're very good at that," Rose said as he lay on top of her.

He found her earlobe and started again. "You should see my other tricks." His arms came around her, squeezing her tight as their mouths met again. Their legs wound through each other's, and Rose felt the next wave of need ignite in her.

She finally ranged her hands over his back, firm with muscles, and felt him smile again as she grabbed his ass.

His grin was quick and hot as his eyes met hers. She found the buckle on his belt and, without leaving his gaze, undid his belt and slid down his zipper. She felt his breathing go shallow as he held himself off her.

Holding his gaze, she licked her palm and wrapped her hands around his cock. She triumphed as his eyes rolled back in his head.

"God," he ground out. He threw his head on her shoulder. She stroked his length and felt him exhale against her. Feeling the same need, she pulled his pants down, and he kicked off the rest of them. He grabbed a condom and rolled it down over his cock, she clenched her pussy, wanting him inside her.

His cock pressed into her, and their bodies molded against each other. Rose reveled in the skin-to-skin contact against him as they stilled. His hand came up to her face, and he wrapped his other arm around her, holding her close. She felt like she'd found the other part of her she didn't know was missing. The part that maybe loved her just like this entwined with him. She sighed into the curve of his muscular shoulder and inhaled that scent that felt like home, placing kisses as she went.

So this is what making love was like, she thought. *Mind-wrecking, soul-bending love.*

He caught her mouth in a deep kiss, tongue playing with hers as he thrust slowly against her. Her nose drew down the length of his, feeling a sparkling spun web of tenderness so foreign to her.

"I need you, Gray," she said into his mouth. She wrapped her legs around him tighter and pulled him closer so she wouldn't ever have to let go.

He locked eyes with her and dove a hand between them. "Say it again," he growled. Hunger in his eyes clawed at her, and he drove her mad, stroking her clit slowly.

"I need you," her voice barely a whisper. She felt tears tug at the edge of her eyelids as their eyes met, searching one another. His lips captured hers before his head fell to her shoulder. His fingers interlaced with hers as they moved slowly, grinding each drop of pleasure out of each other.

Each brush of his chest against her tits felt like a stroke of happiness, of acceptance, as he thrust harder and harder into her. His thick cock stretched and filled her.

"Spread your legs, honey. I need all of you," He grabbed her leg around his arm, spreading her wider and thrusting deeper. He kissed her, picking up speed. His mouth took hers as he seated himself, and she felt the breath leave her body at the fullness.

He ground against her hard with each thrust, and finally, Rose felt the surge of white-hot pleasure rip through her as Gray's thrusts went hard and long against her. They tumbled over the edge together, and Rose felt a piece of her heart attach itself to the man she loved.

~

GRAY

A BUZZING PULLED at the edge of Gray's lucid dream. He relived last night with Rose as she lay safely tucked in his arm. *She needed him.*

The buzzing stopped, and he shifted her closer to him, his cock hard again for her. He pulled her soft curves against him. He let his hand wander along her stomach, and it made its way up toward her breast as the buzzing started again.

Fuck. My phone.

He turned over and grabbed for it on the marble nightstand. It was barely seven. Sleep was doused from his body as he saw six missed calls and three frantic texts from Violet. He swiped to answer.

"Violet?" he croaked in a sleepy voice. "What's going

on?" Rose was still fast asleep in his arms, out like a light.

"Gray." He heard a tremble in Violet's voice through the phone. "Someone's padlocked the store."

He sat up, extricating his arm under Rose's neck and giving her a gentle shake awake. "What do you mean? Bloom's locked?" He rubbed a hand over his face.

"I came in early to get a head start for the Lopez consultation, and every door has a giant lock on it with Do Not Enter tape over it. There are fliers posted all over town about us going out of business. It's so embarrassing."

"Okay, Rose is still asleep. We'll be there in ten. Get in your car, lock it, and don't say anything to anybody. Got it?"

"Okay." She let out a shaky breath, and he hung up the call.

He turned to Rose. "Honey," the term of endearment escaped his lips before he could stop it. "Rose honey, you gotta wake up." She was out cold but groaned and started stretching with a harder shove. "Something's happened with the store."

She sat up instantly. "Everyone okay? Vi? Lily?" She cracked open her eyes.

"Everyone's fine, but the asshole is back. Someone put a padlock on the door to Bloom. They can't get in. Violet said there were notices everywhere. We've got to go."

"Fuck." She tossed over the covers and grabbed her phone. "Twenty-seven missed calls." Rose threw on her clothes.

Gray grabbed a shirt and threw it over his head. They were yanking on clothes as fast as they could. "Duke, come on. I'll meet you down at the car."

"No, you don't have to go." Rose shoved her hair and grabbed her stuff. "Stay. It's fine. I'll handle it."

"Rose, I'm coming with you. Our problems, remember?" The steely glint in his voice caught her attention.

She nodded quietly.

"Let's go." Gray thundered down the stairs, let Duke out to do his business, and they were off on the road two minutes later.

"Fuck. The Lopez meeting," Rose remembered the appointment Violet mentioned. "She called—oh, wait. No. Looks like Lily already handled it." She scrolled through a wall of missed texts.

"You don't always have to be the one to handle everything, Rose."

"I'll handle that fucking debt collector."

They drove into town a few minutes later. There was a small crowd gathered outside of the Bloom front door.

"Well," Gray muttered. "So much for keeping it quiet."

They hopped out of the SUV and walked to the front door.

There was a giant padlock on the back and front doors. Lily stood off to the side, mouthed "Nash" to Gray, and pointed to her phone. He was no lawyer, but he would at least have experience with debt and how it's collected.

Mrs. Maroo stormed down the street, walking from Pop's Diner. "Can you believe this?" She waved a handful of flyers she snatched off the light poles.

Rose had started shooing people away, telling them this was a misunderstanding. "And don't forget to put in your

Father's Day order," Rose said half convincingly as people sent her worried looks and wandered away.

"Rose, they could have helped us," Violet said. Her arms were wrapped around her body so tight that Gray worried for her circulation.

"How?" Rose put her hands on her hips. "Playing a tug of war with a deadbolt lock?"

"This is all my fault." Violet's hands came up to her face.

Gray gave her a quick hug, but Rose was in no mood to comfort. "Vi, I need your game face on. We can have feelings later. Mrs. Maroo, we need council."

"Rosie, these debt collectors will do anything they can to get money from you. If we can prove you are operating in good faith and you're trying to pay, then they should back down. If not, I'll wallop their asses so hard in court, they won't be able to sit down for two weeks."

"I sent the money transfer yesterday, but it hasn't cleared yet. I just literally can't get the money to them any sooner." Rose bit her top lip, thinking. "We have to move two client meetings today. Cancel a bunch of orders."

"You can have the meetings at the farm," Gray offered.

"I'll handle it." Rose sent him a stern look. "Aren't you busy today, anyway?"

Fuck. He was supposed to drive across the state to Lancaster today. A grocery store had placed a huge order for his hothouse pansies, and he was already behind on his day. It was four and a half hours there, one way. He'd have to leave Rose in the middle of this mess.

Gray's phone rang. His eyebrows leapt to his hairline when he saw the caller ID. He swiped to answer it. "Allison.

How's it going?" He locked eyes with Rose as she whipped around to him.

"Gray, I heard about Bloom. They're going out of business?"

"You heard?" Gray sent an eye over to the lock, and all three Parker sisters did a simultaneous facepalm. "News travels fast."

"My sister lives in Fairwick Falls, and she knows Rose and I have been talking about me taking over the store."

Gray's heart plummeted.

"I tried to get ahold of Rose, but I only have the store line."

"I'll put you on speaker. She's right here."

"Allison, hi," Rose said in a warm, calm voice that completely hid the chaos in front of him.

"Look, I was on the fence about expanding into Fairwick Falls, but I know you're in a terrible bind, and the shop is so great. I don't want anything to happen to the business you've generated, so I'm happy to make an offer and start negotiations with a down payment this week."

Rose blinked up at her sisters and then at him. "I'm going to take you off speaker, Allison."

He handed Rose his phone and felt like he was handing over his heart as well.

Rose paced as she talked to Allison. "Two hundred and fifty thousand for the building and the business name as it stands today with a deposit of fifty thousand in a week," Rose repeated, staring at him.

His heart hit the pavement.

She was going to leave.

Chapter Twenty-three

ROSE

Rose's mind raced in every possible direction as she talked to Allison. *Stall stall stall.*

"I'm so glad news travels fast, but..." Her heart clutched. This was everything they'd worked for. The best possible scenario, really, so why did it feel like her future was being snatched from her? "I need to discuss this with my sisters. We're all an equal partnership here at Bloom."

They agreed to talk the next day, and Rose hung up.

Violet and Lily's shoulders slumped, and tears gathered in their eyes.

"So, that's it then? We're selling already?" Lily asked in a small voice.

"I mean, that was the plan, right?" Rose crossed her arms, hating every minute of this. She was at war with two versions of herself.

How could she change so much in only six weeks? March

Rose would have agreed to the deal before the terms could be polished, spoken for the four of them, and smoothed things over if necessary. But May Rose?

May Rose loved the store. Loved her life here.

She looked at the view of the town square she had every morning at Bloom. Even now, somebody played fetch with their dog on the spring green lawn, and a small family was going from the coffee shop to the playground. Birds chirped, and the end-of-spring breezes ruffled Violet's and Lily's hair as they stood outside their cozy, adorable little shop.

It felt like the most beautiful, spring-themed knife was turning a circle in Rose's stomach.

"I mean, it's Rose, right?" Violet shrugged. "We're going to do what is best and most logical, even though that makes me really," Violet's voice caught, "really sad."

"Sadder than a padlocked store?" Rose gestured to the handle, trying one more time to move it. "We don't have the money for this, Violet. This will happen again and again."

"I know. It just..." Violet trailed off as Lily rubbed a hand on her back.

Fuck, why do I always have to be the bad guy?

A tear ran down Violet's face. "We love doing this. And we knew it couldn't last forever, but I kind of hoped it would."

Lily wrapped her arms around Vi. "We just know you, Rose, and you want whatever's best for us and most efficient. That's why you get shit done."

Rose felt her stomach drop. "I don't want to ruin everything, but we have to be practical."

God, she hated being practical. She was always the party

pooper, always the person who made sure everything was handled perfectly.

She had a raging case of Oldest Daughter Syndrome she hadn't been able to shake for thirty-five years, and she wanted the antidote more than ever.

Her heart thudding a million miles an hour, she met Gray's gaze and felt a stone wall come up between them. He knew she'd be gone when they sold. There was no reason for her to stay, right? Recruiters had already reached out since word got out she wasn't at CMG anymore. It was time to get back to her real life.

Gray walked toward her. "You gotta do what you gotta do, Rose."

"I just need time to think," a sadness echoed in her voice.

He nodded back at her, not meeting her eyes. "Let me know what you guys decide." He placed a quick kiss on the side of her cheek. "I'll always be here," he whispered in a ragged voice and slowly walked back to his car.

Did she *want* to leave Fairwick Falls? Could she abandon everything they'd made? She peered through the store window into the little piece of heaven they'd created together. The shop had been in Fairwick Falls for over a century, and generations of her family, now gone, built and cared for it. Was she the single link that would break that chain?

"Just give me a day, and we'll talk about it, okay? I just need to think."

"We could do it, Rose. If you wanted to." Lily offered, seeing the conflict brewing inside her.

But did she want to?

"You guys drive home. I'm going for a walk."

Rose's walk turned into a two-mile meander, which left her even more confused than when she woke up that morning from the best sleep she'd ever gotten.

Thirty minutes later, Rose threw her purse down on the bed in her room and changed into her workout gear as fast as possible. She craved a run to escape all the thoughts in her head.

This is how my parents screwed me up. Any time something potentially good happens, I think about how it could go wrong. Protect myself.

Rose remembered the letter from her dad still buried in her purse and stopped dead in her tracks. She hadn't had the mental energy to read it yet. She wasn't sure if she even *wanted* to hear from the man who'd turned her life upside down.

All the runs, all the venting, all the late-night pie with Vi had only scratched the surface of her anger at her father. She'd been denied a childhood she could never get back, and the unfairness raged through her veins.

She pulled out the letter from her purse and fought the urge to rip it to shreds. *I could control this one last thing. I could get the last word.*

But no matter how much she wanted to rip it into confetti, she couldn't.

She tore into the letter with fury. *I can always shred it later.* Her cheeks blazing with anger and an unsteady hand, Rose sat on the bed to read her father's chicken scratch handwriting.

Rosie,

Someday, you'll read this, and I guess I'll be in the great beyond. I know you carry a lot of hurt about how your mom died. Your childhood wasn't perfect, yet you were always my little rock.

No adult man should depend on a child, but you were there when I needed you most. I've spent the rest of my life trying to be someone else's Rose, their rock, to make up for it.

You always wanted to know why I never kicked your mom out. It's the same reason I never stopped loving you, even when we didn't talk. I never stopped loving your mother for her problems because true love never quits.

I believed in her goodness every day of my life. I couldn't leave the other half of my heart to fend for itself when it needed help the most. When you lost your mother, I lost the love of my life. My bright spark. That day at Canon's Diner, you said you wished I had died with her. I want you to know I forgive you because I failed you when part of me did die that day.

But remember, Rose: words have power. Use your power wisely.

One day when you were a tiny thing, we were at the Donnelly's when he ran for town council. Bob Donnelly asked you who you thought would win. You said, "You, Mister D. Cause I bet on smart people with good hearts." That pure-hearted logic stuck with me for the rest of my life.

I'm sorry for all the dark days but know you carried me through on your strong little shoulders, and I've been forever grateful. Even as you're reading this letter, I still love you to pieces. I love you and never will quit.

I'm so proud of my little Rosie, the strongest little girl who made me a better man.

Love, Dad

Rose heaved sobs as she read, each tear falling onto the page. She paced around her room, trying to process. She'd run until she had a decision.

She was strong, right? She could handle this. She just had to think.

GRAY

GRAY'S PULSE thundered in his ears as he drove the back roads to his house. This morning he'd had a dream in the palm of his hand: Rose in his bed, a future with her as his business partner. And it was all about to crumble between his fingers.

His fingers rubbed his lips in frustration. She needed to choose what she wanted. He couldn't and wouldn't guilt her into staying with him. Pain reverberated in his chest as he thought of her getting back in that old fucking rental car, on a plane to LA, and never seeing her again. Moving to LA was out of the question after his past, and he was tied to his land, his business.

Gray glanced at the clock. He had to make that delivery today, but it couldn't have come at a worse time. It was a massive order to one of the first mom-and-pop stores that had taken a chance on him. He was building a legacy he wanted to pass on to Alex one day, and he couldn't risk the relationship he had made with his customers.

It would be a ten-hour round trip if he didn't run into rush-hour traffic through Philadelphia. He felt a clawing urgency to be with Rose, to protect her from Lenny, but he couldn't be in two places at once. He wished Frank was here. He'd throw the keys at him, say he'd buy him a piece of pie later, and hit the road back to Rose.

Gray pulled into the driveway of his greenhouse and saw Marco, his new full-time employee, loading one of the box trucks for delivery. Marco would drive the first truck, and Gray planned to drive the other. Josh, his part-timer, wheeled another pallet toward the truck.

"Hey, I'm glad to see you guys. Thanks for getting started early." Gray walked over to them.

"We heard about Bloom. That's messed up." Marco wiped his brow and took a breath from loading.

That wrench in Gray's gut was back again. "Yeah, I think we'll get it worked out." Gray shrugged, not wanting to talk about it, or he might get emotional. As Josh walked up, an idea sparked in Gray's head.

"Hey, Josh. Would you be up for some extra hours this week? Could you drive the other truck with Marco?" Josh was only part-time, but he'd been great. Gray should have given him more responsibility ages ago.

Josh leaned on the dolly he wheeled over. "Normally, yeah. But today I got a thing at my kid's school I can't miss. It's her first choir concert." A twinkle in his eye had Marco and Gray smiling back.

"Yeah, of course. Family comes first." He'd heard himself

say those words a hundred times. Why hadn't he put his family first? What good was business growth when you missed your kids' recital? *Or his first steps*, Gray thought with an ache. He'd lost so much with Alex already. He hated being responsible and feeling like the bad guy because of it.

Maybe someday he'd have his shit together and could be a better father and a better partner. He'd made his bed, though, and it was pretty fucking uncomfortable having to lie between a rock and a hard place. He bit his lip and shoved the disappointment in himself down.

Today? He'd sacrifice what he wanted one more time to prove he wasn't a fuck up, drive across Pennsylvania, and leave his heart here.

~

ROSE

Rose sent a flurry of texts as she caught her breath from her run and charged through the front door of Violet's cottage. Lily and Violet were already on their way back to the cottage after Rose texted them that she had a plan.

She'd already told her followers there was an emergency session of the SmartGirl SmartMoves podcast, and she desperately needed their help.

Rose realized she'd maybe never used the phrase "I need your help" before. What did that say about her?

Maybe she was changing. And maybe that was a good thing.

Rose smiled for the first time in what felt like forever as

she heard the cottage door slam. “I’m up here,” she called from her bedroom.

Rose glanced at the clock; she had fifteen minutes before it was time to finally be honest with her listeners, finally be honest about who she was, both to herself and to them, and spill her guts.

Rose didn’t even bother to have a fancy backdrop for this call. She just decided to cuddle up on the bed. She felt so perfectly safe here, which helped ease the thundering beating of her heart.

“What’s going on?” Violet said as she came up the stairs. “You look like you’ve seen a ghost.” Violet’s big eyes were magnified behind her glasses, and she looked like a very concerned owl.

Rose took in the sight of her little sisters and realized deep in her heart she’d made the exact right decision. She loved working with them more than she’d ever expected. Rose let a laugh out, allowing one sliver of happiness to escape.

She stood up, pacing her bedroom. Twelve minutes before the podcast started.

“What’s wrong?” Lily asked, her brows furrowed.

“Nothing...in fact,” Rose laughed, “I think it’s all really good. Like, really *really* good.”

Lily and Violet glanced at each other in wary surprise.

“So, I was an absolute dummy. I assumed being in a big city, back in consulting, making as much money as possible would make me happy at some point if I got high enough in the ranks. I thought that’s what I wanted.”

"You were never happy there. You were always miserable when we talked to you," Violet said with concern.

Rose chewed her lip as she paced. "I mean, I realize that *now*. It's easy to forget what happiness feels like when you've been in an overworked fog for ten years. And I'm happy now."

"That's great, but...about what? The business?" Violet asked, her eyes crinkling with hope.

Rose dove in with a vengeance. "I want to stay here. And make something with both of you. Keep making something. I think what we have here could be big. Not a single store; a lifestyle brand."

Lily's eyes lit up with possibilities, and she wiggled with excitement.

Rose continued. "I've learned how to build and position a brand from the very best, and I want to make something that's mine—ours, with the rest of my life." She practically hummed with energy. "Vi, your landscape designs are amazing, but your real love is your plants, right?"

"Yeah," Violet said slowly.

"Great," Rose said with building excitement. "Be the Chief Plant Officer for us. Build our stock of florals and plants so we can expand." Rose was pacing now up and down the length of her floor.

"I thought small because we were in a small town. But plenty of brands have started with a smaller target audience and expanded to regional and national chains. We can turn Lily's personal social media accounts into business accounts. Let them have a look at three sisters creating beautiful things."

Lily danced side to side with excitement. "Oh! Vi, how fun would it be to work on enormous wedding designs together?" Lily practically jumped on Violet.

"Wait!" Violet flung her arms out. Rose and Lily stopped in their tracks. "I can't think with you both walking everywhere." Violet shoved her hands through her mass of auburn curls.

She turned to Rose. "You'd stay? Like, stay forever?"

Rose hadn't realized how much this was weighing on her sister. Violet had quietly and diligently worked for so long, never asking for much.

"Really stay," Rose said, taking her hands.

"What finally changed your mind?" Lily asked.

Rose glanced at the clock. Eight minutes until the podcast. "I went for a run to think and ended up at Dad's grave. I yelled, no, screamed at him. I'd been running for miles and miles and couldn't take it anymore. I was—still am—so damn mad at him for dying. At leaving me with everything again. I screamed until I was hoarse. And as I knelt to scream directly at his headstone, I saw that he was fifty-eight when he died."

Violet scratched her head in confusion. "But you knew that already."

Rose's heart thudded in her chest, remembering how her mortality smacked her in the face. "What if I only have twenty-three years left?"

Six minutes left. "What do I want to do with my last twenty-three years? Stare at PowerPoints and drink bad coffee from a communal kitchen? Fall into bed alone every night, exhausted from work I don't even like?"

The more she talked about it, the dumber it sounded. How had she spent so many precious years of her life wasting them away?

"I want to make a go of this. I want to stay here, and I want sister hang sessions, and lattes from Fox & Forrest, and friends, and..." Rose took a gulp, "a super-hot flower farmer."

ROSE

Lily gathered her in a fierce hug, her eyes shining. "I'm so damn proud of you."

Rose squeezed her back. "I want to try to make something real with both of you, but only if you're both in."

"I'm in." Violet hardly waited for Rose to finish her sentence.

They both waited, staring at Lily.

Lily hated commitment. She'd lived in eleven different apartments and eleven different areas of the city since moving to New York.

"Lilybug, we know you hate being tied down, but maybe for a year so we can get it off the ground?" Rose bit her lip, hoping she'd say yes.

"What we've made is amazing. I can never leave you guys, at least..." Lily's smile bloomed, "Not for a year." She shrugged and sent them a laugh.

Rose glanced at the clock; three minutes left.

"So, we're going to do it for real?" Rose looked at them across her tiny twin bed.

They all glanced at each other and held their breaths. It felt like they were on the precipice of something amazing. "We're going to do it," Rose said. Lily and Violet leaped across the twin bed and launched themselves at Rose.

Rose caught them, laughter and happiness bubbling up out of her, and, for the first time, didn't hold it back. "But first, we've got to get our flower shop back."

Two minutes until the podcast.

"What about Gray?" Lily asked.

"No time. I'll text him to listen to the podcast." Rose hoped he'd be happy, and if he wasn't...well, they'd handle it together. Rose whipped out her phone.

ROSE

No time to talk – but I have news. Listen to the podcast? 🩶

GRAY

Dortha, you're killin me. But of course, I'll listen.

Rose sent him the link to the livestream.

"What are we gonna do?" Lily said, looking at both of them. "We have arrangements in the shop wilting as we speak."

"I'm hoping for a miracle for now," Rose said as she threw on her headphones, sat on the cozy bed covered in her family's handmade quilts, and nodded to her co-host.

Rose dove in once they were live "Hey, all. Thank you so

much for joining us for this emergency session of the podcast. I have so much to tell you," she said, getting serious, "and a big confession. I'm so embarrassed about it, but I need to be honest."

Dread filled her body as she prepared to be, *ugh*, vulnerable. Her stupid fight-or-flight response gripped her, and she breathed through it.

"I told you I relaunched our family flower shop because I wanted to be an entrepreneur. What I didn't tell you is that it's because I failed first. I got fired from my full-time job before coming back to my hometown." She willed her eyes not to look at the comment box so she didn't lose her nerve.

"When I lost my job, I was so embarrassed. My sisters and I started the business to pay off a family debt. I never shared this, but my father passed a few months ago." Unexpected emotion clutched at her throat. She cleared it to keep going. "I hope you'll forgive me for lying by omission. I should've been honest and not continued the narrative that women have to be perfect to be valuable. And know that if you've ever been let go or fired, it doesn't mean you're not a boss; it just means that wasn't the right path for you.

"I think I've found the right path because I've never been happier working alongside my sisters and my," she took a gulp, "boyfriend, I guess?"

She saw chat comments coming in from the hundred or so listeners who were tuned into the livestream. Many comments were about how they'd been fired at one point and how it led to better things.

"Launching a business has been so hard, but it's made me better. I've found my passion, working with people I love in a community that is part of my DNA. I want to spend the next twenty-three years of my life making it the best it possibly can be.

"And I've learned," she took a breath, "I was wrong about so much of what I told you. It's not just about making money; turning a profit as quickly as possible. The best part of all our work is spending time with people who matter to you, doing things you love." Rose saw her two BFFs for life leaning against her dresser.

"You guys want to come say hi?"

Violet's eyes widened, and her head shook "no" as Lily raced toward Rose.

"Oh c'mon, Vi!" Lily pleaded, reaching out a hand to Violet's arm. Lily popped into screen and waved. "Hi, guys!" she said way too loudly.

"Oh my god, they're not on Mars," Rose said, rubbing her ears under her headphones. A series of laughing emojis came across Rose's screen. "This is Lily, and...come on," she said, nodding at Vi. "...this is a very shy Violet." Violet peeked her head out for a minute and then popped back off-screen.

"Our late father couldn't pay his back taxes, and a debt collector is threatening to close down our cozy little flower shop. I have no business asking for your help after I wasn't honest with you, but I don't have anywhere else to turn. If you were in my position, how would you raise one hundred thousand dollars in the next twenty-four hours?"

Angela popped in, "Brittany from Rochester wants to hop in."

Rose braced herself for a negative onslaught.

"I've been there," Brittany said. "I was fired last year, and it was fucking brutal. Just wanted to say it's nothing to be ashamed of; we've all been there."

A chorus of support came through the chat, and Rose felt some part of her finally relax after all these months. With her launching the podcast, building her brand, and somehow feeling like if she wasn't perfect, it would all fizzle away. Sure, she'd probably lose some subscribers, but it felt so good to just be herself for once.

Angela put another caller through.

"Hey, boss besties!" a quirky voice popped into the broadcast. "So, I don't know if this is helpful, but in my new candle business, I needed to raise money for supplies, so I took orders ahead of time and then delivered them later. Anyway, good luck, Rose! We still believe in you!"

"Oh my gosh, that's exactly it. You're a genius. Angela, can you wrap up the session? I owe you one. I've got to go. You guys are the best boss besties a girl could ever have!" A chorus of good lucks rang out in the chat, and she slammed down her laptop.

"Lily, I need you to sketch the most beautiful flower arrangements for every holiday you can think of. Valentine's Day, Father's Day, Earth Day, whatever you can think of. Vi, I need you to text Mrs. Maroo and say there will be an event outside of Bloom this evening that is absolutely VIP only. Secret."

"So she'll tell everyone? Got it." Violet started tapping away on her phone, sending messages.

Rose bounded down to the kitchen and snatched one of the envelopes that Violet had kept in a pile from the debt collection agency.

She punched in the number emblazoned all over the envelope, and the greasy, hacky, coughing piece of scum answered. Rose was going to make a deal.

GRAY

GRAY PULLED the box truck to the side of the country road and caught his breath as the livestream of Rose's podcast ended. She was staying. He was her...boyfriend?

Best news he'd heard all day.

And she took his advice and told her listeners everything. She was so fucking brave.

He looked down at his shaking hands. *What the hell am I doing? My dream girl is staying and fighting for our business, and I'm driving across the state?* How stupid could he be?

If Rose could ask for help, so could he. He dialed Nash's number and held it to his ear, chewing on his lip. It wasn't a handout if he asked a friend, right?

The phone rang and rang. Gray punched it in again, feeling more desperate by the ring. He couldn't trust anyone to drop off tens of thousands of dollars of product across Pennsylvania in his work truck.

Pop's voice echoed back through his head. *What are you willing to risk for it?*

He blew the strands of hair out of his eyes as he realized the only people he could think of who would drop everything at a moment's notice. The people who he'd trust to not fuck it up. Despite the pit of dread in his stomach, he dialed a familiar number and picked up the phone.

"Hey, Mom. You and Dad busy today?"

An hour later, with a small detour to his parent's house, the keys had been tossed to them. His mom looked happier than he'd seen her in a long time, and though his dad huffed and puffed like the self-important windbag he was, he seemed genuinely happy to get behind the wheel of the cab.

"I'm just so glad you called, Graham." His mom ran her fingers through his hair and wiped off a speck of mud she found along his cheek. "Your father hasn't been this excited in a long time. We're going on a road trip for the first time in twenty years." Her arms wiggled with excitement.

"Thanks. I know it's inconvenient."

"Nonsense," she said, patting him on the arm. "That's what we're here for. All we wanted to do this whole time was help."

Gray's eyes hit the floor as he shoved his hands in his pockets. He nodded. All they wanted was to help.

Why did it feel so hard to let them?

"This woman you need to help. You love her?" His mom's appraising eyes roamed his face.

"Very much so." He hoped like hell she could love him back someday.

"Good." His mom gave him a hug and walked to the truck. "It looks good on you." She sent him a happy wave and got in.

He jogged over to his SUV as they pulled the truck out of the driveway.

Concern and turmoil rumbled through Gray's stomach as

he thought about how to protect Rose and how he could help.

A text came through on his phone in a group chat with Lily, Vi, and Rose with the details for an event they were throwing together that evening. Lenny had agreed to let up if they could prove they had over half the money in hand today.

He tapped Rose's face and hit the call button. He needed to hear her voice.

"Hey," she practically purred in his ear, and he felt a knot of tension relax between his shoulder blades.

"Is my *girlfriend* there? I heard my *girlfriend* on a podcast earlier, and I was hoping my girlfriend might be able to talk for a minute." He had the widest shit-eating grin and thought he might burst from happiness as Rose's laughter rolled through the speaker.

"Thanks for listening," she said. Background voices came through, almost drowning out her voice. "Sorry, I can't talk long. I know we're partners, but I made a decision without you. I hope that's okay."

"Rose, I trust you. Here's how I'm going to help, and I want to see if it works for you: I'm going to drive to every watering hole in the county and tell them about the event tonight and text all my floral contacts so they put in bulk orders."

"That's...perfect. Thank you." She sounded happy, and Gray physically ached to see her face.

"Thank you...?" he teased.

"Thank you, boyfriend." She laughed, and there wasn't a

better sound in the entire world. "I've got to go. See you tonight?"

"Couldn't keep me away."

They hung up, and Gray had to stop himself from ending with "I love you." If he didn't tell her soon, he was gonna burst.

First things first, though. Whatever happened at the auction tonight, whatever the future would be between him and Rose, Lenny would finally leave the Parkers the hell alone, even if Gray had to risk everything. He'd stop by a familiar grease stain and tell him to stand the fuck down.

Fifteen minutes later, Gray pulled up to the dingy, yellow house that was all too familiar to him. The memories of getting his haul of pills and cocaine as a drug dealer in high school flooded back.

Lenny ran a debt collection business but hadn't upgraded himself, which made Gray wonder how desperate he might be to deliver this large deal on Frank's estate.

Gray weighed whether he should go in or not. He was flirting with disaster today, that was for damn sure. He got out and surveyed the houses around him. Everything was the same since the last time he'd been there. Dirt was etched into every surface, and broken appliances and toys were scattered throughout the yards.

He wondered if Lenny would even recognize him now; grown up, filled out, no hollow red rings around his eyes. He had to do this; he had to figure out what the hell was going on.

He knew that Rose would hate that he was getting involved,

but sometimes you just had to do things for people you loved. He stopped on the sidewalk as the irony hit him. Maybe this is why his dad always fucking meddled. Because he loved him.

Ugh, no time for feelings right now. Gray took a deep breath and walked up the crumbling cement stairs. He hoped this wouldn't go south. That Lenny still remembered him.

And that Lenny wouldn't shoot him.

He knocked hard on the door. "Lenny, open up." He pounded again, this time letting anger come through.

"I'm comin', I'm comin." He heard a man hack and spit before he got to the door. Gray heard several locks flip, and the door opened, a screen still separating them.

Lenny's eyes narrowed in recognition. "Why you at my house before fuckin dawn, man?" Gray could smell Lenny from where he stood. He looked like death warmed over with his long greasy, balding hair and several teeth missing.

"I need to talk to you about a friend of mine you're fucking with."

"She hot?" Lenny scratched his protruding belly under his stained white shirt.

"Can you come out here?" Gray was never going back into that house again.

"Gimme a minute." Lenny let the door slam and came back out with a hoodie on.

"Why the fuck are you being so hard on Frank Parker's girls? They're just trying to do what's right, and it takes time to find three hundred grand."

Lenny lit up a cigarette. "It's between them and the IRS. I'm just the muscle."

"Just the muscle? Bullshit. I have never seen anybody's

business be padlocked because they were a little late in paying their taxes."

"Well," Lenny sent him an oily smile, "that was just a present from me to you."

"A present? You're just screwing with Bloom because of me? Because of what happened twenty years ago?"

"Yep," Lenny snorted, so proud of himself.

When Gray was caught dealing in high school, his parents forced him to give up the name of his supplier. He'd always been waiting for how Lenny would get him back.

Lenny didn't have significant criminal charges, just a few weeks of jail time because he was smart enough to cover his tracks. But Gray had always felt it would come back to haunt him, and he had least expected it to hurt the woman he loved.

"The fuck, man?" Gray pushed off the railing he'd been leaning on and shoved at Lenny.

"Now, now. Don't want to get the law involved. Again. You know what they do to rats." Lenny eyed him with a scowl.

"Don't fuck with them. Fuck with me."

"I am fucking with you. That's why this is so fun." Lenny's evil smile sent a chill down his back.

"Everyone is coming to the event tonight, and they'll raise the money, so your little game is over."

"Eh, we'll see," Lenny said. "But for now, watch your back." He slammed the door in front of Gray's face.

Of course, this would happen. Of course, Gray would take something so pure, so lovely—a small-town flower shop—and fuck it up. Could he do nothing right?

How could anybody love him? Just one fuck up after another.

Well, he considered, *like I told Rose, when I fuck things up, I like to be thorough about it.*

"Lenny, I'll make you a deal," Gray said, hoping his idea would work.

Chapter Twenty-five

ROSE

Several hours later, Rose stood on the patch of grass in the town square across from Bloom as their impromptu pledge drive came together.

She'd never felt nervous like this before any of her consulting presentations. She took her job seriously in corporate consulting, but the fallout of any bad decisions never hurt her personally.

This? This was so personal.

In the last seven hours, Lily sketched like a maniac, Violet told everyone she knew in town about the event, and Rose coordinated livestreams and posted online about their fundraiser that evening. A small crowd started congregating, and Rose waved to Nick and Aaron as they walked over from Fox & Forrest.

"Is this the appropriate dress code for an urgent flower fundraiser?" Aaron said, gesturing to his stylish outfit.

"You could wear a paper bag for all I care as long as you buy some flowers." Rose gave him a quick hug.

"Here's your shabby chic stage," Nick said, setting down a small low bench for Rose to stand on.

"We also brought over leftovers from today." Aaron nodded at the gazebo next to them filled with croissants, muffins, and coffee cake from the cafe that morning.

"You guys," Violet said, putting her hand on her hips. "You didn't have to do that."

"We need all the help we can get, Vi." Rose sent her a chastising look. "Lily, are the live streams ready to go?" Rose hustled to where Lily had a bevy of devices propped up. They were stationed along the rickety card tables they'd borrowed from Mrs. Maroo's law office.

"Yeah, I think they'll be able to see me when I hold up my sketches."

Lily had sketched designs for Valentine's Day bouquets, Father's Day arrangements, bridal shower centerpieces, Thanksgiving, and about a million other holidays, including National Houseplant Appreciation Day. They'd try to get enough pledges to make a deposit that night. Lenny had agreed that if they could prove they had over half the money - $147,000 by the end of day today, he'd unlock the store. After the greenhouse and house sale, and Rose throwing in her own savings, they had to get $70K from the fundraiser tonight, an unthinkable amount of money in flowers for a small town.

"Have you heard from Gray?" Violet pulled out folding chairs for guests.

Rose grabbed chairs from her and set them in front of

the makeshift stage. "He was making the rounds to tell people about the event, but I haven't heard from him since."

People wandered in and started taking their seats, and their fundraiser would start any minute. Lily had sketched a flower-laden thermometer to track their pledges on the best poster board they could find at the last minute.

Rose huffed out a laugh thinking how amateurish it all was, how homespun. They would hold up pieces of paper and ask their friends and community to pay them on trust alone. Any other time, Rose would be completely mortified by what they were doing. She'd always needed things to be polished and top-of-the-line production quality.

The next hour wouldn't look expensive and perfect, but this somehow felt better because it was honest. It was them, and it was authentic.

It was so much more nerve-wracking to be authentic.

Butterflies somehow multiplied in her stomach as she thought of possibly failing, of asking all the people she loved most in the world for help, and it still not being enough. It was terrifying to think she wasn't enough; that she could do her very best and still fail.

Rose's heart almost burst from how much she wanted this. Numbers turned over in her brain. *$70,000 was just $50 1,400 times, right? That's not so scary; 1,400. Everybody could use flowers a couple of times a year. That's just a couple hundred people.*

Rose scanned the growing crowd for signs of Lenny. She spotted the unkempt, pissed-off man across the square as he shuffled toward them. They wanted to pay; he just wouldn't listen to them. She hoped she ruined his night because he'd upended her life in such a stupid way.

"Hiya, sweet cheeks." He took a hit on his vape and puffed out a cloud of sickeningly sweet cotton candy smoke toward her.

"Did you murder a unicorn and then smoke it?" Rose waved her hand at the cloud.

"Talkin' real big for a girl about to lose her boyfriend's business."

"Wait, what?" Rose towered over the sweat stain of a man in front of her. "What do you mean 'lose my boyfriend's business'?"

"Let's just say I'm getting even." He shrugged and grinned.

"He doesn't have anything to do with this. That's not what we agreed to."

Lenny puffed out another cloud at her. "Grudges are a bitch. Just like you."

Lily lunged at him, and Violet caught her around the waist. Nick and Aaron walked up, ready to step in.

"You're right." She'd been preparing for this moment her whole life. She articulated every syllable like shards of glass shooting into his forehead. "I *am* a bitch, Leonard."

Rose stepped toward him with a threatening smile and saw his face fall. "A bossy, know-it-all bitch. I'm done apologizing for outsmarting and outworking lazy, incompetent," she glanced down at him, "disgusting men around me. Our deal still stands, correct?"

He took another step back from her. "Yeah, whatever." He waved a hand at her as he walked away. "Just don't fuck it up, or the IRS'll get a brand-new flower farm." Lenny laughed.

Rose took a few steps back and rubbed her chest. He'd put his farm up as collateral for her. She felt like she was having a heart attack. It'd been so long since she had her last panic attack she forgot how much they could sneak up on you when you least needed them to.

"Rose, just breathe," Violet said, letting go of Lily. She looked at her watch. "We'll be fine. It's time."

Rose took a deep breath. "We can do this." It was all going to be okay. Her crazy idea would probably work. She probably wouldn't destroy their businesses. She probably wouldn't get her sister's house taken away. She probably wouldn't ruin everything.

She really fucking hoped people wanted to buy flowers today.

Rose scanned the crowd for Gray one more time. Why wasn't he here? She needed him. She needed his calming presence and his charm working the crowd. Rose had business savvy, but she'd never be connected with the community like he was.

She took a deep breath and stood up on the bench. "Hi, everyone. Thank you for joining last minute. You know that we're in a bind. You might have heard through the unofficial town newsletter, aka Mrs. Maroo," everyone chuckled, surprising Rose, "that we have some large bills to pay today. I feel completely embarrassed coming to you after all the support you've given us, but we have nowhere else to turn.

"We have some friends joining us via the internet," Rose sent a wave at the table of computers and phones currently live streaming, "and anything you all can offer would be much appreciated."

A smattering of applause interrupted her, and she felt a sliver of hope. "Let's start the bidding for Lily's first amazing design: a Father's Day arrangement."

She looked over as Lily held up a large, gorgeous sketch of bright flowers interspersed with tropical greens and accents of roses. The peach roses Lily included were her father's favorite, and Rose's eyes welled up suddenly without warning.

Rose's voice caught. "This," she trailed off. *Get it together, Parker*. "This features my father's favorite flowers: roses," she said, sending a lopsided smile toward the crowd as she twisted her mouth, trying to keep it from turning into a sob that was hiding somewhere right behind her control.

"This arrangement is forty-five dollars. Any takers?"

Fifteen hands flew into the air, and Rose's eyes widened in shock.

"All right." She smiled back at the beaming faces she would have ignored only two months ago. These people had saved her time and time again with their friendship and their loyalty. She'd find some way to pay them back someday.

"I think that's..." She punched the numbers in on her phone.

"Six hundred and seventy-five!" Nash called up from the back as he jogged toward her. "Here. Let me help." He grabbed a marker from her and stood next to Lily, coloring in the large tracker.

"And we have an additional twenty orders between the live streams," Violet called out.

"All right," Rose said, rubbing her hands together. "Any last calls for the beautiful limited-edition Father's Day arrangement?"

A few more hands shot into the air, and they moved on to the 4th of July picnic arrangements. An hour in, they were doing well. They'd miraculously raised forty-four thousand dollars between the live streams and the community but were running toward the end of their available designs.

Rose called out arrangements for St. Patrick's Day, anniversaries, and even Mother's Day, which was now almost a year away. They crept toward fifty thousand dollars, but hope started sinking in Rose's stomach.

It would be fine if Gray didn't make that stupid agreement with the oily slimeball. The only thing she'd lose is her business, not his.

"Did I miss the chance to order the 'I'm in Love with You' bouquet?" a voice called from the back. A small gasp sounded through the crowd.

It was turning dark, and though the gazebo lights barely illuminated the square, her heart jumped into her throat. She'd know the voice anywhere.

"Did you hear that doll? He said he loves you!" Margie croaked out from the crowd. A chuckle ran through it, and Rose felt her cheeks blush.

"Thanks, Margie," she said, trying to muster a crumb of patience.

He loves me. Even through everything. Even though he knows all the worst sides of me.

"How many of those bouquets do you want to order?" She put a hand on her hip and let hope blossom in her heart.

Gray came into focus. He'd worn a crisp white button-up with the sleeves rolled up, showing his tattooed forearms, rippling as his muscles clenched. The sight sent trembles of need through her.

Why was it always the fucking forearms?

"Put me down for one every week until I die." A serious gasp sounded through the crowd as he slowly walked toward her.

She kind of loved that he was so cocky.

"How long do you plan on living?" Nash called out, doing the math in his head as he colored the tracker.

"Let's say...twenty-three years."

Rose could feel her heart in her throat as her eyes locked with his. She wanted all those years with him. She loved him so much it hurt to look at him. How could she have thought even a day ago she could leave all of this behind? He wandered through the chairs up to the bench.

"All right, whiz kid," Lily said, cocking her head over to Nash. "What's the math on that?"

"It's twenty-three thousand and nine hundred dollars at twenty bucks a pop."

"Round it up to twenty-four for inflation." Gray walked up, not breaking his stride. He caught Rose around the waist, hauled her against him, and Rose kissed him with every fiber of her being.

"And we have seventy thousand dollars!" Nash yelled.

The crowd cheered, but it all fell away in the cocoon of Gray's kiss. His mouth pressed firmly against hers, and his arms around her felt like safety. His hand held her jaw as his arm ensnared her waist, pulling him toward her. He gently set her down, his mouth still on hers.

Rose desperately wanted to stay in the cocoon of his arms, but she had a crowd to handle. She pulled away slowly. "No one's going to take me seriously in this town if you keep coming in and sweeping me off my feet." She smiled at him, her thumb brushing against his lips.

"I just want everyone to know you're mine," he said, his eyes searching hers, and his thumbs stroked her back.

"Gray, you didn't have to do this." God, it felt so good to be in his arms, the weight of the day behind them. The crowd stood and walked towards the tables with a makeshift money box.

"Of course, I had to do it. You mean a lot to me, Rose. I don't know if you heard earlier, but—"

"Where's my money?"

Rose turned around to see Lenny scratching his stomach behind her. "You'll have it by the end of the day." Rose broke away from Gray, all business again. "Give me those keys."

"Your boyfriend has them."

Rose looked over at Gray quickly. He dangled them in the air.

"He gets to keep his farm as long as I see the money transferred today."

A line formed in front of Violet and Nash as they collected the funds. Rose pointed to them. "Go see Violet."

Violet waved nervously at Lenny as he let out a disgusting chuckle. "Don't mind if I do."

Gray started toward him. "You son of a—"

"It's fine," Rose said, pressing a hand to Gray's chest.

"Lily will be right there. She'll kick his teeth out if he tries anything."

Gray clasped her hand on his chest, holding it tighter. "I have a surprise for you."

"Nash, Lily," Rose called as Gray tugged her hand toward the flower shop. "Hold down the fort." They sent her waves and went back to the throng of people surrounding them, ready to write a check or give them their credit card. "We have to make this quick."

"Those folks aren't going anywhere," Gray said, tugging her even faster to the flower shop. "I'll happily drive you to their houses to collect every last dollar tonight, but I need five minutes with my girl."

His girl.

ROSE

Rose wrapped her arm through Gray's as he interlaced their fingers.

"So, I know we've only been on one date... yesterday." Gray placed a kiss on her hair, and Rose thought she might melt with happiness. "But I'm in it. I'm in it for however long I can trick you into staying with me." He looked down at her as they crossed the green lawn of the town square.

The last twenty-four hours had been a complete marathon, but she finally felt on solid ground again. She stared into stormy-green eyes that looked like the color of her future. "There's no tricking here."

He'd said he loved her, right? Or was that just a one-time thing? Should she say it now? Would it be weird? She hated being bad at new things.

He stopped in front of their store, and Rose took in his

features, shaded in the twilight dusk as he pulled the keys out of his pocket. He shoved the key in the padlock as it broke apart, and Rose felt a weight lift off her shoulders.

"How did you get the keys from Lenny?"

"I threatened loss of his property, his life, and his manhood, but it helps that we knew each other."

"Knew each other?"

He walked around the back door and unlocked the padlock on the employee entrance. "I dealt in high school, and he was my source." Gray bit his lips in embarrassment. "That's why he was fucking with us, with Violet. Normally he wouldn't go that hard, but it was because I gave up who my supplier was when I was a kid. He did some time for it."

She wasn't sure what to say. "So all his harassment..."

"Was one hundred percent my fault. I made everything worse and didn't even know it until a few hours ago. I'm so sorry I fucked this up for us. That's why I had to put up my place as collateral."

Rose's head whirred, thinking about their narrow escape. "But what if we hadn't raised the money?"

Gray chewed his lip. "I was willing to risk it for you. And I wanted to make it up to you with what's inside."

Rose reached for the back door handle, eager to get back inside her sanctuary, to the pride and joy she'd built with her three favorite people on Earth.

When had Gray gone from being her worst nightmare to her favorite person? The best person to spend time with, make her laugh, and have her back through everything?

"Wait," Gray put his hand over hers, "let's go to the front. I have a surprise."

"I do not like surprises, Graham Roberts."

"I know," he wiggled his eyebrows, and a cheeky grin bloomed on his face. "But trust me, you'll like this one."

He tugged her to the front of the store. Rose glanced over the town square and saw the party still going on around the fundraising tables. Violet and Nash were taking money hand over fist, and the realization of how much she'd changed hit her. March Rose would insist on handling it herself, but now she was so happy for her squad to handle it. Lily stood guarding a very grumpy Lenny sitting in a chair. He rubbed his chin, and Rose hoped her spitfire sister had decked him.

"You ready?" Gray brought Rose back to the moment.

Is this what it would always be like? Nestled between her family, found and blood, and this gorgeous, annoying, adorable, loving man in front of her?

"Ready."

GRAY

NERVES GRIPPED Gray's chest as he looked down into Rose's face. She hated surprises, he knew that, but maybe just this once, he could sweep her off her feet and not fuck it up.

"Close your eyes."

"Gray, it's my store." She huffed, sticking out her bottom lip in irritation, but she closed them after a brief eye roll.

"I saw that, Parker." He pulled her in for a quick kiss on her temple. It was very unfortunate she was so adorable when she was irritated. He'd never get enough of that pout as he teased her incessantly. He wondered if she'd still make that face in twenty or thirty years as they grew old together.

First things first, though. He turned the antique door handle and led them both inside the cool chilled air of Bloom. The smell of fresh flowers was stronger than usual, smelling like it was perfumed just for them. He flipped on the lights and dragged her hands down from her face to finally let her see.

She gasped, and his heart leapt in his throat. Her eyes widened at the site in front of her. Thousands of peonies filled every single surface of the store. He brought them in buckets and baskets and whatever he could find. He laid them on the tables, in vases, in the candles display, the chocolate display, in heaps on the check-out counter, and there was barely any spot visible on the floor that wasn't taken up by bundles of milky white, vibrant fuchsia, pastel orange, and ballerina pink peonies.

"Gray, when did you... how..." she trailed off, not able to compute. "When did you do this? Why did you do this? How did you do this?"

He brought her in close and smiled into her hair. Of course, he should know that she would want all the answers. "Rose, just—"

"Take it in, yeah, yeah. I got it." She waved her hand at him. "I am. I'm just—my brain is on overdrive." She leaned down to smell a bouquet of fuchsia peonies in front of her.

She looked like an absolute picture, leaning down with her chestnut hair falling against the petals. He wished he could take all the flowers out on the floor and make love to her like he wanted to, surrounding her with beauty.

He saw her breathe in the scent of flowers, close her eyes, hold them closer, and breathe deeply again. A shimmer of a tear threatened at her eyelashes, and he leaned down beside her, placing a hand on her back. She fluttered them open.

"Why would you do this?" Her eyes searched his. "I'm not..."

His heart sank. Was this it? Was she going to tell him she didn't love him back yet? They had the one date, the one deal, the one partnership, and it was over? Had he gone too far? Fuck, he could never read the room.

Her eyes went back down to the fluttery petals. "I'm not worth it," she whispered.

What the actual fuck? "You're worth ten times this, honey. A thousand times this."

She shook her head and fought her lip from quivering. "I'm too much. I'm bossy. A know-it-all. You said so yourself."

"You are bossy." He grabbed her arms as they stood up and brought her close. He pressed her head to his chest and wrapped his arms around her.

"And I have to have things a certain way."

"Yep," he nodded, running a hand down her hair as his thumb stroked her waist. The thud in his stomach built into warmth when he realized where her head was at.

"Rose, I know all this about you. Those are all the things I love about you." She pulled back to look up at him, and his hand came to cup her cheek. "I love that you're fierce and stubborn, you're ambitious, and you're smarter than anyone else I've ever met. I love that you want things a certain way because it turns out usually they're the best way, which is very annoying but also pretty cute."

She leaned into his hand and laughed.

His hand grasped the back of her neck, and he threaded his hands through her hair. "I love that you fight fiercely for your family and for what you believe in. And most of all, I love who you are. But..." The tension came back. He needed to ask how she felt. "The real question is..."

Her mouth tilted into a nervous frown. "Falling for you was...an accident. I tried to stop it, I tried to logic it away, but goddamnit, I love you." Her brows drew together as she said the best, sweetest words he could hear.

Of course, his grumpy girl would scowl at him as she made his every dream come true.

"You said it in front of all those people," she talked rapidly, gaining speed. "And then here, again and again, and again, and—"

He brought her mouth to his to shut her up. He wondered if this would ever get old, having her right here, safe in his arms. If it would still give him a thrill, just the same way that it always had. He pulled back, and his thumb ran along her cheekbone, flush from the chill of the night air. "I had to show you I'm so fucking glad you're staying. I want those next twenty-three years. I want every single bit because I don't think it will be enough for me."

"They're yours," Rose said, looking up into his eyes. Her hand grasped at his wrist as his hand held her face.

It wasn't a proposal exactly, they weren't ready for that, but it was a promise. Hell, they'd only been on one date, but like Pop said, when you knew, you knew. And he'd known about five seconds after meeting her that she would drive him nuts for the rest of his life.

ROSE

"Wait," Rose remembered, coming out of her fog of self-centeredness of the last twelve hours. "I thought you had a big delivery?"

"My parents took it."

Rose's eyebrows shot up.

"I took your advice," he said, his thumb tracing her bottom lip.

"And accepted some help?" Her eyes narrowed on his lips that she desperately wanted back on her mouth.

"And accepted some help." He brought her to him, pulling her in for a hard, quick kiss. He peered around the corner, looking back at the crowd still chatting under the lights of the gazebo.

"I think we have time." He pulled her hand, weaving through the baskets of peonies.

"Time for what?"

He pulled her into the supply closet, shut the door, and pinned her against it. "I think we have about five minutes until our friends and family—"

Because they were a family, she realized. All of them. Not just her sisters, but Nash, Mrs. Maroo, Pop, everybody.

"—invade the store and celebrate your success." His mouth came to her neck, and she was pinned to the door with the hand on her waist. His arm bracketed beside her head as he towered over her.

"Rose, I need two things from you."

"Anything," she whispered as his hand slid underneath her skirt. His large rough palm ran along the edge of her panties.

"I need you to move in with me," he said, pulling back slightly, still pinning her between him and the door, his eyes searching hers.

Get this every day? Yes fucking please. She nodded dumbly.

"Yeah?" A youthful light brightened his eyes as hope bloomed between them.

A smile curled her lips. "I mean, I'm *mostly* moving in to see my boyfriend every day."

"Me or the one who has four paws?"

"Take your pick." She nipped at his jawline. His hand dipped underneath her panties.

"I need to see you every day. I need to wake up to you. I need to roll over and know you're right where you belong every morning," he said into the curve of her neck. She was completely enveloped by his scent and the wall of muscle surrounding her.

His mouth worked along the column of her throat. She gasped from pleasure.

"What was the second thing?" she muttered.

"Always have to be on task, don't you?" he chuckled into the curve of her shoulder. Her knees started to buckle as his hands gripped her ass. He pulled back and locked eyes with her.

"The second thing I need is to be inside you right fucking now."

Chills ran down her arms. *His mouth was going to get him out of a lot of trouble.*

Gray stepped back suddenly, holding her hand out.

Rose was confused. "What?" She looked down at her dress.

"I want a good look before I muss you up," he said, spinning her around. He let out a low whistle as she turned her back to him. "I need a minute to admire this view."

Rose smiled over her shoulder at him. The back of the dress went *very* low, falling well below her waist. It was probably scandalous for Fairwick Falls, but she felt thankful for wearing it right now.

Gray's hands landed hot on her skin as his fingers curved inside her dress. His fingers traced their way up from her hips, gently moving along the sides of her back. "We're going to stop right here." He placed a kiss on her bare shoulder. His lips trailed along her spine, and his hands crept under the sides of the dress, running along her ribs, until he found her breasts.

Rose leaned back against him, needing more of him. His fingers roughly grasped her, squeezing her tight against him, and she wound her hands up through his hair. He teased her, circling and pulling her nipples as need pooled in her pussy.

"I want twenty-three more years of you. Of your perfect tits," he growled in her ear.

She pressed against him, feeling every hard inch of his cock pressing against her ass.

He stepped back and slowly unzipped her dress, pushing

it past her hips so it fell to the floor. She stood in her heels, and little else, and his hands roamed her backside, tracing her curves and lingering in the dips and valleys.

He pressed her back to him, his mouth landing at her ear while his hand made its way down her back, over her ass, as his foot edged her leg out to spread her legs. "Arch your back for me, honey."

Honey. She'd do anything for him. His hand curved under her, and he slipped a finger inside her wet pussy, spreading her from behind. "I've dreamed about taking you in every room of my house. Fucking you against any door I can." He whispered in her ear as she felt a rush of wetness and wanting inside her.

"Spreading you out on the kitchen island and licking every inch. Seeing you hold our headboard as you ride my face."

Our headboard. God, she wanted all of that immediately. Yesterday. Always.

He pulled out his fingers and wrapped his arm around her to reach her clit. His fingers traced slow, lazy circles around it. She heard a mewl. Had it been her? Desire curled through her, and she'd do anything he wanted at that moment as long as he didn't stop.

He turned her around suddenly, a wolf-like smile on his face. His mouth was on hers, and his hands fisted in her hair. She tugged on his shirt to feel his chest and ran her hands against his abs.

He was rock hard against her. She needed more.

His hands grabbed her ass territorially as he backed her up against the door. She loved being taken, made his. Her hands slowly unbuckled his belt, rubbing him as she went. He nipped her shoulder as she grabbed his cock.

"Show much how much you want it, honey. How much you want this cock in you." With one hand, she stroked him and pushed the end of him against her wet panties, now soaked. She pushed them to the side so he could feel how wet she was as she stroked him.

Their tongues danced, and he barely breathed as she slid the end of his cock around her clit, seeking the barest of touches and teasing him with the delicious feeling. A growl rumbled from him, and Rose saw his eyes go feral. He pulled a condom out of his pocket and sheathed himself in it in record time.

He yanked her to him for a crushing kiss, stealing her breath. She felt his full strength as he strained her against him. She wrapped one leg around him, and he lifted her up to wrap the second around him, needing him as close to her as possible for more friction.

He lifted her up, his mouth never leaving hers. She ripped off the rest of his shirt. She needed his skin against hers. He hooked her leg under his arm and pressed her against the door, spreading her legs and sending jolts of need straight down.

He sank into her to the hilt, his body pressed against her. They stilled at that moment, savoring it.

"God, I love you." He was breathless, straining to keep himself back.

Her heart could burst from wanting him in every way. "I love you more." She smiled through her grinding need. "Now fuck me like you still hate me."

His eyes turned dark, and a fierce grin broke his face in two. "I love it when you're a brat." He thrust hard into her, pushing her up the door. "Now, take all of this cock into that tight little pussy."

Yes.

"Harder," her head rolling back to the door as she clenched around him.

"I will break this fucking door down with how much I want you. Grab one of those perfect tits for me, honey."

Holy hell, she wasn't going to last long. She grasped her breast and squeezed as his eyes scored her body with heat.

"You know what I want. Show me." He thrust into her again and again.

She pinched her nipple hard, twisting it, and moaned at the possessive look in his eyes. He'd eat her up, and she'd enjoy every minute.

He leaned up to capture her mouth in a long, slow kiss. "Good girl." He slammed into her again, his hips grinding against hers as goosebumps ran down her arms. Each trying to wring more pleasure than the other. The sound of their breaths and moans mixing together made Rose's blood rush, and she felt the delicious build-up crest inside of her.

His hand wrapped around the back of her neck possessively as he increased his speed, a torching heat building inside of her.

She bit her lip, enjoying the torture.

Gray's eyes went to Rose's lips, and he groaned a breathless curse. All his need burst at once. He rocked them harder, faster. Their breath mingled, eyes never leaving each other until she finally came into a white-hot release and screamed as pleasure ripped through her like a fire.

Gray stilled inside her as they caught their breath, panting from the effort. His head rested on hers, and she already couldn't wait to do that again. She pressed herself closer to him, needing to remember every physical piece of this moment.

Seconds later, the shop's front door was thrown open, and voices bounced around the inside of the high-ceiling showroom.

Gray sat her down, bent his legs, and she gently placed her shaky legs on the ground. He eased out of her, and she noted with pride his chest was still heaving almost as hard as hers.

"Christ," he said.

"You were right on when they'd be here," Rose pulled on her dress and ran a hand through her hair.

"It's no use, honey," he leaned in to kiss her jawline. "It looks like you just got fucked in your storage room. Though it looks pretty good on you." His hand cupped her chin.

She batted it away and laughed. "Get yourself together, Roberts. We can't be known as people who don't support their community. I don't know if you know this, but it's important to form a genuine connection with your customers in a small-town shop." She bit her lip to keep from giggling as he gave her the largest eye roll she'd ever seen.

He zipped himself up. "Go ahead out. I need a minute." She stared down at his pants and was proud of herself that, even now, he was still hard. She put her hand on the door and unlocked it, ready to make a covert escape into the showroom.

"Hey," she said, turning around as he dealt with a condom in the waste basket.

"Yeah?" He turned around, eyes curious on hers.

Her heart had shattered into pieces and reformed into something that looked like a future with Gray. "I love you."

"Even though it was an accident?" His hand reached out to hers in the small supply closet.

"Especially because it was an accident." She grabbed a quick kiss from his mouth, opened the door, and walked out to greet her future in Bloom.

Epilogue

One month later

GRAY

Gray threw his truck in park outside Bloom as a chattering Alex sounded through his phone. Rose answered back in a mix of English and French, the two of them somehow managing to communicate.

"Bonjour!" Rose waved through the phone at the beaming little face.

They'd just returned from two weeks in Montreal, and in that time, Alex had managed to wrap Rose around his tiny little finger. They had a shared love of dogs, bubble-blowing, and drawing flowers poorly. They'd spent an enjoyable visit with Giselle, Andi, and Alex, and he was thrilled to see how easily Rose slid into the rest of his life.

Gray had taken an unprecedented two weeks off, even though it was the busy season on the farm. He wanted to show Rose and himself that it was important to make time for family. He'd realized that he could work himself to the bone, but it wouldn't matter unless the people he loved knew how he felt and felt cherished by him.

He looked over at her, making silly faces at Alex to make him laugh, and realized he was going to marry the fuck out of Rose Parker.

They'd only been *together* together for a month, and it was too soon even to broach the subject, but he knew. He wasn't sure how long he'd be able to wait to ask her. Why would you wait if you knew what your forever was?

They both said bye to Alex and hopped out of the SUV.

"What's this big reveal you have lined up?" He grabbed Rose's hand as they walked across the parking lot.

"You'll see. It's a surprise." She tapped away on her phone one-handed as they headed into Bloom.

It was a gorgeous early summer day, and the door to the flower shop had been propped open. Moving boxes littered the front stoop, and a sweaty Nash waved hello as they approached.

"Figures you'd get here right as we finish up." Nash picked up a heavy box.

"It's good for you, Lord Donnelly, to do some manual labor like the rest of us peasants," Gray shot back.

Lily was moving into the loft apartment above Bloom, and the others had already started moving her in since their flight from Montreal had been delayed. Gray picked up one of the boxes on the stoop and brought it inside.

Lily, Violet, and Nash stood at the foot of the staircase, panting and guzzling water bottles.

"There you are. I've missed you." Lily ran toward Rose and caught her in a monkey-style hug, wrapping each leg around her.

"Lily, you're tiny, ugh, and sweaty, but we're too old for this," Rose laughed as she grabbed her sister on the waist and set her down.

"I am never too old to attack my sister with love."

Violet walked over at a slower pace but still with a beaming smile on her face. "It's so good to see you. I'm so glad to have help." Vi wrapped Rose in a hug.

"With the store or with the boxes?" Gray said.

"Oh my god, both." Violet stretched out her hips and legs as she spoke. "Anyone who thinks they need a gym to work out is dumb. Just help somebody move up two flights of stairs. Lil, I still don't know why you need to move up here. I'm going to be so lonely."

"How's Lily gonna get lucky at her sister's house?" Gray asked as he sat the large box next to Violet.

"Ewwww." Violet punched Gray in the arm.

He loved that he essentially had two little sisters now to endlessly tease. Gray waggled his eyebrows at Violet. "Now you can get some action too."

"If you have any hot single friends, send them my way before Lil's. I am older, after all." Violet guzzled from the water bottle again and shoved at the halo of humidity curls around her head.

"A friend is visiting in a few weeks. Maybe your car can break down, and I'll send him over," Gray shot Rose a wink.

~

ROSE

Rose smiled back at Gray, his wink reminding her of what they'd done that morning before their flight. He placed a quick kiss on her cheek as he and Nash went out to the truck to get Lily's dresser.

In the two weeks Rose had been gone, Lily had made a quick trip to Brooklyn to empty her apartment and move to Fairwick Falls. This was a new beginning for all of them.

Rose had moved into Gray's house after their emergency fundraiser and was getting used to both the quiet of the countryside and the luxury of waking up next to Gray each morning.

Still, though, she felt a pang of loss. She already missed living with Vi and Lily. They'd had their cozy evening chats and Violet's decadent breakfasts. It had felt like old times, but better.

"You okay?" Lily asked as she grabbed another bottle of water.

"Just going to miss having you around all the time." Rose extended her arms to gather her sister into a big hug.

"Rose, I will see you literally every day," Lily quirked an eyebrow at her.

Rose heard heavy breathing as Nash and Gray carried a chest of drawers through the doorway and sat it down.

"This is the last of it," Gray said.

"Lilypad, you're not allowed to move again," Nash said, wiping his brow. Gray and Nash both bent over, catching their breaths.

Lily stuck her tongue out at him.

Rose practically vibrated with the itch to tell them the good news.

Lily rolled her neck. “C’mon, we still have some big pieces to haul upstairs.”

“Wait, I have news,” Rose said. “With the fundraiser, the sale of Dad’s house finally going through, and two months of success in Bloom that finally posted to the account, I am happy to announce,” she whipped a piece of paper out of her pocket, “that we have two hundred and fifty thousand dollars paid off!”

Lily and Violet both yelled, “What!” in unison, as they jumped to hug Rose.

“Rose, that’s over halfway,” Violet beamed. Rose could see the enormous weight taken off Violet’s shoulders.

“I know! I’ll sell my car when Gray and I go to LA, which should give us some extra cash toward the last ninety thousand dollars.” After Rose sent the money from the fundraiser and house sale, they’d reported Lenny’s harassment, and the IRS had officially ended the collection agency’s relationship with him. They were now on a payment plan for the remaining amount they owed.

They were mostly out of the woods, but she’d feel much better when everything was paid off.

They all took turns hugging each other, though Rose noticed Lily and Nash’s hug was more of an arm pat.

“And,” Rose said, interrupting the cheers, “I’ve secured a new client interview tomorrow to pitch a huge event this summer—landscaping, floral designs, the whole nine yards—for the Fairwick County Wine Festival.”

"That's the biggest event of the year," Violet's eyes widened.

Rose was practically bouncing with excitement. "And it's just the first step. First, the Wine Festival, then a product line, then a magazine spread, and then next—"

"The world," Gray chuckled as he grabbed her waist. He met her mouth in a tender kiss, their eyes never leaving each other. What could stand in her way with him by her side and her sisters at her back?

Next, the world.

A chorus of cheers echoed in the small floral shop as the extended Bloom family celebrated their wins and the exciting things yet to come.

THE END

More from Elise Kennedy

***Love in Fairwick Falls* Novels**

Wallflower in Bloom - Coming Fall 2023

***Only One Cozy Bed* Novellas**

Pumpkin Spice & Pour-overs

Apple Cider & Subterfuge

Hot Cocoa & Mistletoe

Snowed In & Snuggle Weather

NEWSLETTER

For small-town romance freebies and news about upcoming books, **subscribe to Elise's newsletter elisekbooks.com/newsletter,** or join the Small Town Romance Patreon for early access to the next story!

ACKNOWLEDGMENTS

This book wouldn't have happened without three essential ingredients:

Friends.

I wouldn't be here without the unending support of the Romance Mafia including Molly Nesbitt, Kat Sterling, Astrid Forge, and Avery Gnilk. I Zoom'd with them more than my own mother during COVID, and meeting such like-minded friends from around the world was such a twist of happiness during a scary time. Between them and the fantastic romance writer friends I've met at The Ripped Bodice and the Romance Writers Club, I feel like I've finally found my people.

Love.

A huge thank you to my husband, Mr. Kennedy, who heard the phrase 'I have an idea for a scene/book/character' a million times...and always responded with '...Go write it!' Very annoying, but helpful advice, as it turns out. When I think of what I want for my characters and my readers (like you, friend!), I think of Mr. Kennedy. A good soul down to his atoms who wants the best for everyone he meets. I couldn't write HEAs without my own HEA snoring in bed beside me every night.

Fate.

When it knocks, listen the fuck up. Picture this: it's Aug 2020. You signed up for an Editor/Agent pitch event at a romance writers' convention...but then chickened out because, like so many other things...you overcommitted and lost interest (HI ADHD!). You cancel your spot so someone else can have it...only a month later, the organizer e-mails you and says, 'Here's your time slot.' You end up pitching two editors who want to read the first five chapters only...YOU HAVEN'T WRITTEN THEM YET. ::scream:: So you scramble for a weekend and pull together a passable five chapters (v1 of 27), and though they pass...you want to keep going. Someone liked your idea! You hold onto that hope and write a whole freaking book, one bite at a time.

It would have been so easy for me to lose interest in another hobby...(the amount of abandoned projects I have is LOL-worthy)...but the three combined are why Rose and Gray got a happy ending.

I can't finish acknowledgments without the AMAZING team of Beta Readers (Cristina Markarian, Harper Thomson, Kat Sterling, Alexia Diaz, Megan Marshall), my editor Jennifer Herrington at Fresh Look Editorial, and transcriptionist Jordan Wichern, who is a saint for listening to all my mumblings. The book would be a pile of mismatched Post-it notes without you all. Thank you!

ABOUT THE AUTHOR

Elise Kennedy is an author of cozy, spicy, heartfelt small-town romances. She lives in California with her (very) patient husband and two perfect pups.

Made in United States
Troutdale, OR
06/08/2023

10510301R00202